D0344840

CLEAN HANDS

Also by Patrick Hoffman

Every Man a Menace

The White Van

CLEAN HANDS

A NOVEL

PATRICK HOFFMAN

Atlantic Monthly Press
New York

FIRST EDITION

Published simultaneously in Canada
Printed in the United States of America

This book was set in 12-pt. Adobe Garamon Pro
by Alpha Design & Composition of Pittsfield, NH.

First Grove Atlantic hardcover edition: June 2020

Library of Congress Cataloging-in-Publication data is available for this title.

ISBN 978-0-8021-2953-6
eISBN 978-0-8021-2954-3

Atlantic Monthly Press
an imprint of Grove Atlantic
154 West 14th Street
New York, NY 10011

Distributed by Publishers Group West

groveatlantic.com

20 21 22 23   10 9 8 7 6 5 4 3 2 1

For Reyhan, Edgar, and Lois

1

LOOSE IN THE WILD

The footage appeared to show two men bumping into each other, exchanging a quick word, and then moving on. The pickpocket had been skilled enough to hide the theft; all you could see was the bump. The camera—mounted in a dome on the ceiling of the passageway in Grand Central Station—didn't have an ideal angle, but the picture was clear. It had been early in the morning; rush-hour commuters passed in both directions across the screen.

Michael D'Angelo—in-house investigator for Carlyle, Driscoll, and Hathaway—had been tasked with examining the video. He sat at his desk and watched the footage again and again, backing it up and playing it over, step by step. D'Angelo had spent eighteen years in the FBI; he knew this kind of thing took time and patience.

The victim of the pickpocketing, Chris Cowley, was a junior associate attorney at the same law firm that employed D'Angelo. He reported that the cell phone had been stolen from the inside breast pocket of his jacket. Upon discovering the theft, Chris had rushed to work and waited for his boss, Elizabeth Carlyle—the head of the firm—to emerge from the elevator. When she did, he told her that his phone had been stolen, and—far more alarmingly—that he had hot documents from the Calcott case on the phone.

Walk. Step. Bump. D'Angelo tapped the space bar and paused the video. He backed it up, this time a little further, and watched again. After the bump, the video showed Chris continuing toward the

3

turnstile, where a slight bottleneck of morning commuters had formed. This had slowed his progress. Once through the turnstile, the footage showed Chris patting his pants pockets for the first time. Two seconds later, the patting moved up to his jacket and became more urgent. Chris then turned and looked in the direction he'd just come from.

D'Angelo sighed, took a sip of coffee, and backed the video up again. He noted the time of the bump—08:12:41—and let it play right up until Cowley turned and ran after the thief. Sixteen seconds. He jotted the time down on a yellow legal pad along with his other notes. He watched the whole thing again. Something about it didn't sit right with him. For one thing, the lawyer and the pickpocket appeared to exchange a glance a few steps before the bump.

But that wasn't it—after the glance, they appeared to be drawn toward each other. Still, that wasn't it, either; it was the bump itself that bothered him. D'Angelo paused the video, closed his eyes, and tried to put himself into the young attorney's shoes. Would he, under similar circumstances, ever bump into someone like that? He didn't think so. Could he imagine performing an awkward dance? Sure. Maybe touch a hand to an arm? Yes. But to actually bump into another man, to have your legs, torso, and shoulder make contact with another person in the midst of rush-hour traffic? It didn't seem likely.

He paused the video; his mind drifted back a few hours and replayed the events of the morning. He'd just settled in at his desk when Elizabeth Carlyle stopped by and asked him to come to her office. She'd always been tough, but her voice sounded particularly flinty that morning. "I need you to come with me right away."

It wasn't every day that Elizabeth Carlyle came to summon you. In fact, D'Angelo couldn't remember it ever happening before. She wasn't the type to drop by in person; she'd usually send someone to get you.

She was in her late fifties. She dressed in tailored power suits, and always—except when she was in court—seemed to be in a hurry. She was cold, but it was hard not to be impressed by her. D'Angelo studied her for a second and saw that she was stressed. Without asking what she needed, he pushed himself up from his desk, touched the knot of his tie, and followed her.

When they entered her office, D'Angelo observed Chris Cowley sitting on a chair in front of Ms. Carlyle's desk. D'Angelo didn't know him well; they'd never worked on anything together. Now D'Angelo looked at him as though for the first time. He was in his late twenties but was still skinny, like a teenager. He had a full head of light brown hair, and his face appeared to only need occasional shaving. A petulant expression hung on his face, and for a moment it made D'Angelo think that he, himself, was about to be accused of some misdeed. Before he could even begin to imagine what that accusation could be, Elizabeth spoke: "Michael, Chris's cell phone was stolen this morning."

So what? thought D'Angelo.

She then told him that Cowley had been carrying the Calcott hot documents on the phone, that the phone had been unlocked, and that his password had—inconceivably—been turned off. The hot documents were the most toxic emails, memos, chats, text messages, and other evidence at the center of the Emerson v. Calcott case. That case, a federal civil suit between two banks, represented the largest portion of Carlyle, Driscoll, and Hathaway's billable hours. It was, to put it plainly, their biggest case. Without the Calcott Corporation, the firm would not exist.

Anger rolled through D'Angelo. He found that kind of sloppiness personally offensive. It didn't take long for the anger to transform into suspicion. What the hell was this kid doing carrying hot documents on his phone? And what in the name of God was he doing walking around with his phone unlocked?

He studied Chris. The lawyer sat there with his elbows on his knees, bent over like a man waiting for news. His ill humor was still apparent. D'Angelo was in the middle of wondering whether it was genuine or not, when Elizabeth asked if he could wipe the phone remotely.

He thought about it. "Sure," he said. "If it's turned on and has a signal."

"It's not on," said Chris. "It's off. Fuck." He looked like he might cry. "I checked."

Hoping for some kind of guidance, D'Angelo glanced toward Elizabeth Carlyle. He didn't have a particularly warm relationship with her. She wasn't the type of person who joked around—it was a quality he actually admired—but her vibe right then was downright hostile. It scared him, and for a moment he patted at his own pockets, making sure he hadn't lost his phone. "I'll see how we can do it," he said.

"Good," said Elizabeth. "I need to tell Scott. I'll be right back."

She left the room, and D'Angelo again turned his attention to Chris. The younger man shifted in his seat and stared out the window. He kept shaking his head—a gesture D'Angelo interpreted as an attempt to express disbelief.

"It's a company phone?" D'Angelo asked.

"Yes."

"Verizon?"

"Yes."

"iPhone?"

"Yeah."

"Tell me the number," said D'Angelo, taking a notepad off Elizabeth's desk.

Chris told him the number. After that D'Angelo had him run through the basics of the incident. The thief had been Asian, maybe Chinese, midforties, wearing a black suit. Chris said that after he noticed his phone missing, he tried to chase the man to a downtown-bound 6 train, but he missed him. He said he was 90 percent sure the man had boarded the train.

D'Angelo took out his cell phone and scrolled through his contacts looking for someone who would know how to wipe a powered-off iPhone. He called Emily Nolan, an ex-colleague from the FBI. The call went straight to voicemail. He left a message. Next he called Jerry Lamb, another colleague from the Bureau. D'Angelo—outlining the general scenario for Lamb—moved toward the window and looked down at Madison Avenue. Eighteen floors below, he saw people shuffling to their jobs. A feeling of well-being settled on him; he felt focused.

The feeling was short lived. First, Jerry informed him that as long as the phone remained off it couldn't be wiped—not without putting something on there first. *Yes, he was sure of that.*

Elizabeth, now trailed by Scott Driscoll, her closest ally in the firm, came back into the room. As D'Angelo tried to end the call, her face showed impatience.

He told her the bad news. He tried to soften it by saying the phone would probably end up getting shipped to China, where it would be wiped and sold on the black market. That didn't comfort her.

When she asked again, he confirmed that it couldn't be done. He watched her eyes close; she rubbed her temples. D'Angelo glanced at Scott Driscoll. He was skinny and normally walked around with his arms out like a weight lifter, but he now stood—arms crossed in front of himself—like he was going to throw up. He looked ashen. He was roughly the same age as D'Angelo, midfifties, but he looked older now.

Calm down, thought D'Angelo, forcing himself to take a steadying breath. In his mind, he began forming a sentence; the message was going to be that he should get over to Grand Central, contact the NYPD, and begin trying to track the thief. See if the cops knew this dude. Start working.

Before he could speak, Elizabeth had opened her eyes, turned to Scott Driscoll, and asked, "Valencia Walker?"

Driscoll nodded.

D'Angelo felt a pang of jealousy. He was standing right there—what the hell did they need to call her for? He knew better than to protest. Instead, he looked away, nodded like he agreed, and told himself they were calling her in because they were going to ask her to do things that they wouldn't ask someone from their own firm to do. They needed a buffer. By the time his eyes went back to Elizabeth, she had already placed the call.

A moment later she spoke into the phone: "Valencia, we have a situation," she said.

Valencia Walker was twenty-one blocks south of CDH's office. She was glad to excuse herself from the meeting she was in. She'd been expecting a call from Elizabeth and acted amused that it would be about a lost phone. What would she think of next?

After hanging up, she sent a text to two of her colleagues and told them she had a job that needed immediate attention. Were they in the city?

Milton Frazier responded instantly: *Affirmative.*

Me too, replied Billy Sharrock a moment later.

On the elevator ride down, Valencia texted them that the billing name for the job would be Hopscotch. She told Billy to go to Grand Central and contact the NYPD sergeant on duty: *Have him stand by.* She asked Milton to pick her up in front of Credit Suisse as soon as he could. Then she texted her assistant Danny Tsui and told him to drop everything, sit at his desk, and wait for further instruction.

As soon as the elevator doors opened, she stepped out and called Wally Philpott, an NYPD detective she paid for jobs like this. "How busy are you?" she asked, when he answered.

"Never too busy for you," said the cop.

"Can you meet me at Grand Central in half an hour?"

"Oh boy," said Wally. "Here we go."

Now it begins, thought Valencia as she made her way toward the building's exit. All of the men in the lobby—the security guards, couriers, and men in suits—watched her. She could feel it. She knew she was good-looking, and she dressed the part. She wore tailored suits, chic and expensive. But it wasn't her looks or clothes they were gaping at. They were staring at her because she carried herself like the most powerful person in the building, no matter what building she happened to be in.

That sense of power had been developed during her ten years as a case officer in the CIA. Her path to the Agency had been unusual. She had gone to college (University of Pennsylvania), bummed around New York for a bit after graduation, went to law school (NYU), and joined The Bronx Defenders. After five years, wanting to make more money and needing a change of scenery, she applied for a position on the legal team of a large consulting firm. They had offices in Istanbul. She'd spent her junior year of college studying abroad at Boğaziçi University and spoke some Turkish. The job seemed like a natural fit.

One of her first jobs in Turkey involved handling some negotiations with a large communications technology company. Her counterpart at the company was a man named Hugh Loftus, a loud, big-bellied Texan. He had a red face, and he drank constantly, even during business hours. They spent months working together.

One night, they were in Emirgan, a neighborhood on the Bosphorus, having drinks with some of their Turkish colleagues. They were seated outside, and the sun was setting. Valencia looked across the table at Hugh. His face had become serious, something that rarely happened. He asked her to join him for a cigarette. She didn't smoke, but she stood up and followed him to the sidewalk.

When they were away from the group, he lit his cigarette, looked over his shoulder, and pulled Valencia by the arm so she was closer. They walked away from the outside tables. She worried that he was going to hit on her.

"You know, I used to work for the government," he said. "Would you ever think of doing that?"

Valencia told him her last job had been with The Bronx Defenders.

He smiled, shook his head, and looked down the river. "I'm talking Government with a big G, you hear me, right?"

Valencia smiled and raised her eyebrows theatrically. "You mean spy?"

"I'm gonna recommend you."

She asked why, and he told her he liked the way she carried herself. "You seem comfortable in your skin," he said. "Your Turkish is decent. You don't have any damn relatives here. And you brought me a Killen's steak when you came to negotiate."

She smiled.

"You flew it all the way in from Houston."

She reminded him that she'd also brought a bottle of bourbon.

"And that," he said, tapping her shoulder with his fat finger.

Still, she thought he was joking, and she paid him no mind.

Two weeks later, he called and said that a friend was in town. Maybe she'd like to meet him? She didn't need to ask what the meeting was about. She understood now. Before then, she'd never thought of being a spy; she had never even considered it. But just like that, it all made sense. Her life clicked into place. She couldn't sleep that night. She was too excited.

She met Hugh's friend—a thoughtful man who introduced himself as Cunningham—took a walk with him, answered questions about her life, asked him about his. The CIA was never mentioned. It all seemed very informal. A month later, Hugh met back up with her. "It's time to take a leave of absence," he said. "It'll be good for you."

She returned to the United States and spent the next year taking tests, being polygraphed, psychologically profiled, and waiting for her background to clear. She did contract work to pay her bills. On February 21, 2000, she received a generic envelope in the mail.

When she opened it, she saw it was from "the Office of Personnel." It didn't say anything about the CIA, but it told her to report for duty in three weeks.

In March of 2000, she began her two-week orientation. From there she was assigned to a desk in the European Division, Turkey section, of the Clandestine Service. She spent her days reading intelligence reports, serving as an interagency liaison, and doing whatever her branch chief—a skinny, unassuming man, called Culpepper—asked.

After three months on the desk she was sent to The Farm for operational training. Her assessment had flagged her as a natural recruiter. Her charts showed that she was exceptional at winning people's trust. She would be trained to spot, assess, develop, recruit, and run foreign agents. Her training, of course, would also include all things operational: countersurveillance, weapons, disguise, counterfeiting, and communications.

Beyond normal spycraft, her lessons also included more esoteric things: acting (taught by an ex-Broadway actor), somatic regulation, and interpersonal manipulation (both taught by a husband-and-wife team of Rice University psychologists).

The ten months at The Farm was the happiest time of her life. After The Farm she did a monthlong crash course in Turkish at CIA University in Chantilly, Virginia. From there she did four two-year postings abroad (and one in the United States). Her first was at the legal office in the American embassy in Turkey. Officially, she was working for the State Department. Unofficially, she was recruiting and running agents, Turkish and otherwise.

She arrived in May of 2001. Four months later, on September 11, America was attacked. The world changed quickly.

Milton Frazier, one of Valencia's men, had also been an officer in the Agency. His path there had been more standard; he'd joined after being in the Special Forces. They had never met while they were overseas. He had heard of her, though, and he read her reports.

Milton joined Valencia's firm four years ago. He'd been sleeping with her for the last six months. She had initiated it. It was a strange affair. She was almost ten years older than him. They barely talked about what they were doing—which was fine with Milton, since he was married and had two kids.

As he pulled up to Credit Suisse, he saw Valencia standing near the door. She had her phone to her ear and her lips were moving, but her eyes tracked his approach. Right when he stopped, she ended her call and hopped in the front seat.

"Some kid had his phone stolen," said Valencia.

"What?"

"A lawyer at CDH."

"What kinda shit was on this phone?"

"The kind they'd rather not have floating around the toilet," said Valencia.

Milton watched her pull the visor down and check her lipstick. She cleaned her teeth with her tongue and then looked at him. The look told him to stop staring at her. His eyes went back to the road; he checked all his mirrors and noted the plate numbers behind him.

When they arrived at Elizabeth Carlyle's office, a security guard accompanied them in the elevator to the eighteenth floor. Elizabeth's assistant stood there waiting; after a quick greeting, he ushered them back toward a quiet conference room. Milton walked slightly behind the group so he could sanitize his hands without being observed.

When they entered the room, Milton saw Elizabeth Carlyle—who he'd met a dozen times—leaning on a table tapping at her phone. Elizabeth hired Valencia's firm whenever she needed a sticky situation taken care of. These jobs, by their very nature, usually fell into ethically gray areas. Standing there, Milton thought about the last thing he'd done for them. He'd been tasked with explaining the downside of testifying to a witness in a securities fraud case.

Milton had laid out exactly what refusing to testify would look like. The witness would be held in contempt of court. He might end up sitting in jail for the duration of the trial. But that was extremely unlikely, and still, wouldn't that be less bothersome than ending up on the wrong side of a lawsuit?

Milton delivered this message in a friendly way; he smiled and spoke like a buddy offering advice. It was, strictly speaking, witness tampering. And if any of it ever came back on them Milton knew he'd have to take the fall. Elizabeth Carlyle certainly never asked for him to do anything like that. Neither did Valencia Walker. He'd acted on his own. That's why he got paid the big bucks.

Still, with all the jobs they'd done for the law firm, Milton had never exchanged more than vague pleasantries with Elizabeth. Valencia always dealt with her. The two women didn't email. They'd meet for lunch, and Valencia would come back with the job.

Right then, when they stepped inside the conference room, Elizabeth looked up and shook her head as though trying to impart what a mess they were walking into. There seemed to be a shared bad mood in the room. It seemed worse than normal.

Seated at the table was an exhausted-looking young man Milton assumed was the lawyer who'd lost his phone. The third person was a white man in his fifties who stood up, walked over, and offered Valencia his hand.

Milton watched Valencia smile warmly and ask about his old boss in Newark, Donnegan. *Always working the crowds*, thought Milton. The woman was like a damn politician.

"Michael D'Angelo," said Valencia, motioning toward Milton. "You've met Milton Frazier? He works for me."

"Pleased to meet you, sir," said Milton, shaking hands.

"Is this the kid?" asked Valencia.

Elizabeth closed her eyes and nodded. "Chris Cowley," she said, barely able to hide her distaste.

Milton walked around the table and leaned against the far wall to watch. He knew that's where Valencia would want him. It also allowed him to keep his eyes on the door, a remnant from his years abroad.

"Okay, sweetie, let's sit face-to-face so we can talk," said Valencia, smiling at the young man. "Pull your chair out." Valencia then set a chair directly in front of his and sat on it. Their knees were a few inches apart. "That's good."

Milton watched her stare at the young man in silence for a long moment. It was a two-step process: first she wanted to raise his blood pressure and then she wanted to see how he'd react to direct attention. The performance wasn't just for her interview subject, though; she was telling everyone in the room—particularly Elizabeth and her investigator—that she was in charge. This was her case now.

Milton's gaze returned to the kid. He didn't look particularly impressive. He was definitely young: a blonde lawyer, a little baby. A little white boy. Milton watched Valencia lean in and sniff the air between them.

"Have you been drinking?" she asked.

"Last night," said the lawyer.

Valencia took hold of his wrists. While she did this, Milton stole a quick glance at Elizabeth and the investigator. They both watched with rapt attention. Elizabeth was blinking, as if she had allergies. D'Angelo crossed his arms, apparently aware that Milton was looking at him.

Holding the kid's wrists in each of her hands, Valencia let an uncomfortable amount of time pass. She stayed still. Later she told Milton that the lawyer's pulse was fast—somewhere around ninety-five beats per minute. But she didn't say anything about it then.

Finally, she let his wrists go, and leaned back. The young man was nervous, Milton could see that from where he stood. But nervousness could be expected; at the very least, the kid was going to lose his job.

Valencia asked how he'd gotten to work that morning.

"I took the A train to Fulton, then the 4 to Grand Central." The words had a rehearsed quality. Milton marked it in his mind and filed it away.

Valencia made Chris Cowley run through the whole trip: where he boarded, where in the car he rode, where he got off.

When Chris finished, D'Angelo handed Valencia a manila folder. "This is the subscriber information, if you want that," he said. He then filled in a few more details: the location and the time of the incident. From the notes he'd taken, he read the description of the thief.

Valencia opened the file he'd given her, looked at it, and handed it to Milton. "I'm going to ask you all to stop doing anything more from here on out," she said. She turned to D'Angelo. "Nothing. No Find My Phone app, no calls to the target phone. No police. No nothing."

D'Angelo dropped his head.

Valencia turned back to Elizabeth. "Liz, sweetie, I want you to go on with your day. Go to the meetings you have to attend. If you have a lunch date, go to it. We'll keep you posted. Hopefully we'll have it all sorted out in a few hours."

She turned back to Chris. "All right, you're going to come with us," she said. "Show us exactly what happened." She stood, offered Elizabeth a small smile.

Milton nodded his goodbye to D'Angelo and shook Elizabeth's hand. "We'll get it back," he told her.

"I was right here," Chris Cowley said, pointing at the ground. He was showing Valencia Walker and Milton Frazier where the theft had occurred. They stood in one of the tiled hallways of Grand Central Station, where a seemingly endless crowd of pedestrians walked past without paying them any attention.

"I was walking this way, and the guy just bumped me. I said, 'sorry,' because I thought it was my fault, and kept moving." He pointed in the direction they'd just come from.

"Don't point," said Valencia. "Just talk."

"Right here, then."

"And after that?"

"Then I exited—sorry—I exited, noticed what happened, hopped that turnstile, and ran back over this way. First I went over there"—he pointed toward the 7 train platform—"'cause I thought I saw him down that way. But he wasn't there, so I ran over that way to the 4-5-6, and missed a 6 train." He pantomimed banging on the door.

"Downtown?" asked Milton.

"Downtown."

"Did you see the man?"

"I think I saw him on the train when it passed, but I can't say for sure."

Chris then led them to where he'd missed the train.

"It was right around here." He turned and surveyed the area for a moment. A few commuters watched them with a kind of grumpy midmorning nonchalance.

Chris wondered if anyone else was watching them. He pointed toward a movie poster. "After I missed him I looked at that poster, and then I walked toward that exit."

Feeling suddenly hungover, Cowley stared that way before he glanced back at Valencia. He couldn't place her exact age; she appeared to be in her late forties or early fifties. She watched him with a slightly amused expression on her face. She wore eyeliner and lipstick, but no other makeup. She seemed extremely capable, and Chris couldn't help being impressed.

He then looked at her associate, Milton, who was listening with his hands behind his back. The dude dressed well, Chris gave him that—expensive suit, perfect shoes. He was black and had a shaved head. His face, to Chris, looked skeptical—a kind of professional skepticism. Even under the circumstances, Chris couldn't help noticing how attractive he was. The man clearly worked out.

Their eyes met for a moment, and Chris tried to psychically convey his romantic feelings without being obvious. *I'm here*, he said to Milton in his mind, *if you're interested.*

"Call Danny Boy," said Valencia to Milton. "Tell him to contact Arty Jacobson at Metro Authority. Tell him to pull the tape from—where are we? Downtown 4-5-6, approximately sixty-something yards north of the south wall. Tell him this gentleman here"—she pointed at Chris—"ran for the train, missed it, and you said you hit the door?"

"Yeah," said Chris.

"Hit the door. And were you in that suit?"

"No, I was wearing a black leather jacket and jeans," said Chris, feeling slightly embarrassed as he said it.

"Black leather jacket. Track it all the way back to when he gets off the train here in Grand Central. Tell him we need the video right this moment," said Valencia, dropping her chin to emphasize the point. "Money is not an object. I don't care if he's in a meeting with the governor, we need it now."

"Got it," said Milton.

Right then another man in a suit approached the group. Valencia introduced him: "Chris, this is Billy Sharrock, one of our other associates."

They shook hands. Billy Sharrock, like Milton Frazier, appeared to be in his early forties: *a white version*, thought Chris. He looked more dangerous; he had rough skin and his brown hair was gelled straight back. His suit, like Milton's, was well cut, but he seemed somehow uncomfortable in it.

"We'll find your phone," said Valencia. She punctuated this by smiling at the group. Chris wasn't sure if anyone knew what that smile was supposed to mean. "Billy can find anything," she added, looking at her watch like she was pointing out his tardiness.

Suddenly bashful, Billy stood there gazing at his feet.

A Chinese man named Ren Xiong stole the phone. Forty-four years old, he'd been in America for less than eighteen months. Just as Chris Cowley reported, he had jumped on a downtown-bound 6 train and ridden six stops from Grand Central to Bleecker Street. From there he exited on foot and headed west toward Washington Square Park. He'd already practiced this route, and was familiar with it, but today, after the theft, everything seemed to stand out with more clarity. He felt intoxicated, as if he were on amphetamines.

There was a camera on the corner of Broadway and Bleecker above the doorway of a shop. Xiong turned his head as he passed, but he didn't fully avoid it. Up to a point, he was supposed to be seen; then he would vanish.

As he walked, the incident played through his mind. It had gone well. Nobody had seen him. He could still feel the inside of the pocket against the back of his hand. He could feel where their shoulders had touched, a kind of physical memory of the event.

He carried the stolen phone, powered off, in his front pants pocket, tapping it every few steps to make sure it was there. A white woman walked by, and he couldn't help glancing at her. It was a beautiful day, the weather was still cool, but there was a hint of warmth in the air. Spring was coming. It would be his second American spring.

At that early hour, the park wasn't crowded. Students walked to class with their eyes on their phones. A few homeless people slumped on benches. A maintenance man fussed with a trash can. Pigeons looked for scraps of food.

Xiong made his way to the west side of the park, where the first few games of chess had already started. He approached a table and watched a Nigerian man he knew—Malik Abdul Onweno—make quick work of an older Russian. Xiong watched Malik's rook chase the Russian's king. The Russian retreated hastily. After each move, the men slapped at a timer. Malik's queen jumped to the back rank, and Xiong—unlike the Russian—could see the match would be finished in two moves.

"That's it. Lights out. Checkmate," said the Nigerian, standing up triumphantly. He noticed Xiong for the first time.

"Wassup with it, man?" he said, stepping toward him and laying a hand on his back. Xiong had told him to be here at this hour, and he was. He studied the man's face and read a hint of nervousness.

The Nigerian turned to a friend of his, raised his hand to his mouth like he was whispering, and called out, "God Save, take my spot." The younger man, God Save, jumped up and took his spot at the table.

"Wassup with you?" asked Malik. He escorted Xiong away from the chess players, one hand on his arm like a jail guard.

"I have the phone I spoke about."

Malik guided him to a park bench where they sat. Xiong handed him the phone. The Nigerian made a show of rubbing his thumb across some scratches on the back and then made another show of picking at a scratch on the screen with his thumbnail. "It works?"

"Yes," said Xiong.

Malik, as though he was breaking bad news, said, "I can give you sixty for this."

Xiong frowned and nodded. He didn't care about the money. His eyes shifted to the park in front of him, and he looked for cameras. Now was the time to start avoiding them. How long did he have until someone came looking for him?

The thought caused a small wave of apprehension to pass over him. He ignored it by staring at the ground. His mind drifted to a memory of being in the Hai River Park in Tianjin. The image of his father passing out ear-hole fried cake came to him for a moment. It vanished when Malik tapped his arm and held out three twenty-dollar bills between his index and middle finger. Xiong took the money, folded it, and put it in his coat pocket. For Malik's benefit, he formed his mouth into a smile, and then leaned close to his ear so he could whisper: "You don't want to hold this one. Tell your guy the same."

Malik leaned forward and whistled to another young man. When the young man rode up on a bike, he held the phone out like a ticket. "Take this to the Jew," he said. He then pulled a roll of Scotch Tape from his pocket, ripped off an inch, and put it on the back of the phone. He held it up so the young man could see the tape. "This one, don't hold on to it," he said. "Don't sit with it, man. I'm not playing. Don't eat your lunch—you got to move this one. Tell him the same."

Youssouf Wolde, the young man who took the phone, was an eighteen-year-old Somali. After Malik handed him the phone and gave him his instructions, he put it in his backpack with the others. He glanced at the man sitting with Malik and wondered how his friend knew so many people. Then he put his earphones back on, fussed with his own phone, and pressed play. He was listening to Bobby Shmurda.

The man they called the Jew kept his office in the Diamond District.

Youssouf rode his bike up Sixth Avenue all the way to West Forty-Seventh Street. When he got there, he turned against traffic and pedaled to the middle of the block. Before he'd finished locking his bike to a light pole, two large Israeli men approached him. One wore a tracksuit and looked like a Tel Aviv gangster; the other wore jeans and a sweater and a Bluetooth earpiece. Youssouf recognized their faces but didn't know their names.

"Brother, you looking to sell?" said the man in the tracksuit.

"Nah, I'm good," said Youssouf.

"Where's Omar?" asked the other man.

Youssouf wasn't sure which Omar he was referring to, so he just shrugged his shoulders and told him he didn't know.

Centered between all the jewelry shops was an electronics store called Asia Model, filled with tall stacks of merchandise. Discordant beeps and bells rang out from the toy section. Youssouf made his way toward the back of the shop, stepping around an old man, who was squatting to see something at the bottom of a shelf.

A clerk at the counter, a man Youssouf was friendly with, saw him and called out, "Opa, where's my lunch?" Youssouf didn't know what he was talking about, either, so he just laughed him off and kept moving.

Before reaching the back of the store, Youssouf went through a doorway on his right that led to a quiet hallway. He passed through another doorway and then skipped up the stairs, two at a time, until he reached the third floor. As he walked, in his mind he repeated the rap lyrics he'd just been listening to: *Making all this loot 'til it stacks. Boy call me real 'cause I'm racks.*

At the end of the hall, he came to a door with a piece of paper taped to it that read *American iPhone Repair.* He walked in. True to the name, inside he found four men seated at their desks repairing iPhones. Three of the men glanced up at him, and one, Ohad, an Israeli, rose to his feet.

"Wassup, player?" said the Israeli.

"Is Avram here?"

Ohad sat back down. "Yeah, yeah, go," he said, seeming sad that Youssouf wasn't there for him.

Youssouf proceeded forward and the next door was buzzed open. He entered a second room, brightly lit, where six additional men sat repairing phones. A few of them glanced up and nodded. Techno music played from a small speaker in the middle of the room. Youssouf continued to the back, where another door buzzed open.

This room had a window and was nicer than the other two. Seated behind a desk cluttered with paper was Avram Lessing. He wore a blue oversized New York Giants hoodie. The top of his bald head was partially covered by a yarmulke. His face, despite the baldness and his age, was chubby and youthful. He wore glasses.

He was talking on the phone. "Mommy, I have to go now," he said, gesturing to Youssouf to sit. "No, no, tell Aba I'll call him back." He ended the call, and with a cocky expression looked over. "So?"

"I got six," said Youssouf.

Avram picked up a bag of toffee candies and offered them to his guest; Youssouf took a small handful, opened a toffee, put it in his mouth, and put the others in his pants pocket.

"Six 7s, any 8s?" asked Avram.

"Man, they iPhones, that's all I know."

"So, break 'em out, fam."

Youssouf smiled; he liked Avram.

He was about to get up when he remembered the instructions Malik had given him. He opened the bag, dug around in the phones, and pulled out the one with the inch of Scotch Tape on the back. After holding it up and showing Avram, he spoke in a whisper: "This one—you don't want to hold on to this one."

Elizabeth Carlyle sat at her desk and considered the calls she could make. For starters, she could try Edwin Kerins, the most reasonable of Calcott Corporation's in-house counsel. She'd explain to him that one of her junior associates had taken a copy of the documents out of the office. *He had them on his phone,* she'd say. *Yes, the phone was stolen.*

Then she'd have to call Charles Bloom, Calcott's CEO. She pictured him for a second, saw his saggy-skinned face, and felt sick. She'd call all the partners of her firm, of course, even the ones who were out of town. She'd tell them all what had happened. The calls would be miserable. There would be yelling, confusion, and long, predictable silences as people tried to understand exactly what she was saying. Recriminations, finger pointing.

Worst of all, though, someone would try to soothe her, someone would try to minimize the damage, tell her it wasn't her fault. Fucking idiots. A Rolodex of idiots played through her mind. All of them. Every single one.

The fact of the matter was that after thirty-one years of practicing law, Elizabeth Carlyle was burnt out. Her twelve-hour days should have become shorter long ago. She was a named partner; she didn't have to work the hours she did. But that wasn't how she operated. She needed to touch every facet.

Elizabeth had known she was going to be a lawyer since the sixth grade. Her father had been an attorney, but he wasn't her inspiration. It was another classmate's father, a man called Mr. Holland, who made a presentation on constitutional law to Elizabeth's sixth grade class.

"If you know the rules," he said, standing in front of the class, and looking right at little Lizzie Ording, "and you prepare, and you come to court, you will win the case."

The theory, of course, turned out to be false. Still, something about it stood out. If she prepared more than anyone else, she would win. If she knew the law better, she would win. If she learned how to act and carry herself in the courtroom, if she learned how to charm judges and juries, she would win.

In other words, there was a way to bring order to the universe. She started, right there and then, to think of herself as a lawyer, and told her mother and father that night that she would study the law.

She went to Georgetown, graduated summa cum laude, and headed straight to law school at Yale. From there she jumped into a clerkship with the honorable Edward R. Monroe at the Third Circuit Court of Appeals. A year later she was scooped up by Heller, Bromwell, Burgess, Drake—which, at the time, was the most prestigious law firm in New York City.

She specialized in Chapter 11 reorganization, and then shifted to white-collar crime, and then finally settled in civil litigation. After six years she was poached by a rival firm, Mooney, Driscoll, Hathaway, Evans, Miller. A decade and a half later, in the midst of the 2008 meltdown, that firm dissolved and reorganized as Carlyle, Driscoll, and Hathaway. She'd made it.

It didn't feel that way now. She looked at her hands. They looked suddenly older than they had the day before. The veins seemed more pronounced, the skin more scaly. They reminded her of her grandmother's hands. A tiny sliver of unpainted nail could be seen peeking from the bottom of her sensible red polish. *Not my fault*, she said in her mind. *Not my fault.*

Her thoughts shifted to the Calcott case. The thing was like a cancer that kept spreading. The case had started after a failed merger between the two banks. During the due diligence period, Emerson's accountants had discovered an irregularity in Calcott's records. Elizabeth had been tasked with looking into it. She discovered that a small group inside the bank's special opportunities fund had been funneling large sums of money to a shell company in Oman. It was a mind-boggling violation of FCPA rules.

When she reported it to the CEO, Charles Bloom, he told her that the fund was experimental. He frowned. "Bury it," he said. "Just bury it."

"Excuse me?" she asked.

"Bury it," he repeated. "Tell the fund they're gonna have to gas up at the Middle East Section from now on. Tell them to make this right."

"I'm not telling them anything," she said.

"I'll do it," he said, smiling as if she were making a big deal out of nothing—like she was some kind of prude.

The question of the irregularities in the fund's books wasn't going to just go away. A week later, Elizabeth convinced Calcott's in-house attorneys that the best way out was to walk away from the merger. She warned them that Emerson would sue for breach of contract, but the claims involved in that lawsuit would be far less toxic than this Oman bullshit.

Elizabeth outlined their response: They would countersue with enough claims that Emerson would be forced to back down. Emerson wouldn't want to have a nuclear war over this. Nobody did. They would back down. The board took Elizabeth's advice. They walked away from the merger.

Elizabeth ended up being right about everything—except Emerson backing down.

Chris Cowley was glad to have a moment to himself. He'd been in the front seat of Valencia's SUV for the past ten minutes. They'd told him to wait there. He didn't have his iPhone, so he sat rubbing his forehead and watching pedestrians come and go. A mellow, post-adrenalized feeling had settled over him; it reminded him of how he'd felt as a child, after a good cry. The worst was over.

Time would wash the details of this memory away. *Temporary problems*, he told himself. In ten or fifteen years, he would have a hard time describing the vehicle he was sitting in right then. His eyes moved around the front of the SUV and settled on the glove compartment. Did the woman keep a gun in there?

He studied it for a moment, then leaned forward and tried to open it. It was locked. He was just beginning to wonder how hard it would be to pick the lock when someone banged on the passenger window right next to his head. When he looked out, he saw a thin-haired, white guy looking down at him. The man was dressed in an ill-fitting suit; he had cop written all over him, head to toe.

"NYPD, kid—open up."

Chris, upset about being startled, didn't roll down the window. "Can I help you?"

"Open the door."

Chris dug in deeper. "They said they'll be right back. It's not my car. I can't move it, Officer."

The two men locked eyes.

"Come on kid, open up. Valencia called me. She wants me to sit here with you." The cop smiled halfheartedly. The whole thing seemed like some kind of game. Chris opened the door and stepped out.

The cop coughed into his left hand and then held out his right. "Wally Philpott," he said.

"Chris Cowley," said Chris. They shook hands.

Even during this simple exchange, the cop seemed to be measuring him in some way. He seemed to believe he could read a man's mind by looking at his face. It almost made Chris want to laugh.

The cop gestured at the vehicle. "Let's wait in the car," he said.

"I can't let you in there, I'm sorry," said Chris. "It's not mine." He took another step away from the car.

"Gotta be careful these days," said the cop, shifting his head inquisitively from one side to the other. "Thieves everywhere, right?" He tapped at what must've been his gun under his coat. "They pay all right, though," he added, nodding back at Grand Central, almost as if he were speaking to himself.

Chris turned his gaze past him, hoping he'd see Valencia and her associates. He was getting impatient.

"This guy get you with a bump and brush?" asked the cop.

Chris knew what he was asking, but he still wasn't sure he should be talking to him. "You work for Valencia?" he asked.

"She hires me sometimes," said the cop, looking away for a moment as though he shouldn't be admitting so much. He coughed again, looked back and continued, "Lawyer?"

"Look," said Chris, raising his hands apologetically, "I'm sure you're a good guy, but until Valencia gets here, I'd rather not talk about anything. You understand, right?"

"Yeah, I got you kid. I'm just shooting the shit, don't worry about it." He reached forward and slapped Chris on the shoulder, a gesture that was both friendly and not. The cop's eyes continued to search Chris's face.

Remembering that he'd snorted a little cocaine the previous night, Chris gave his nose a quick rub with his right index finger. He sniffled. The idea of sex passed through his mind. He looked at the cop and imagined being fucked by him. It brought a small level of comfort.

"You watch the playoffs?" asked the cop.

Chris rubbed his nose again. "I'm afraid not."

The cop exhaled. A moment passed. "There she is," he said, nodding toward Forty-Second Street.

Chris saw Valencia walking in their direction, her eyes directly on him as she approached. It took effort not to look away or drop his gaze down to the ground like a man with a guilty conscience; instead, Chris scratched at his head and then rubbed his eyes.

"Good, you met Wally," Valencia said when she arrived. Chris watched her shake hands with the cop and pat him on the back.

The cop then quickly shook hands with the other two men, and Chris watched Milton pass the cop a white envelope. The cop put the envelope in his inside jacket pocket without looking at it and Chris assumed that it contained money.

Valencia moved closer to Chris and held her phone up for him. He had to lean in, but when he did, he saw an image of the pickpocket grabbed from a surveillance camera.

"Is that him?" asked Valencia.

Chris squinted at the image. "I think so."

"Okay, good," said Valencia. She took the phone and squinted down at it, just as Chris had. For a moment he wondered if she was making fun of him. "Good," she repeated.

Her phone rang. She plugged one ear and answered. "Yeah, Danny?" She listened. "Okay, Bleecker Street. Six train"—she nodded and lifted her eyebrows at Milton—"8:26 a.m., northwest exit onto Bleecker."

Phone to her ear, she turned and nodded at her companions. She looked happy. "Very nice work, Danny. No, thank you. Okay call me then." She ended the call. "Bleecker Street," she said.

After wasting almost an hour and a half on Facebook, Avi Lessing was feeling frustrated with his lack of workplace discipline. He placed all six of the phones he'd purchased from Youssouf Wolde in a canvas tote bag, pushed himself up from his seat, pulled out his set of keys, and unlocked a door in the back of his office.

Behind the door was a fairly large walk-in closet. Avi had repurposed it by lining the walls, floor, and ceiling with copper sheeting. Inside what he called the Gold Room—his employees called it the Wank Room—was a desk, a chair, a desktop computer, a fan, and a lamp. The copper sheeting prevented Wi-Fi or cellular signals from leaving or entering. No GPS, no remote cameras, no calls. No Find My Phone: Avi could snoop as much as he wanted.

After turning on the lamp, he closed the door, locked it, and sat down. He turned on the computer, and then, one by one powered up each of the six iPhones. *I'm tired*, he thought, while he waited for the phones to boot up. *I need to stop eating that bullshit for breakfast. Can't eat sugar cereal, gotta eat fruit and lean proteins.*

When the first phone was ready, he grabbed it, pressed the home button, and saw the prompt for a passcode. He turned the phone off and set it aside. The same thing happened with the second and third phones.

The fourth phone was Chris Cowley's. Avi pressed the button and saw a home screen, with some kind of painting of a pool. It looked like Miami. White water splashed up where someone had just dived in. He saw the time and date in white. He turned the phone over and saw the piece of tape on the back. This was the phone Youssouf had said not to hold on to.

The battery icon showed three-quarters of a charge. He pressed the home button again, and quickly scanned the apps and programs. There were no social media apps, and no bank apps. He thumbed around for a few moments, wondering where to look first.

Credit bitch, gimme that credit shit, he said in his mind, thinking, like he sometimes did, in the voice of a rapper. *Wassup mommy? Wassup mommy? You wanna ride on my Ducati? You wanna ride in my Bugatti? I'm about that passcode shit.*

He pressed the phone's photo icon and looked at the pictures. Nada. A few selfies; a dinner; a long-haired man; a sunset; a shot of Manhattan taken from Brooklyn; a group of drunk men laughing in front of a bar. No girls. Nothing good. He made little clicking noises with his tongue while he looked.

Next he tapped the documents folder. Inside was a single file, titled *Calcott Hot Docs_1_36*. He squinted at it for a moment, and then tapped on it. A trove of hundreds of files appeared. He felt himself frown, and leaning forward in his seat, he began fingering around in these files.

The first few batches seemed to be financial records of some sort. Spreadsheets, they didn't mean anything to him. Next, he came across what seemed to be an archive of old emails. *What is this shit?* he wondered. He skimmed and skimmed: *Calcott. Calcott. VP. Todd. Careful. Breadth. Magic. Disclosures.*

A quiet, euphoric feeling came over him. *Oh yeah, bitch.* The clicking noises he made with his tongue and mouth increased in volume. These were not normal emails. This was juicy. Some of them were marked *Confidential.* Some were brief, some were long. Some were corporate-sounding, some sounded casual. He didn't know what exactly they were about, but he knew they seemed important.

"Mmm-hmm," he said, nodding and leaning forward.

Over the next few days and weeks, he'd think about that moment. He'd play it over in his head again and again. He had a chance to act differently. There had been a brief amount of time—not more than ten seconds, really—between when he stopped skimming the emails and when he began copying them. Later, he'd look back and wonder whether he had felt any kind of apprehension.

Maybe a small amount of reluctance—a quiet warning, something like, *No, it's too much work.* It wasn't enough to stop him. He plugged his USB cord into the phone. He clicked with his mouse, and a prompt asked him if he wanted to save the files to his hard drive. He clicked *Yes.* He would come to regret that decision more than anything he'd ever done in his life.

When he finished copying the files onto his computer, he stepped back out to his office and googled: "Calcott Corporation" + "New York." One of the first results that popped up was an article in the *New York Times* from a few months ago that mentioned a lawsuit between two banks.

He skimmed through a few paragraphs: *The specter of a trial has Wall Street on pins and needles.* Farther down: *What once seemed unlikely, now seems inevitable.* In the middle of the story was a picture of one of Calcott's attorneys, Elizabeth Carlyle.

He looked at her for a moment, zooming in on the image. She looked powerful, like a senator or something. A quick search and he was on her Wikipedia page. She was definitely a big-time player. This was big. This was the real deal. This wasn't for his homey in Queens. This was way above old Mick the Mook's pay grade. These weren't small-time matters. These documents were valuable. This was real shit. He knew just the person for this.

He'd sell them to Yuri Rabinowitz.

Yuri Rabinowitz, Yuri's brother Isaac, and a third man, their friend Moishe Groysman, were riding motorcycles back from Manhattan when the call came in. Yuri was thirty-one years old. His brother was twenty-eight. Moishe, at thirty-eight, was the oldest of the three. Their bikes were dark and loud. All three men wore black leather jackets; their helmets had mirrored visors. They looked macho and futuristic.

They had just visited a club in Chelsea. One of their associates—another Russian—had wanted them to invest in it. They had not been impressed. The place needed repairs. The walls in the kitchen were rotted. The ceiling in the main room hung low. There would be no investment. They could say as much to each other without words—a look was enough.

Still, they said no. They told their friend the place was a dump, and they asked him what the fuck he was wasting their time for.

Their friend, in an effort to seem important, had brought along an American real estate agent. The agent, a woman in her thirties, seemed a little nervous around the men. She held a paper file over her chest and kept her eyebrows lifted the entire time, as though her face had frozen in shock.

"What kind of club are you going to make here?" Yuri asked his friend in English.

"Ultra lounge," said the friend, with a shrug, as though the question were too obvious to answer.

Still, as bad as the club was, they weren't upset to have made the trip. It had given them an excuse to ride their motorcycles into Manhattan. They were on their way back to Sheepshead Bay, stopped at a light, when the call came in. Yuri didn't answer, but when he saw it was Avi calling, he pointed to the corner, and when the light changed, the three men turned right onto DeKalb and then backed their bikes up against the curb. Yuri, still seated on his bike, took his helmet off, hung it on his handlebar, and returned the call.

"You called back," said Avi.

"Avi—"

"Where are you?"

"Brooklyn."

"Listen . . . I have some documents, that you . . . that you might . . ."

"What the hell are you talking about?"

"Legal documents."

"About me?"

"No! Not about you. How do I say this—just—you would be interested in seeing them."

"Documents about who?"

"They're not about anyone, Yuri. I'm telling you: I think you might want to see them."

"Am I reporter? Why would I be interested in this?" He turned and made a *What-the-fuck* face for his brother and friend to see.

"It's better we talk in person," said Avi, clearly trying to stress how important these so-called documents were. "You need to come to my office. This is big. Trust me—this is big. I guarantee you."

"Avi, I swear to God—I'm going to break your fucking neck."

"Come to my office and break my neck if you want."

The line went dead. Yuri looked at his brother and, speaking in Russian, reported what Avi had said. His brother shook his head and smiled. Their friend Moishe had taken off his helmet and was staring at Yuri with a flat expression.

They headed back to Manhattan.

Ren Xiong stood outside a fruit and vegetable market just down the block from his apartment building. He stood with the posture of a man searching for produce, but his intention was to examine the street. He didn't expect to see anything amiss, but it would have been foolish not to stop and look.

Will I ever see this street again? he wondered. After a moment of watching, he picked up a red apple and examined it for bruises. *I need a drink, not an apple*, he thought. His gaze returned to the street; he paid special attention to every car on the block. Only one of the parked cars was occupied. He watched the car for a few seconds and then entered the store. The apple cost seventy-five cents; he paid with loose change.

Crossing the street with his shoulders slumped, Xiong headed toward his building. He took a bite of the apple and then slowed his pace so he could finish it and throw it away before he went in. As he passed the car, he glanced in and saw a young girl, probably not more than fifteen, sitting in the front passenger seat. She looked like she was daydreaming.

Xiong's apartment was above a Chinese meat market on Mott Street. The five-story building was filled with mostly Fuzhounese tenants. Country people. Tiny apartments, dirty hallways, bright fluorescent lights. Xiong stopped outside the meat market and threw his half-eaten apple into a trash can. He had his keys out before he reached the door. After entering his building, he closed the door in a manner that allowed him to take a final look at the street behind him. Nothing.

He took the stairs, two at a time, to the fourth floor. In the hallway, one of his neighbors, an older woman, was just entering her apartment. Xiong pulled out his phone and slowed his pace by pretending to send a text message. When he was alone in the hall, he squatted down and examined the kit he'd set at his door. It was a small thing, just a sewing needle he'd cut down to the size of a thumbnail. He'd leaned the needle against the door near the doorframe. If anyone opened the door, the needle would fall. The needle stood.

He still opened the door with caution—the kit didn't address the issue of the window. Once inside his room, he exhaled, scratched his scalp, and let his eyes wander over his small space in search of anything out of the ordinary. He did this every time he entered his room, even when he'd been drinking. Everything seemed to be in order. The place looked fine.

The act of standing near his bed brought on a desire to sleep, but he ignored it and took off his suit coat, zipped it into a black garment bag, and hung it in the back of his closet. He changed into a different pair of pants, a different button-up shirt, and a windbreaker. He wanted to look like everyone else in Chinatown. He found a wool baseball hat in the closet, put it on, and looked at himself in the mirror. He looked old, and this made him depressed.

Xiong pulled two different suits and two shirts out of the closet and set them on the bed. He set four pairs of underwear and socks on the bed next to the suits. He pulled three T-shirts from a dresser, and one pair of polyester sweatpants. There wasn't much else in his small apartment, but everything that remained would be picked up and disposed of tonight. The place would be scrubbed, bleached, and vacuumed by professionals.

He set his suitcase on the bed, folded his suits into the bottom, and put the shirts and underclothes on top. He then grabbed the Chinese paperback he was reading and slipped it into one of the zip pockets. In the other, he put his toothbrush, toothpaste, and razor. He unplugged his digital clock, wrapped the power cord around it, and placed that in the suitcase too.

After zipping his suitcase closed, he went to his tiny bathroom, filled a glass with water, and watered the two plants on his windowsill. While watering the plants, he heard the distinct sound of the front door clanging shut. He moved to the wall that ran perpendicular to the hallway and placed his ear against it. A flaw in the building's design allowed him to hear footsteps in the stairway. He closed his eyes and listened. One person, climbing the stairs without haste.

He returned to the bathroom, wet a piece of toilet paper, and after cleaning the dust off the sink, and a few dried drops of yellow pee off the toilet rim, he threw the paper into the toilet and flushed it down. Then he wet another piece and quickly dusted the bedside table where the clock had been.

Rolling the suitcase behind him, Xiong stepped into the hallway and locked his door. He squatted so he could reset the needle, just in case he needed to return. Before he stood back up, his across-the-hall neighbor, a young boy, opened his own door and looked at him. Xiong had always liked the kid. He spoke to him in Chinese: "*Remember, if anyone comes looking, you don't know me.*"

"*I'll say, I don't know you,*" the kid said sleepily, like he'd just woken up from a nap.

Elizabeth Carlyle couldn't sit still. Every time she tried a feeling of panic began to concentrate itself in her midsection. If she stayed seated, the feeling would spread from her guts to her face and pull at her lips and temples. The area around her hairline had become damp with sweat. She didn't feel well.

She was walking down CDH's hallway with no particular destination in mind; it took effort to look natural. In her mind, she tried to find some comfort by telling herself that nobody could see the way she felt. As she walked, her eyes scanned the beige carpets; they were perfectly vacuumed, but that didn't bring the sense of comfort it sometimes did. Neither did the Corbusier furniture. The place looked dead to her.

Right then, Jennifer Jennings, a young associate, stepped up beside her and began filling her in on one of their other cases. "Sujung said she'll finish the motion by four p.m.," said Jennifer, as though they were already in the middle of a conversation. "Judge McEwan's clerk is waiting for it—thank God. Oscar Lim and Mary Ellen are doing cross prep and claim they'll be ready by Monday."

"Perfect," said Elizabeth, nodding her head and pursing her lips. *Perfect*, she repeated in her mind. She understood what the younger lawyer was saying but more by tone than by content. Jennifer drifted away and entered another office. She was replaced by another young associate, Vishal Desai. He was dressed in shirtsleeves.

"On ABSOL, the judge has continued the hearing until the four-teenth and says—"

"Why?" asked Elizabeth, not stopping, but turning her head and looking at the lawyer.

"He says he has a personal family event that will interfere with—"

"And we objected?" asked Elizabeth. This she understood. She felt her temperature rise another degree.

"Strenuously," said Vishal, looking appropriately nervous.

"So, there is nothing else we can do," said Elizabeth. For half a second she allowed her mouth to form the approximation of a smile. She was done with this conversation. Vishal was smart. He fell back as the other attorney had and entered his own office.

Elizabeth brushed her hair back with both hands. She did it once, twice, three times. Her mind bumped around what the two attorneys had just told her, and then it drifted back to Chris Cowley and his lost phone. Instead of visiting him, she continued walking to the north side of the building where Michael D'Angelo kept his office.

His door was closed. She knocked on it softly with the back of her hand like she was shaking dice.

"Come in," said the investigator.

She stepped in and let her eyes sweep over the place. It was devoid of any signs of a personal life. No family photos, no art, no plants, not even a calendar.

"Let me show you something," he said. He looked down at his computer, then made a pained face at the door. "Sorry, do you mind closing that?"

She closed his door, then walked around his desk to see the monitor. A nervous feeling bloomed in her belly. It felt like she was invading his space. She couldn't help sniffing the air as she stepped behind his desk—it smelled like soap. The man had a thick head of salt-and-pepper hair, which she examined, looking to see if he had dandruff. She didn't see any.

"Valencia's guy sent us the tape," he said.

She wiped at the corners of her mouth. "Excellent."

"Okay, so—" A silence fell over them while he backed up the video. She wondered if anyone had seen her go into his office. Her eyes went to his shoulders and she felt a fleeting sexual attraction. What would he do if she reached out and massaged him?

"So, look at this," he said.

She leaned closer to the screen.

"That's him," said D'Angelo, hovering his cursor over the paused image of Chris Cowley. He pressed play. Elizabeth squinted and watched as Chris proceeded down a hallway inside Grand Central. She watched him bump into a man and saw both men continue on their way. The investigator backed it up again. "What'd you see?"

"He picked his pocket?"

"Sure, but what else?"

"A talented thief?"

"What else?"

Her patience was running thin. "That they bumped?"

"Exactly," he said.

Elizabeth frowned. "Play it again."

They watched again, and she asked what he was suggesting.

"That they're looking at each other."

"Play it," she said.

He hit play. They watched the bump, and then he backed it up again to the same spot where Chris appeared to look at the man he was about to bump into; the man looked at him.

"Just tell me what you are suggesting," she said.

"That you should fire him."

Her mind replayed the calculations she'd already made. For the time being, Chris Cowley was more dangerous outside the firm. The math, once you removed the emotions, was simple. For now, she'd take him off the Calcott case and put him in a place where he couldn't do any more damage. They'd watch him. As soon as the case was concluded, they would fire him. But she didn't say anything; she just shook her head and frowned.

The investigator hit the space bar and the video played again. They watched the two men bump and then go on their way. "Would you ever bump into someone like that?" he asked.

"There are a million things I wouldn't do," said Elizabeth.

"Okay Billy, today your name is Morgan D. Hallinan," said Valencia, passing an FBI badge and photo ID forward to Billy. The photo on the identification card showed Billy's face and Morgan's name. The name Morgan Hallinan, if anybody checked, would trace back to a real agent with that name. "Foley Square. You remember him, right?"

"Sure," said Billy.

They were in the SUV. Milton was driving, Billy rode shotgun, and Valencia sat behind them in the middle row. She'd sent Chris Cowley back to his office, telling him to sit by his desk phone and not talk to anybody. Wally Philpott had his own car and was going to meet them in the Village.

She handed another badge forward. "And Milton, you are Alonzo J. Jones, Newark office, on special assignment with Special Agent Hallinan. Got it?"

"Lonzo Jones," said Milton, glancing in the rearview mirror.

They were driving under the large, middle-class tenement buildings on Third Avenue. Pedestrians standing at crosswalks watched them pass. Valencia cupped her hand, smelled her breath, and looked at an NYPD van parked on Thirty-First Street. She put two fingers on her left wrist and measured her pulse, a leftover childhood habit.

"We have fresh paperwork from Danny Boy," said Valencia, turning and reaching for a stack that had come out of a printer in the back of the SUV. "It looks decent. Signed, stamp, judge, blah, blah, warrant, obstruction—you know the deal."

She handed the forged paper work to Billy. "Anybody asks, you show them that. We'll start on Bleecker and head west from there." She was leaning forward now, with both of her hands resting on the back of both men's seats. "You'll take the first shop on the northwest corner, I'll jump forward one block, and we'll continue leapfrogging until we find a deviation." She looked at the traffic in front of her, leaned back in her seat, and breathed deeply.

Right then, her cell phone rang. It was Roger Dewey, an old associate from her government days. He worked for the DEA now, a high-level position. She'd left a message for him ten minutes ago. "Roger, how are you, my darling?"

He told her he was fine and laughed in a familiar way.

"Listen, I got a real situation here," she said. "I mean a real one. Remember Abu Dhabi?"

She heard the sound of an exhale, a mix of grunt and laugh. He asked if this would make them even.

"Even-steven," she said. She dropped her voice to a seductive level: "You guys are set up with a StingRay in Grand Central, right?" she asked.

He confirmed they were. He sounded a little uneasy with where this call might be headed.

"Okay, I need a list of all the cell phones that travelled from the 6 train platform—"

He cut her off and told her he couldn't get platform-specific information in any kind of timely way.

"Fine, so Grand Central, from 8:05 a.m., to the 6 train, Bleecker Street stop exit, 8:26 a.m."

He cursed and told her she was literally talking about Grand Central at rush hour.

"I know," she said. "Ha, ha, right?" She looked at the two men in front of her and raised her eyebrow theatrically for Billy, who had turned in his seat.

Roger Dewey then informed her there could be thousands of numbers.

"I've got someone to sift through all that," said Valencia. "When can you get them to me?"

Again he asked if they'd be even for Abu Dhabi—Valencia confirmed they would—and he told her he'd get the list to her within ninety minutes.

"Thank you," she said. "Hi to the wife."

After ending the call, she looked out at the street in front of them, shook her head, and said, "That guy, Jesus Christ."

Yuri Rabinowitz and his brother Isaac had been negotiating in Avram Lessing's office at the American iPhone Repair shop for ten minutes. Their friend Moishe was downstairs on West Forty-Seventh Street watching their bikes, which were parked in a no-parking zone.

"Why would I do that?" asked Avram.

"Because my uncle is not going to buy some shitty piece of paper without reading it first," said Yuri. They spoke in English.

His Russian friends were criminals, but he had no intention of being bossed around. Avram let his lips jut out—an expression he employed when he wanted to look serious.

"Look," he said, turning his monitor to the brothers. "*New York Times.*" He scrolled down to the picture of Elizabeth Carlyle. "You know her?"

The brothers shook their heads no. "Listen to me, this woman is major."

He let that sink in. "I'm saying five thousand dollars. Come on— your uncle is going to think twice about five thousand dollars? Yuri, be reasonable." His eyes went to Isaac to try to appeal to the younger man. Isaac, impassive as always, didn't respond.

"Is it reasonable to buy a suit without trying it on?" asked Yuri, sounding tired, like they'd been negotiating all day. "Do you go to the market and buy tomatoes without squeezing them? Do you buy a car without—"

"I mean in some situations, yes," said Avram, cutting him off. "If I buy a suit online, I don't try it on. Sometimes in the store, I just grab tomatoes, no squeezing, especially if it's a good store, you don't squeeze at my dude's place. A car from an auction? How many cars have I bought at auction?" He pretended to count on his hand. "You know what they call this?"

"Save it," said Yuri.

"Listen, Yuri, I brought this to you because you are my friend. Because of that I will offer these documents to you and your uncle for five thousand dollars."

"This is one of the worst offers I've ever heard," said Yuri. He turned and glanced at his brother, who was sitting with his eyes closed.

"And because I respect your uncle, I will offer you—and him, mind you, and *him*—a money-back guarantee on these papers. You pay me, I give you the thumb drive. If you don't like what you see, you get your money back."

To show how generous he was being, Avram frowned and held both hands up. "But with this special guarantee that I offer you now, today, because you're a friend, then I must say, if your uncle ends up liking what he sees, you give me another twenty-five hundred."

Yuri had to keep himself from smiling. He could take the thumb drive, burn a copy of whatever had been on this so-called top-secret phone, and tell Avi he didn't like what he saw. Americans were so simple-minded. "This is how you negotiate?" he asked.

"With the special money-back guarantee, yes, the price goes up," said Avram.

"Money-back guarantee?"

"Money back," repeated Avram, defeated.

"Okay, we have a deal," said Yuri.

Avram sniffled, wiped his nose with the back of his fingers, and opened his desk drawer. He shuffled things around for a moment and then produced a small thumb drive. With a bent back, he stood and held it out for Yuri.

Yuri grabbed the small device and examined it as though he could read the data with his naked eyes.

"My house is made of money, and my house is made of bricks," rapped Avram, wanting to appear less nervous than he felt.

After dropping the phones off at American iPhone Repair, and eating a cup of noodles at a bodega where a friend worked, Youssouf Wolde had started back toward Washington Square Park. He rode slowly and kept his earphones around his neck. Before he got to the park he stopped at a coffee shop on East Twelfth Street. He stayed on his bike and looked in the window. When he saw his friend Lonnie, he knocked on the glass lightly until she looked up from her book.

Lonnie was a nineteen-year-old NYU student. She was from Minnesota, a state he knew about because one of his cousins had settled there. She dressed like an American hippie, in baggy pants, handmade hats, and string necklaces with shells. They'd met in the park. She'd just walked up to him one day and started talking. She was the only non-crazy white person that had ever done that to him in the six years he'd lived in New York.

She hugged him when she came outside, and said, "Dude, where have you been?"

"Got sick," he said, touching his stomach.

"Poor Poobie," she said. That was her nickname for him. She rubbed his shoulder. "Why didn't you tell me? I would've brought you soup."

"You can't bring soup to the Bronx."

"Why not?"

"'Cause it would get cold on the subway."

"You're hella stupid," she said. She punched him on the shoulder. "You ready to get high?" she asked.

"I gotta go give my partner something," he said.

"Look at you," she said. "All gangster: 'Gotta give my partner something.'"

"Nah," he said. "I'm a delivery boy."

"Let's go," she said.

Lonnie was always down to hang, and she smiled all the time. He liked her for that. She didn't care that he was poor. She didn't care that he came from Africa. She liked to smoke weed and listen to music, just like him.

While they walked toward the park, Lonnie told him about her struggles with teachers, and how they weren't grading her properly. Youssouf listened, nodded when he thought he should, made his face sympathetic, elbowed her in the arm and laughed when she said something funny. But his mind was distracted. A sad feeling had settled over him. He wanted to be her boyfriend. He wanted to move back to Minnesota with her. Move into an American home. Buy a car. It was all a fantasy, though. She didn't want that. He was just a delivery boy, and not even a real one at that.

"What's Malik's deal?" asked Lonnie.

"With what?"

"With what he's got you doing?"

"Just running shit."

"You get paid for that?" she asked, with her head bent in a slightly flirtatious way.

"He'll give me twenty," said Youssouf, pulling on the handlebars of his bike to pop the front wheel in the air. "Wish I was old enough to be an Uber driver, though. My cousin could make like a hundred

43

dollars in one night. No boss. Just drive around, listen to the radio, smoke weed. Pick up girls. I'd get rich that way."

Lonnie's face became serious. "Uber's messed up, though."

"They all are," said Youssouf. "But you gotta work. Can't just be out here running phones for dudes."

"You should deliver weed."

"I'm Somali! Cops'll be all over me. They checked my bag on the train last week. Terrorist shit. Look at me, I'm brown skin—African man."

"It's not fair," said Lonnie. She rubbed his back. "We'll get you a real job. A safe job. I'll hire you as soon as I start my business."

"What business?"

"A plant store."

"That's wassup, though," said Youssouf. "That's it. We can do it in Minnesota." He looked at her. Her face looked like she'd just heard bad news. Youssouf's face became hot. His mouth became dry. *Too much*, he thought.

"I'm never moving back there," she said.

"Why?"

"'Cause it's fucking boring, and everyone's white."

"Okay, so we'll start it here," said Youssouf.

"Yeah, in Chinatown. We'll call it Poobie's Plants."

Less than half a mile away, Milton Frazier was backing into a parking spot on Mercer Street. Both Billy and Valencia had turned in their seats and were watching to see if he'd bump the car behind them; it was a Porsche.

"Do you want me to jump out?" asked Valencia.

"I got it."

And he did. He swung the car in, pulled forward, backed up, and they were good. Less than six inches on either side. Milton had long ago conquered his most obsessive traits, but he still couldn't help taking a moment to remind himself that the vehicle was off, the lights were off, and it was fine to leave the car.

The three of them walked to Bleecker Street without much talk. They made a left and walked two blocks to the subway's exit. A jackhammer on Broadway pounded away at the pavement. A bearded man selling paintings of what appeared to be graffiti watched the three of them pass.

It had been almost five hours since Milton had eaten his oatmeal and breakfast sausage. He had two hard-boiled eggs, a packet of salt, and two oranges in the SUV. He hadn't eaten them because he knew Valencia wouldn't like the smell of the eggs, and she'd love to tell him all about it. But he cursed himself for not bringing them with him. He shook his head while they walked.

"Danny said he got out right here," said Valencia, nodding toward the exit. "8:26 a.m." They all took a moment to look around. "Let's assume he knew where he was going and start this way." Valencia pointed west on Bleecker in the same direction that the exit flowed.

They walked west, each of them scanning buildings for obvious cameras. On the next block, they came to a designer clothing store. Above the door, and on the corner of the building were two security cameras. "All right," said Valencia, nodding at the store. "I'll keep going."

As she walked away both Milton and Billy stared at her for a moment, and then looked at each other.

"Stupid job," said Billy, raising his eyebrows.

"It'll keep the lights on," said Milton. "You ready?"

Billy took a breath, and told him he was. "Let's do this," he said.

The store was a fancy place: the floors and walls were white, the light was muted, and house music played quietly from hidden speakers. There wasn't a single customer. Two female employees, both African American, stood in the back and watched the two men approach. *If my daddy could see me now*, thought Milton.

"Hello," said one of the women, in a singsong voice.

"Are you the manager?" asked Billy.

"Yes, I am," she said, offering a fake smile. "Can I help you find something?"

"Yeah, we need to see the video from that camera," said Billy, pointing outside.

"I'm sorry, it's not public," said the manager.

"I'm sorry, we should've introduced ourselves," said Milton, stepping forward. "I'm Special Agent Lonzo Jones, FBI." He showed his badge. "This is Special Agent Hallinan."

Billy smiled, showed his badge.

"We're not going to copy anything, but we need to see it," said Milton.

The manager's eyes narrowed. A clock inside Milton's head continued counting how many seconds had passed since they entered the store. He turned and looked at the street behind them, a hint that he wanted the woman to make haste.

"Donald, can you help these men?" said the manager, calling to a suited guard standing near the door. The guard walked toward them holding his chin up as if he'd been challenged.

"Video," said the guard. "Come on." He led them to a door in the back of the store. Behind it was a hallway with clothes hanging on movable racks. A plastic trash can sat overflowing with take-out boxes. At the end of the hall was a small office containing a desk with a computer on it. Donald hit the light switch and the room became bright. "Do you need me to do it?" he asked.

"I think I can handle it," said Milton. He stepped to the computer, pulled out the chair and sat down. He moved the mouse and the monitor came alive. There was dust on the keyboard, and he had to restrain himself from cleaning it. He looked at the home screen and found an icon for Sony 7X00. He was familiar with that system. "Okay, let's see," said Milton, talking to himself quietly.

"Computers," said Billy, shaking his head, playing the role of the friendly one.

A live feed of the store appeared on the screen. Milton compared the time on the feed to his cell phone's clock and noted that it was a minute and twenty-two seconds slow. "One twenty-two," he muttered to himself.

He punched in 8:25 and clicked the a.m. icon on the search box. The computer worked for a moment, and then the screen changed, and he was looking at nine camera views, four of which were blank. He clicked on the one that was above the door, then clicked on the one he'd seen on the corner of the building. The corner camera provided a better view. He let it play for a moment, and then sped it up so it played at double speed.

The security guard, Donald, stood above him watching with his hands on his hips. He seemed happy to help the FBI. Billy stood near the door with the manager, who looked worried she might get in trouble for something.

"Bingo" said Milton. "There he is."

He stopped the tape, backed it up, watched it. Walking down the sidewalk, moving directly toward the camera, was a thin man in his thirties or forties. He wore sunglasses and a dark suit. His hair appeared to be gelled back. The man walked straight toward the camera, but—and Milton appreciated him for this—kept his face angled away from it. He paused the video. *8:27:52 minus one minute and twenty-two seconds would put it at 8:26:30.* A peaceful feeling came over Milton; the perfect roundness of the numbers made him feel like the universe had clicked into its rightful place. He stretched his neck and studied the man on the screen.

He pulled out his own phone and looked at the picture they'd received from the MTA surveillance in Grand Central. Neither picture was perfectly clear. In the earlier shot, the man hadn't yet put on his sunglasses. Milton's eyes, like a computer, compared the two images and looked for any deviations that suggested it was a different person. He looked at the man's hairline, his skull-to-body-proportion, the width of his shoulders, the cut of the suit's lapel, the length of the suit coat, the length and fold of the newspaper. Nothing suggested this wasn't the same person. Milton felt 99 percent sure it was.

After that, he performed a quick series of commands, his fingers striking the keys and moving the mouse. He clipped the video and set the clip on the computer's desktop. Then he pulled a small thumb drive from the inside breast pocket of his coat, and without asking permission, plugged it into the computer and copied the file onto it. Approximately four minutes and fifteen seconds had passed since they'd entered the store.

He pulled out his cell phone and called Valencia on speed dial.

"Talk to me," she said.

"We have visual confirmation, 8:26:30, headed west on Bleecker."

"Perfect," said Valencia. "Skip two blocks west."

Yuri Rabinowitz, his brother Isaac, and Moishe Groysman were just arriving at Daba's Teahouse, a Russian restaurant on the boardwalk in Brighton Beach. They'd been told their uncle Yakov Rabinowitz was having lunch there with a few of his friends. A cold wind blew in from the ocean and all three men walked with their faces turned away from it.

The restaurant had an open-air dining patio that stretched along the boardwalk. Just then it was completely free of customers. Moishe sat at one of the tables, pulled out his phone, and began looking at Instagram. The two brothers left their helmets and told their friend they'd be right back.

Upon entering the restaurant, Yuri felt self-conscious about his clothes. He pulled at the collar of his leather jacket as though that would somehow transform it into a suit. He stole a glance at his younger brother, who as always, seemed perfectly unbothered.

A broad-shouldered host, wearing a black jacket and bow tie, raised a hand, smiled, and let his head dip in greeting. Beyond the host's station was the restaurant proper. It wasn't particularly fancy, and at this hour, apart from their uncle and his associates sitting toward the back of the room, there were no other diners.

In the space between their uncle and the host's station, sitting at a table alone, holding a cell phone to his ear, was their uncle's protector, Grigory Levchin. Crag-faced and massive, he pulled himself up from his seat when he saw the two brothers, covered the phone with his hand, and said in Russian, "*Your mother was looking for you.*"

"*Tell her I was at your mother's house,*" answered Yuri.

Grigory grumbled, patted a heavy hand on Yuri's back, and then leaned in and kissed both him and Isaac on their cheeks. He held his hand toward their uncle's table, allowing them to pass. His breath, Yuri noticed, smelled like cough drops.

Their uncle Yakov Rabinowitz sat facing them. Seventy-one years old, skinny, bald, Jewish—he didn't look like a gangster at all. He had a benevolent face and dressed in casual and comfortable clothes appropriate for his age. The other three men seated at the table, all roughly the same age as him, were dressed slightly more formally in jackets and ties.

"*You boys look like Saturday Night Fever,*" said their uncle. His eyes then shifted to Grigory. "*Grab chairs.*" He looked back at his nephews; his eyes went up and down their outfits. "*We're Jews, we don't ride motorcycles,*" he said. "*What is all this?*"

The brothers walked around the table, shaking hands and patting the older men on their backs. "*Uncle,*" said Yuri, glancing at the other men, "*we have to tell you something.*"

"*They want to hear what you've been doing with yourselves,*" said their uncle. The other men at the table nodded and shifted in their seats as if someone was squeezing past them. The two brothers sat.

There was a bottle of vodka in the middle of the table. It was almost unheard of for their uncle to drink during the day. Yuri figured it must be one of the other men's birthdays. He looked around but couldn't tell which one.

"*We've been given some documents,*" said Yuri, turning back to his uncle. "*Corporate stuff. Secret material. It's been sold to us. We think the law firm would pay us to return it.*"

Their uncle looked like he'd just heard a bad joke. "*What document? Why would they pay for it?*"

It was Isaac's turn to speak up. His eyes, as he did so, had a humorous glow that captivated his audience. "*Uncle, we looked it up online. This is a very big case.*" He smiled at one of the men to his right. "*There are newspaper stories. Lots of money. The Southern District, a civil case. Big banks suing each other. We wanted to bring it to you. See if you think Katzir should look at it. If Katzir says it's worth money then, well, we proceed.*"

Yuri heard the sound of clanking dishes coming from the kitchen. He felt suddenly foolish. "*Uncle,*" he said, "*this is something we thought we should ask your permission before doing. That's why we came here with it—*"

Isaac cut in: "*And of course we will give you a piece of what we make with this deal.*"

Their uncle smiled, looked at his friends. "*These boys—don't let their clothes fool you. They are good boys!*"

After swapping out her low heels for a pair of black running shoes, Elizabeth Carlyle set out on foot for lunch. There was a place on East Thirty-Fifth and Lexington that served salade niçoise in the style she preferred—composed and drizzled, not dressed and tossed. The walk would do her good. She could breathe deeply and stretch her legs. The restaurant was just far enough away to guarantee no chance encounters with any colleagues. The last thing she needed was more talk.

As she walked, she began to imagine newspaper stories related to the missing documents. The *New York Times* would cover it. She wrote the headline in her mind: "Rise and Fall of a Great Lawyer." The *Wall*

Street Journal would be all over it: "Calcott Brought Down by Own Law Firm."

The stock market would react. Pensions would be lost. There would be whispers in Chappaqua, where she lived. Gossip at the country clubs. Pointing, talking, muttering.

She pulled out her phone and checked for missed calls. There were none. After slipping her phone back into her pocket she watched two young women—wearing heavy makeup and dressed like they were going clubbing—walk right toward her. They were deep in conversation. "I would lie to protect her," said one of the girls. "But that doesn't make me a liar."

The two girls made Elizabeth think of her own two daughters, both of whom lived in California now. Elizabeth had hoped they would return to the East Coast after college. Neither did. With each passing year, the chance of them moving back became less likely. But Elizabeth didn't want to think about that. Instead, she repeated the phrase, *But that doesn't make me a liar*, and turned it into a joke: *It makes me a lawyer.*

Right then a young man in a suit walked past. Her mind returned to Chris Cowley. Hadn't someone recommended him? Who? The hiring committee had settled on him without much debate. Why? What had been so special about him? The other candidates had been perfectly capable.

She remembered one Yale graduate, a young woman, who had seemed smart. Why hadn't they gone with her? Her mind jumped back to Chris Cowley—he'd been born, grown up, gone to college, gone to law school, looked at all the jobs in the world and settled on her firm. How many chances to deviate from that path had there been? He could have done a million things that would have kept him out of her life. Instead, he had applied to her law firm, been selected, done his background research, showered, shaved, gotten dressed, and come in for an interview.

She'd interviewed him—that was the worst part. It hurt to think about. She'd had a chance to stop him, and she'd missed it.

Right then, a taxi driver leaned on his horn, and a chorus of other cars joined in. Elizabeth looked toward the next intersection. She told herself that she would keep pitying herself until she reached the near corner—after that she'd have to start pulling herself together.

At the restaurant, the waiter, a Frenchman, recognized her and made a show of leading her to a table near the window. After she'd taken her seat, a look of concern appeared on his face.

"Where have you been?" he asked.

"Working," she said.

"Maybe a glass of wine?"

A glass wouldn't be enough. She wanted a bottle. She wanted more than that. She wanted the waiter to pull her by the hand, lead her back into the kitchen, and kiss her. "Just a salade niçoise," she said. "And an espresso. Bring the espresso first, please."

"Of course, madam," said the waiter.

Left alone, sitting near the window, watching the pedestrians on Lexington Avenue, Elizabeth took a deep breath. *You'll be fine*, she told herself. She noticed a strap of muscle around her belly gripping and she consciously tried to let it unwind. *You'll be fine.*

Her thoughts shifted to Valencia—specifically to the first time they met. It had been at a gala for a breast cancer charity about eight years ago. Elizabeth had noticed Valencia standing near the bar. There was something about her that drew the eye—the way she carried herself, a kind of confidence. She was laughing loudly and telling two men some kind of raucous story. Elizabeth looked her up and down and ran through the first of what would become a regular series of comparisons. Elizabeth was white, the kind of white that didn't age well.

Valencia, on the other hand, once described herself to Elizabeth as "ethnically vague." She could have been Arab, Jewish, Italian, Turkish.

They were roughly the same age, at least the same generation. Elizabeth kept herself in good shape, but she'd always been a slim woman. Boney shoulders. She had dull skin, too, even back then. On the other hand, Valencia had beautiful skin and shiny hair; she wasn't skinny. She was filled out in the right way. The only flaw that Elizabeth could find in Valencia was her crooked teeth, but even that added to her charm.

Whenever they met, Elizabeth always ran through the same comparisons, and she always came to the same conclusion: she was simply genetically inferior. She was less attractive. There was nothing she could do about it.

Her mind stayed on that first night: A friend of Elizabeth's husband pulled both women together and drunkenly insisted they meet. Standing there—holding Valencia's hand in her own—Elizabeth turned to the man and asked, "Why must we meet?"

"Two strong women," said the man.

They squeezed hands.

"I'm very pleased to meet you," said Valencia.

The man then took great pleasure in leaning his big head between them. "C-I-A," he whispered, nodding at Valencia.

"Is that so?" said Elizabeth.

"Ex," said Valencia. "I've been—"

"Biggest lawyer in town," said the man, interrupting, and now nodding in Elizabeth's direction.

"I know who she is," said Valencia.

And Elizabeth, at the time, had accepted that. She'd allowed herself to be charmed by it. Thinking about it now, eight years later, it seemed absurd. Elizabeth wasn't yet known outside her legal circles. Not like that. Nevertheless, she allowed herself to be charmed. Two weeks later she invited Valencia for coffee. Four months after that, she hired Valencia for the first time.

That first job involved an antitrust suit brought by the DOJ against a Silicon Valley software company represented by Elizabeth's firm. At the center of the government's lawsuit was an engineer who had left the company under unhappy circumstances. Elizabeth brought Valencia on board to look into him. A few weeks later, Valencia told Elizabeth that she thought the man was emotionally unstable. Elizabeth asked what she based this on. Valencia smiled, and said, "a feeling."

At the time, Elizabeth suspected Valencia was trying to tell her, without saying it, that she'd read his emails, or listened to his phone calls. The truth was, Elizabeth didn't want to know. She told her to keep going.

Two months later, the government dropped its lawsuit. The engineer had stopped cooperating. Over dinner and drinks that night, Valencia explained that she'd just leaned on him a little. She'd had him followed in a way that would be discovered. She wanted to make him uncomfortable.

Then she sent one of her guys to dig in his trash. "It's legal in California," she said. They didn't care what was in the trash; they just wanted to get caught doing it. That was all it took to make the witness change his mind.

Was it legal thuggery? Perhaps, but it worked.

A friendship formed between the two women. They'd see each other every few months for lunch, or the occasional after-work cocktail. She'd hire Valencia to do something, and Valencia always got it done.

Sitting there in the restaurant, Elizabeth again considered what she found so intriguing about Valencia. It wasn't work related. It was something more personal than that. It was the way she kept herself from being bothered. The world never seemed to touch her. The waiter placed the cup of espresso on a saucer in front of her and interrupted her thoughts. Elizabeth stared at the drink and told herself she needed to cultivate that kind of equanimity herself.

"You know what," she said, looking up at the waiter. "I will have that glass of wine."

*   *   *

Valencia Walker stopped under the awning of a pizza place on Bleecker and looked at a camera perched above the doorway. These cameras were often just for show, but this one had a wire tacked and running along the wall for a few feet until it disappeared into a drilled hole. Valencia's eyes shifted to the window of the place and she read the words *Dante's Pizza Pie Zone*, written in white cursive. After taking a deep breath, she pulled the door open and stepped in.

Inside, a slump-shouldered college kid stood shaking Parmesan onto his slice. Rock music played from a small radio. Behind the counter two Latino cooks shuffled pies from here to there. Beyond them stood the manager, a man Valencia guessed was Palestinian. He wore a white T-shirt and white apron and seemed to know something was up. "Can I help you?" he asked, suspiciously.

Valencia stepped to the counter, locked eyes with him, stood perfectly straight, and said, "I need to see the video from that camera." She turned and pointed toward the camera.

The manager's eyes went from the camera back to Valencia. "What happened?"

Valencia put her left hand on her heart, leaned closer. "Something important was stolen," she said. "I'm trying to find it."

"When?"

"Earlier today."

The manager didn't push back, but the muscles in his face told her that he suddenly felt nervous. In response, Valencia offered a small smile and blinked in a way that allowed her eyelashes to be admired. The manager had a rag in his hand, and he placed it over his shoulder, shuffled to the counter, and lifted it for her. When she got behind the counter, they had to perform a quick dance to let him get in front of her so he could lead the way.

Beyond the front room was a hallway that smelled like bleach. The manager led her to a back room, opened the door, and turned on a light. Valencia leaned her head in and saw unfolded pizza boxes and large white plastic vats of tomato sauce stacked on a metal shelf. Toward the back of the room was a desk with a computer on it. The manager moved toward the desk and pulled the chair out, set it at the side, and offered it to her.

"What time?" he asked.

"If you could start at 8:25 this morning, please," she said.

The manager bent over the desk, fussed with the mouse, and then, keeping his eyes on the screen, stood back up. They both waited while the computer dredged up the video file. Valencia listened to the computer humming and an air shaft blowing air.

Four separate camera views popped onto the screen. Valencia saw that there were two cameras outside.

"There we go," said Valencia. "Thank you."

The manager bent down, clicked the mouse, and the images began moving. Valencia leaned forward in her chair and pointed at the view from one of the outside cameras. "Is that Bleecker Street?"

"Bleecker, yeah."

"Can you enlarge that one, please?"

The manager clicked on it and the view from the camera above the door filled the screen. They watched for about fifteen seconds until someone entered the frame.

"Stop," said Valencia. The man paused the tape. "Is that pointed east?"

"East? Toward Lafayette? Yeah, yeah, east," said the manager.

"Okay, play it."

They continued watching.

A person entered walking west. "Stop," said Valencia.

He pressed a button on the mouse and the video froze. Valencia leaned forward and examined it. It was a woman. "Okay," she said. The video rolled.

"Stop," she said. Another person walking west. Valencia leaned in and looked at the image. The footage was blurry, but she saw that the man was dark-haired; he wore the same dark suit. She pulled out her phone and looked at the image Danny had sent her. She looked back at the screen. "Play it, please."

The manager pressed play and they watched the man exit the frame.

"Can we see the other view?"

"Yeah, yeah," said the manager, clicking over to the other outside camera.

"Is that LaGuardia?" she asked.

"Yeah."

"Right on LaGuardia? Toward the park?"

"Yeah, over toward Washington Square."

That's him, she thought; a warm feeling filled her chest. She breathed in deeply through her nose, felt her stomach expand, and exhaled. "Thank you, that's all I need," she said.

Valencia dialed Milton before she'd even made it to the front of the place; he answered just as she stepped back onto the street. "He went to Washington Square Park," she said, looking in that direction, when he picked up. "Meet me at the little NYPD shack on the south side of the park."

Just then, two German-looking tourists on Citi Bikes rolled by. Valencia watched them and made sure they weren't looking at her. Surely, somebody was watching her, she thought. Somebody had eyes on her, she was sure of that. She called Wally Philpott, her NYPD detective, and told him to meet her at the same place.

For a moment, as she made her way to the park, she felt a kind of rage build in her chest. She saw the man's ugly face in her mind. *You're going to tell me what to do?* He was insane.

Milton and Billy were already standing near the NYPD trailer when she got there. They had similar expressions on their faces—they looked like they were expecting bad news. When she joined them, Milton nodded to the west. She turned and saw Wally Philpott walking toward them with a coffee in his hand.

"What? You wanted one?" Wally Philpott asked.

"Our target came to the park between 8:25 and 8:30 this morning," she said, turning and looking at the trailer.

"All right." The detective pulled up his pants and stepped to the trailer. When he got there, he knocked loudly on the door. A moment later the door swung open and a young uniformed officer poked his head out. Wally nodded, shook hands with the cop, and said, "Let me in, kid." The cop glanced at Valencia and her two associates, then opened the door.

Valencia crossed her arms, reminded herself to be patient, and resisted the urge to tap her foot.

Since returning from Grand Central, Chris Cowley had been in his office with the door closed. His tie was loosened, and his coat hung in the closet. Elizabeth Carlyle had already removed him from the Calcott case, but so far she hadn't fired him.

He'd moved a large binder of discovery for one of his other cases to his desk. It sat there unopened.

His palms were sweaty and every few minutes he wiped them on his pants.

He'd spent the past half hour clicking through various news sites, not looking for anything more than a way to distract his mind. Now he was shopping. He was looking at expensive coats. He knew his Internet activity would be monitored, but he didn't care. If he hadn't been fired yet, surely they wouldn't fire him for doing a little shopping. It might even make him look more normal.

Right then somebody knocked on his door. Before he could say anything, the door opened and Stewart Hillier, another junior associate who'd been hired in the same class as him, peeked his head in.

"Dude, do you have those Plymouth briefs?" asked Stewart.

Chris didn't have any idea what he was talking about. He didn't know what Plymouth was. He frowned and said, "No."

"What's up?" asked Stewart, stepping into the room, closing the door almost all the way, crossing his arms, and leaning against the wall in one awkward movement. Stewart was tall, brown-haired, big-boned and soft-bodied. As dumb as he was, he could still sense something was wrong, and a look of concern—whether genuine or not—appeared on his face.

"Nothing, I'm just burnt," said Chris. His eyes became teary and he used all his mental energy to stiffen up and make that stop. *Stop, you fucking piece of shit*, he told himself in his father's voice. "Need a vacation," he said. Then, he put his hand on his forehead, pretended to yawn, and wiped at his eyes.

"You see that new paralegal?" asked Stewart, dropping his voice lasciviously.

"Dude, I'm gay," said Chris.

"You can still see, though, right?"

"She's not into guys like you."

"How do you know?"

"Because she carries herself with pride," said Chris. His hands—for a moment—went to his pockets again and patted for his phone. "Besides, aren't you engaged?"

"A player gotta play, though—am I right?" said Stewart.

Chris leaned back in his chair and turned his eyes to his computer monitor. He wanted this encounter to end. He closed the window he was on and turned his eyes back to his intruding guest.

"How's Calcott coming?" asked Stewart.

So, this was it? His long introduction, the Plymouth brief, the new paralegal, it had all been a lead-up to this. Rumors were circulating. Someone had probably seen Elizabeth walking him down the hallway. Her face would have been noticeably mad. That would have been enough to get people talking.

Chris looked at Stewart. "It's going," he said.

He took another big breath and nodded toward his computer, but his guest had taken out his cell phone. Using both thumbs, he was frantically typing a message. The droning white noise in the office seemed to have gained in volume. "Anyway," said Chris.

"Ying's motion had like five typos in it," said Stewart.

"That's crazy," said Chris. He opened up his email and began pretending to respond to a message. *Please go away*, he thought.

"Do you think Ying uses Adderall?"

Chris ignored the question and continued to act as though he was emailing. Stewart, finally receiving the message, muttered, "All right," and drifted back out of the room.

When he was gone, Chris went to the door and quietly closed it. The effort he'd spent trying to control his emotions had made his head hurt. He rubbed his temples, but that did him no good. *Everything is temporary*, he told himself. All these problems will end.

He walked to his closet, opened it, reached into his jacket pocket, and made sure he still had the thumb drive. Would that be enough? Would the thumb drive be enough? This thing was never going to end. He was fucked.

Showing no signs of hurry, Wally Philpott made his way toward Valencia. He'd been in the NYPD trailer for fifteen minutes. He carried a few sheets of paper in his hands and read from them while he walked. The uniformed cop who'd helped him also stepped out and now gazed across the park as if he were looking for someone. Valencia, arms crossed, watched both men. In an effort to appear friendlier she smiled.

"Ask and ye shall receive," said Wally. He handed her the first page. On it Valencia saw a printed screen grab from the surveillance system that monitored the park; it showed their target, the Asian man, in high definition. The shot had come from above, as if the camera had been positioned on some far-off balcony. It wasn't a great angle on his face, but she could see clearly that it was their man. A time stamp on the page read, 08:36:42. Below that, printed on the paper, was the NYPD insignia.

Valencia felt Milton approach her and look down at the picture in her hand. Something about him being so close made her feel slightly uncomfortable, and she noticed she had stopped breathing. She handed the page to Milton and shifted a half foot to her left.

"All right," said Wally, "our guy goes up and sits with a dude they know on the west end over there." He nodded toward the west end of the park and handed Valencia another piece of paper, this one showing the mug shot of a black man. The name, Malik Abdul Onweno, was printed on the top-left of the page. Below his name were various statistics about his size, his coloring, his DOB, and other identifying information.

"Dabbles in stolen goods now and again," said Wally, lifting his eyebrows and scratching his scalp. "But they say he's a good kid, some kind of chess master. They say dimes to dozens he's over there right now." Wally looked at the younger cop, who nodded his head. "You want a uniform with you?"

Valencia looked at the cop too. "Yeah, sure," she said. "But keep back."

They split into three distinct groups: Valencia in the lead; Billy and Milton behind her; and the two cops about twenty feet behind them.

The fountain in the middle of the square sprayed water into the air; Valencia looked at it as she walked and made vague promises to herself about vacations and romance. Beyond the fountain stood the arch; it always made her happy to see the arch. Scattered all over the park were college-aged kids who clutched book bags and looked at cell phones. An older man sitting on a bench facing the fountain played the guitar and sang loudly. He looked like a hippie who'd cut off all his hair and shaved his beard. He kept his eyes on Valencia as she walked.

When she reached the path that led to the chess players, Valencia made a subtle circular motion with her fingers up near her ears; Milton and Billy understood she was telling them to split up and cover the north and south side of the area. They separated without speaking.

When she got closer to the chess players, Valencia stopped for a moment and turned away from them. She waited for Wally and the cop to join her. There were eight games going on, and at least half of them involved black players. "Malik is the one at the second table?" she asked the cop.

The cop looked that way and nodded. "Yep," he said. "Dark dude in the blue hoodie, with the little dookies."

"Thank you," she said. As she made her way to the tables, she kept her eyes on Malik Onweno. The game engaged his attention completely. Her training kicked in. She'd been taught to pretend to know the stranger she was approaching. Not to act on that knowledge at all—she wasn't going to pretend they had a shared history or be friendly—but to carry herself with the knowledge that she already knew whomever she was approaching.

Even when she got within fifteen feet of him, he kept his eyes on the board. Players of varying ages and races occupied the other tables. They played speed matches and smacked their little timers after every move. A couple of African men, who weren't playing, watched Valencia.

She walked right up to the table and stood behind Malik's opponent. Malik moved his bishop, captured one of his rival's pawns, and smacked the timer. He glanced up at Valencia and looked back at the table.

"Mr. Onweno, I need to speak with you," she said, feeling proud of the way her voice sounded.

"As soon as we're done," said Malik, without looking back up.

If he'd wanted to piss her off, he'd succeeded. She stepped around his opponent and was about to knock all the pieces from the board, when she changed her mind, and instead, leaned forward and pushed Malik's king off the table. It landed on his lap.

"Are you done?" she asked.

The man reacted like she'd poured water on him; he looked shocked. Valencia thought for a moment that he might cry. She could feel the men around her stiffen up like fighting dogs. The air became electric.

"Let's go," she said, nodding toward a more private area, and sucking in a deep breath.

Malik raised his hand to his opponent, as if asking him not to interfere on his behalf. The opponent, an older Polish or Russian-looking man, hadn't responded in any way. He just sat there with his mouth open, staring up at Valencia in disbelief.

Valencia looked back at Malik and focused all her mental energy trying to send a nonverbal message to him: *It's urgent. Do not resist. This can only get worse for you.* The man made a face, stood, and together they moved toward a bench about thirty feet to the north of the chess games. Without being obvious about it, she matched her posture and stride to his.

While they walked Valencia tried to summon her most empathic self. She told herself that this man—this African immigrant—was probably scared shitless to see a woman wearing a pantsuit come and ask for him by name. That was fine—in fact, it was exactly what she wanted him to feel. It was perfect. A flock of pigeons flew over their heads.

Up the path, Valencia saw Milton sitting on a bench watching them. Just then, another African immigrant walked by and seemed to ask Malik with his eyes if he was all right. Malik ignored him.

When they got to the bench, Malik gestured for her to sit, as if they were in his office. She straightened her pants and perched herself on the edge of the bench. Malik joined her, sitting down slowly, like he had a stiff back. Valencia saw Wally and the uniformed cop standing about sixty feet away. She didn't look for Billy, but she could feel him to her right. The hum of the city's traffic filled the air around them.

"So what is this?" Malik Onweno asked, in an accented voice Valencia guessed was Nigerian.

With her hands resting in her lap, Valencia stared into the man's face. His eyes had gone to the ground. He had long, beautiful eyelashes. It looked like he was busy trying to figure out what he had done.

She let the silence stretch on for a moment, and then finally said, "I'm looking for a phone."

"I don't deal in phones," said Malik, shaking his head. His eyes stayed on the ground. He'd already come up with that line, thought Valencia. He'd been practicing it while they sat there.

Valencia could see a tiny vein pulsing near the man's temple. "Look at me," she said. He turned and looked at her. She touched her own cheek with her hand. "Look at my face. Look at who I am. Do I look like a cop who chases after stolen phones?"

Malik pursed his lips and shook his head a little.

"Do I look like a cop at all?"

"No," he said.

She took a moment to let him think. Then she said, "I'm after a particular phone. It has passed through your hands. I'm not asking about it. I'm telling you."

"Still, sister, I'm being honest, I don't trade in phones."

Valencia reached into the inside pocket of her suit coat. She pulled out a baggie that held about twenty gel-capped pills filled with brown powder. It was her melatonin. "This is heroin, Malik. It's uncut. Do you want me to put it in your pocket and have those cops search you?" She nodded toward Wally and the uniformed cop.

Malik looked at the bag, then over at the cops, who were now openly staring at him. He stayed silent.

"A Chinese man came and sold you a phone today," said Valencia.

Malik looked back down at the ground and continued making his calculations.

"Last chance," said Valencia.

Malik, when he spoke, sounded sad. "A Jewish guy in Midtown, in the Diamond District."

Valencia turned toward Milton Frazier, snapped her fingers once, and waved him to her.

Leo Katzir's law office wasn't fancy at all. It was on the ground floor of an ugly sixties office building in Sheepshead Bay. The walls were paneled in fake wood. Against those walls, leaning and sagging, were stacks of cardboard boxes filled with case files. Two bedraggled-looking Russian immigrants sat in the makeshift lobby waiting for counsel on their DUI cases. Mr. Katzir's secretary, a twenty-two-year-old Russian woman, sat behind her desk with headphones on, watching YouTube videos and snapping gum.

Yuri Rabinowitz, his brother Isaac, and their friend Moishe Groysman had been in Leo Katzir's office for ten minutes. They'd brought the thumb drive and they wanted the lawyer to have a look. Katzir—with his lips moving over words—clicked through various documents and read them. He didn't seem to like what he saw; in fact, each new file seemed to upset him more than the last.

The lawyer was fifty-two years old; he wore a burgundy cardigan over a white shirt with a black tie. He was bald, soft in the stomach, and wore a yarmulke. "Would someone be willing to pay for their safe return?" he asked, leaning back and tapping his pudgy fingers on his desk. "Yes, they would. Do I advise you getting mixed up in this kind of business? No. No—listen to me, boys, I'm serious."

He looked at each of the three younger men. "And I'm not saying that to cover—to *legally* cover—my own ass. I wouldn't do that. I'm saying this sincerely. Do not go down this road."

Yuri sat and listened. He tried to parse the man's English for some kind of deeper meaning. His eyes went from the lawyer's face to the plants on the windowsill behind him. They needed water. The office was very warm; the plants definitely needed water.

"You're a lawyer, though," said Yuri's younger brother. "This isn't lawyers' work."

Yuri raised his left hand to his brother, an impatient, *Be quiet* gesture. He despised it when his brother interrupted him. When he looked back at the lawyer, he saw that his expression had settled into a frown. "What if we asked for less?" tried Yuri.

"It's not the amount that bothers me," said Katzir. "It's the fact that this is a federal crime. The FBI will investigate it. What do you think your uncle will do if you bring the attention of the FBI onto him? Can you imagine?"

"We told him about it," said Yuri.

"And he blessed it," said Isaac.

Katzir's frown turned into a smirk. "I highly doubt that," he said. The lawyer then looked at Moishe Groysman, in hopes that the more mature of his three visitors would talk some sense to the two younger brothers.

"He did," said Moishe, with a shrug.

They were interrupted by Katzir's secretary, who opened the door and stepped inside. "Sophia Kamenka," she said.

"I'll call back in five minutes," said Katzir.

Yuri watched his brother turn in his seat and look the young secretary up and down. She returned the look with a small smile, stepped back out, and closed the door. The smell of her perfume hung in the air. Annoyed, Yuri dropped his gaze to the floor and reminded himself that there were more important things in this world than the ability to flirt. But he didn't feel convinced.

"Boys, you wanted my opinion, and I gave it to you," said the lawyer, Katzir.

"But if our uncle calls, you'll tell him the documents are worth money?" asked Isaac.

"I'll tell him what I told you—do not go down this road."

Valencia stepped through the door of American iPhone Repair and looked at the four men sitting at their worktables. "Can I help you?" asked the one seated furthest from the door. After Milton and Billy followed her in, he rose to his feet. He didn't say anything more; he just stood there blinking.

Valencia's eyes swept over the other three workers. They all appeared to be under thirty, and they looked like they lived with their mothers. "I need to speak to your boss," said Valencia.

The standing man shook his head. "He's not in." The other three stayed in their seats and watched with their heads held back. They all looked nervous.

Valencia stepped farther into the room. "Open that door," she said, pointing at the second door.

"I'm sorry?" said the man who was standing.

"I need you to open that door," she said.

Milton pulled out his fake badge, and he held it up for the men to see. Valencia could feel the energy in the room shifting; she watched the standing man's eyes go from the badge back to her. He then raised both hands like he was pleading. "You guys are gonna need to come back with—"

Billy stepped past Valencia toward the closed door. He set his duffle bag down on the floor, and then took a moment to examine the door, paying special attention to the hinges. He tried the handle and confirmed that it was locked. The standing man had withdrawn a few steps and seemed to be considering taking out his cell phone. Billy then bent over, unzipped his bag, and pulled out a two-and-a-half-foot battering ram—an ATF-style doorbuster.

By the time Billy had straightened up and taken his backswing, the man said, "Okay, okay, we'll call him."

Somewhere, someone buzzed the door; Billy pushed it open slowly and peeked his head in. He stood in the doorway for a moment assessing the second room. Then he turned to Valencia and gestured for her to go first.

She counted six men when she entered. When she walked in, half of them stood. The room was organized in two rows of worktables. There were no windows, and no visible cameras. On the tables were iPhones and iPads in various states of disrepair; the tables were equipped with tripod lamps and magnifying lenses. There were a few Asian workers and the rest, Valencia guessed, were Israeli. They seemed confused and looked scared; one of them smiled sheepishly, as if he'd been caught doing something stupid.

Valencia felt Billy step past her. She watched him walk around the tables on her left. "I need all of you men to please stand on that side of the room," he said, pointing toward the south wall.

Valencia turned and saw Milton shepherding the men from the first room toward her. She then walked past them to the office's front door and confirmed that it was closed and locked. She returned to the middle room.

"Sir, put your hands on the wall and stay there," said Milton, talking to one of the men. The man complied. Milton stepped back and kept his eyes on the group.

Billy, meanwhile, had picked his doorbuster back up; he was approaching the third door when it opened from the inside.

Valencia watched a bald man in a Giants hoodie step out. He wore glasses and loose pants. He had his hands up near his face like an old person assaulted by too much noise. "Everyone, please," he said. This was the boss, Valencia was sure. "What is this?" he asked. "What is this?"

"Frisk him," said Valencia.

Billy pushed him face-first against the wall.

"What is this?" Avram Lessing repeated.

Billy patted him down roughly. He checked his ankles and pockets, squeezed under his genitals, swiped between his buttocks. "He's clean."

"Hold him there." Valencia turned and looked at the rest of the workers again, and held her finger to her lips, raised the finger in the air, and told them, "Gentleman, please, everyone remain calm, and you won't be arrested."

She entered the boss's office, a medium-sized room with a window that looked out on an enclosed space between buildings. The room smelled like canned soup. A large, framed poster with directions on how to help choking victims hung on the wall. She walked around the back of his desk, bent down, and made sure nobody was hiding behind it. She tried a door on the far side of the office and found it locked. She looked around for cell phones but didn't see any.

After stepping to the window, looking out, and then lowering the shade, she called out, "Bring him in."

Billy ushered him into the room, a hand on the man's back.

"What is this?" Avi Lessing asked again. "You can't just charge in here. This is bullshit, we have civil rights. I have a lawyer. You're gonna want to deal with him."

Valencia stepped within arm's length of the bald man, and looked into his eyes. He was terrified. She stayed silent for a moment, savoring his fear. "An African kid brought you some phones today," she finally said, speaking quietly.

"What?"

"A boy named Youssouf sold you some stolen phones today."

"I don't buy phones, I repair—"

"Let me explain something to you," said Valencia, cutting him off. "I'll make it clear. We're only going to do this once. I'm not going to go back and forth with—"

"Excuse—"

"I'm not going to argue," she said. "I skipped my lunch, my blood sugar is low, my feet hurt. If you think I'm interested in your pathetic little stolen phone operation, you're mistaken."

She looked as deeply into his eyes as she could. "I don't care about that," she said. "I care about a particular phone, a phone you received today. One phone. An iPhone. Did you receive any phones today?"

He looked down. "Yes."

"How many phones did you receive?"

"From Youssouf?" he asked. "Six, he gave me six phones."

"Where are they?"

"Right here." He nodded toward a tote bag in the corner of the room. "Right here. No problem."

"Get them, and set them on that desk," said Valencia.

After pulling his pants up, he retrieved the phones and set them down on the desk slowly. Then he turned to her with an aggrieved expression. He looked like an upset teenager.

"Get on your knees, and put your hands on your head," said Valencia.

"What?" asked Avram Lessing.

"Break him," said Valencia.

"Okay, okay, okay," said Avram, getting down on his knees and putting his hands on his head. Valencia glanced at Billy, who closed his eyes and nodded once, admiringly.

Valencia then stepped to the desk and looked at the six phones. They were all iPhones. She picked up the first one and pressed the power button. She then went through the other five phones and turned each one on. While she waited for them to boot up, she went to the door and checked on Milton again.

All ten of the workers still had their hands against the wall; they stood with their heads turned toward her. Milton, sitting on the edge of one of the tables, brushed at the space between his eyebrows. He had the room under control.

Valencia stepped back into the office and picked up the first phone. It was passcode protected. She picked up the second phone: passcode protected. On the third, she clicked the home button, and on the home screen saw the painting of a swimming pool that had been in the packet of info given to her by Elizabeth's investigator. She clicked on the email icon and scrolled through the emails until she saw one from a lawyer at Carlyle, Driscoll, and Hathaway.

She then held it out for the man to see, gave it a little shake. "See, no big drama, no big fuss."

"Take it," he said.

"I will," she answered. She stood there for a moment looking down at the phone. "I have to ask you something, though." She waited for the right amount of tension to develop between them. "Did you snoop around on this phone at all?"

"No, just to see if they work. I don't look, I just turn them on, see if the screen works."

"Did you take anything from this phone?"

"What am I gonna take? No, I'm selling it, I didn't take anything."

She turned and looked at Billy. He raised his eyebrows, let them drop. Valencia stepped toward the man's desk. "Listen to me—we are going to examine the phone forensically. We will be able to see if any files were removed from it. I'm going to ask you one more time, did you take anything from it?"

"No. No, I didn't take anything from it," said Avram, looking to Billy, like he might offer some kind of help.

"All righty then," said Valencia. "Thank you." She clicked the phone again and checked the time.

At that same moment, Ren Xiong was in the middle of taking care of some last-minute details before leaving town. He'd just visited his girlfriend Wan Kin Yi. He told her he had to go on a business trip and that he'd be gone for a few weeks, maybe longer. They had sex in her bed, which had white sheets and a white blanket and pillows and seemed altogether more luxurious than anything else in the rest of his life. Before he left, he gave Wan Kin Yi an envelope with a thousand dollars in it, explaining that he wanted her to be comfortable. She made a funny face but she didn't refuse the money.

He didn't know if he'd see her again, which made him feel sadder than he expected. He spent most of the walk back from Alphabet City thinking about her. Now he looked at his phone, saw it was almost four p.m., and sped up his pace.

He'd left his suitcase at a mailbox store in the hands of a Chinese worker he was friendly with. When he picked it up, the worker asked where he was off to. Xiong told him Los Angeles, and the two men joked about him becoming a famous actor. "*I won't forget you when I'm rich,*" Xiong said.

Upon entering the laundromat he took off his baseball cap. He'd lost the receipt and he wanted the old woman to recognize him. She greeted him in Chinese, and he apologized for not having the ticket. She disappeared in search of his shirts, and Xiong looked around the place and felt saddened by the dirty floor. Didn't the owner have any family who could help with sweeping and mopping?

The old woman returned with his two shirts, and Xiong paid without making any more small talk. Then he set his suitcase on the floor, opened it, and put the two clean shirts—still wrapped in plastic—inside. After zipping it closed, he stood, smiled at the woman, and rolled the suitcase to the door. Before leaving, he looked at his phone again—4:10 p.m.

The laundromat was on Baxter Street. Xiong had been instructed to walk north on Mulberry. If he wasn't contacted by the time he got to Broome Street he was to get into a taxi, head to Penn Station, take the train to Philadelphia, then jump in another taxi to Camden. In Camden, he'd go to a safe house on Norris Street. He'd been once before; it was a place without charm. The television didn't pick up any Chinese stations, and the nearest pool hall was a half-hour bus ride away.

Xiong got to Mulberry and rolled his suitcase north. He passed a fish store and looked at some sea bass laid out on ice. The smell coming out of the place was enough to stop him from breathing through his nose. He walked on and scanned the street for signs of irregularity.

His eyes settled on a Chinese man with a paper bag walking toward him. The man stood out because of his athletic build. He carried the bag from the bottom, as though it might break from its load. If the man had a gun, Xiong thought, he could keep it in the bag and fire without pulling it out. As the gap between the men closed, Xiong reminded himself that if his old bosses from Anquan Bu—the Ministry of Security—ever sent someone, they would come from behind. He would never see them. It would be merciful that way. Still, Xiong kept his eyes on the man, and they passed each other without incident.

Two blocks later, just after Grand Street, Xiong noticed a black SUV parked on the west side of the street in front of him. When he got within ten paces, he saw the back window lower. Xiong leaned down and looked in. Riding in the backseat was his American boss, Jonathan Redgrave.

"There he is," said Redgrave, smiling like a wolf.

The driver's door opened, and Manny Vega stepped out. "You all right?" asked Vega, holding a hand out for a shake. He always had dark circles under his eyes, and today was no different. He was roughly the same age as Xiong, somewhere in his forties. He had small scars on the right side of his face, the remnants, seemingly, of an explosion. He looked dangerous, but he'd always been friendly. They shook hands and Vega patted him on the back.

We've lived our lives and now we're here, thought Xiong, *standing on this street*. For a moment his mind jumped back to the sea bass he'd just seen, the single skyward eye looking like it was shocked at the predicament it found itself in. One moment alive in the sea, the next dead and on ice.

Manny Vega took Xiong's suitcase from him, and the back door popped open. "Come on," said Jonathan Redgrave, waving him in.

Xiong reminded himself to be calm and got into the back.

"There he is," repeated Redgrave. They shook hands, and they didn't say anything more until Manny Vega finished loading the suitcase, and the back door slammed shut.

Jonathan Redgrave, as far as Xiong could guess, was somewhere in his forties or fifties. It was harder to tell with white people. His face looked older; it was sallow and pitted. He was skinny, had dark hair and a receding hairline. He looked like the kind of man who exercised regularly but remained unhealthy. He was, Xiong thought, ugly both inside and out.

"That was good work today. You should be proud," said Jonathan. Manny jumped into the driver's seat and the vehicle began to move.

Xiong licked his lips, nodded, but he didn't feel anything. He'd been smuggled away from China, away from his family, his life, to work for this man. It brought him no joy. A former Anquan Bu operative, Xiong had been compromised by accepting money from the Americans. They'd given him a choice: fake his own death and come to America and work for them, or be exposed. He agreed to work for them. Because of his family in Tianjin, he couldn't run away. His entry into America had been undocumented. There was no record that he existed. In China he was dead. Now Jonathan Redgrave had a man without documented fingerprints, DNA, iris scans, or a known facial pattern. He could do jobs for them. He was a tool in their toolbox. They kept him, he imagined, for some bigger job in the future. Not for these little jobs. Someday he would really be needed, and afterward they would throw him away.

"We're gonna put you in Camden, and then move you to Baltimore in a week," said Redgrave. "Just sit tight."

Xiong nodded again, and then looked out his window at the people walking on Broome Street. He looked at their jackets, backpacks, and hooded sweatshirts. *Sit tight*, he thought—that means sit without moving. His mind shifted to Baltimore—he thought about his gambling options there. The pool hall downtown had games. He could find a new girlfriend. He could start exercising, get back in shape.

"Manny said the kid played it right?" said Jonathan Redgrave.

"Is it a question?" said Xiong.

"I'm saying, Manny said the kid played it just right. Do you agree with that assessment?" said Redgrave, sounding annoyed.

"He seemed sad," said Xiong.

"You hear this?" asked Redgrave, looking at Manny Vega in front. The driver shook his head.

"May I ask a question," said Xiong.

"Please," said Redgrave.

"What are you going to do with him?" asked Xiong.

"He's a good kid. He's played it straight so far," said Redgrave. "Shit, you know better than anyone, once you're in the field . . . you are in the field."

Xiong glanced at Manny in the mirror. The man nodded. They were all in the field.

"So, it is now 4:39 p.m. I told you I'd have the phone back by the end of the day," said Valencia Walker, sounding cocky. She slid the missing iPhone across the table to Elizabeth Carlyle, and then turned her attention back to Chris Cowley. He looked appropriately wrung out.

"Technically, you said 'a few hours,'" said Elizabeth.

"Nonetheless," said Valencia.

"Should I tell him how much you cost?" asked Elizabeth.

"I don't think that would be appropriate," said Valencia.

Chris shook his head and a pained look passed over his face. "I want to thank you," he said, raising his hand and tapping the table with his fingertips. "I don't even know what to say."

Right then the door of the office opened and Elizabeth's assistant, Andy, poked his head in. "Ms. Carlyle, there is somebody downstairs at security who wants to speak to you."

"Take a message," said Elizabeth.

"They say it's urgent. About a phone."

"One person?" asked Elizabeth.

Valencia stood, pulled out her own phone, and began texting her men. She didn't know exactly what was happening, but she knew her night was far from over.

"One man, yes," said Andy.

"Tell security to personally escort him here. Tell them, under no circumstances should they let him go," said Elizabeth.

Valencia and Andy went straight to the elevator and got there before it arrived. When the doors opened, Valencia was surprised to see an Indian or Pakistani man sandwiched between two of the building's suited security staff. The man wore a stained beige shirt, and a loose maroon tie. He had jet-black hair and a black mustache, but appeared to be in his sixties. He was clearly very nervous.

Valencia thought about checking him for weapons but decided against it. "This way," she said, motioning in the direction of Elizabeth's office. She let the guards lead the way. Andy followed behind.

Chris and Elizabeth were both standing when the group arrived.

"Thank you, please wait outside," said Elizabeth, dismissing the guards and Andy. The door closed and the four of them were left alone.

The man raised his hands apologetically. "I'm a delivery man. I don't know what this is. I got a call for a delivery. I met them, they give me paper, that's it."

"Tell us what you've been asked to deliver," said Elizabeth.

"I don't want to get in trouble," said the man.

"I can assure you—you are not going to get in any trouble," said Valencia. She stole a glance at Chris Cowley. He appeared to be as confused by what was happening as she was.

"I'm not with them," said the man.

"We know," said Elizabeth. "Now tell us what you've been told to say."

"They gave me two hundred and twenty dollars. They say, tell them, 'we have the Cal . . .'" The man searched his mind for the word.

"Calcott files?" asked Elizabeth.

He nodded.

"What else?" asked Valencia, in the friendliest voice she possessed.

The man took a folded envelope out of his pocket, unfolded it, and with some difficulty tore it open. From inside he pulled out a plain white page with black handwriting on it. He began to read from it: "They say 'You have until tomorrow, five p.m.' They say 'Seven hundred and fifty thousand dollars cash.' They say 'We'll be back in communication with you.'"

The man looked up from the page, which was shaking, and swallowed. Valencia nodded at him to continue. He looked back down.

"They say otherwise they go to Emerson lawyers. They say, 'We know their address.' They say, '1604 Broadway,' and then they go to *New York Post, New York Times, CNN*, everywhere, news. Emails." He looked back up and took a deep breath.

"What's your name?" asked Valencia.

"Juahar."

"Juahar, we're gonna need the two hundred and twenty dollars that they gave you. We'll replace it with fresh bills." She took a step closer to him. "Did they write that note, or did you?"

"I didn't write it. They wrote it. Not me."

"The envelope and paper? Did they have the paper?"

"Yeah, yeah, it's all them."

"Fine, why don't you set that note and envelope down right there." She pointed at the table. "We're also going to need to take a statement from you, get a little bit more of the details fleshed out. Are you okay with that?"

"Yeah, but . . ." said Juahar. He frowned, shrugged, turned his palms up.

"Don't worry," interjected Elizabeth, her face showing exactly how angry she was. "You'll be paid for your time."

2

YOU WORK FOR US

"That will be all, Chris," said Elizabeth. The message—delivered with raised eyebrows and a cold expression—couldn't have been clearer. Still, for a moment Chris didn't understand what was happening. He stood there blinking, then looked at the deliveryman, as though he might be able to help. The deliveryman offered nothing. *Seven hundred and fifty thousand*—the number passed through Chris's mind without meaning. He looked at Valencia and saw her standing there with her arms crossed. She nodded to him like, *Yes, this is happening*. Chris finally understood; he was being asked to leave the room.

His cell phone lay facedown on the table; a moment passed while Chris deliberated as to whether or not he should take it. His eyes went to a piece of tape on the back, and he wondered if Valencia had put it there. Finally, he picked it up, held it, waited a second for any objections, and then jammed it into his pocket.

Then he looked back at Elizabeth. "I'll be in my office," he said. The words came out at a lower volume than he'd hoped. The walk to the door seemed endless. His ears were ringing, and he felt dizzy.

When he finally stepped out, he saw Elizabeth's assistant Andy seated at his desk. The expression on Andy's face suggested a mixture of disbelief and watchfulness. "Back, to my office," Chris whispered to himself. He pointed down the hall. One of the security guards sat near Andy's desk. His posture and facial expression indicated that he understood something big was happening. He kept his eyes on Chris.

Look normal, Chris told himself. Normal walking feet, and hands in pockets.

As he made his way down the hall his mind went to the beginning of his problems. Just under two weeks earlier (an overcast Saturday), he'd been in his apartment working on an answer to a motion when someone knocked on his door. The building had an intercom system— he figured it was a neighbor knocking.

When he looked through the peephole, he saw three men standing in the hallway. They wore suits and ties. That was the precise moment when all of this started. There'd been nothing leading up to it. One day you're home doing a little work, the next you're involved in a criminal conspiracy.

At first, the men at the door looked like detectives, maybe FBI agents. Keeping his eye on the peephole, and without opening the door, he asked who it was. He couldn't remember the exact words they used when they answered: something about needing to open the door right then.

He remembered some paperwork being held up—some kind of warrant. He leaned away from the door for a second and considered grabbing his phone. His heart was racing. The next thing he remembered was the sound of metal gently bumping against metal; he looked through the peephole again and could see that one of the men was bent over. Chris could only see the man's rump.

It occurred to Chris that the man was picking the lock. Scared that the guy was going to damage his door, Chris pulled it open and tried to make himself stand tall like a lawyer who wasn't at all scared of cops.

The men didn't ask if they could enter. They just walked right in. There were five of them in total: two stayed in the hallway, and three pushed their way right past him. The next thing Chris remembered he was sitting on the couch. One of the men, a tall, skinny white guy with pitted skin, sat down next to him. He had thin hair, and a receding hairline. His eyes were dark, almost black, and set close together. He wore a slightly wrinkled gray suit. He seemed like the leader.

He had a cheap-looking book bag in his hand, and he unzipped it and pulled out a laptop. At that point, Chris still thought the men were law enforcement, at the wrong door, maybe looking for one of his neighbors.

I'm going to have your fucking badges for this, Chris remembered thinking with a kind of bloodlust. *I'm a fucking lawyer.*

The man opened the computer, typed in a security code, and shifted in his seat.

"Okay, so here's the deal," he said. "You've been viewing child pornography. It doesn't matter if you thought they were eighteen, it doesn't matter if you think you can beat the case. It will be in the news."

Chris stayed silent and then shook his head.

The man continued. "I guarantee you. One phone call and it will be all over the place. Fucking BuzzFeed, everywhere."

The man looked at one of his associates as if he were going to ask a question, then he seemed to decide against it and continued talking to Chris. "People love when lawyers get busted with child porn. They love nothing more. It's their favorite thing. You can't get it off you. That kind of shit sticks with you for the rest of your life."

Chris wondered if he was joking; he turned and looked at the other two men. They were busy going through his things. One of them looked Latino, or Middle Eastern, the other was pink-skinned, short, and ugly. Chris could see the darker one at the dresser near his bed. He was pushing the clothes around inside it as if he were looking for something.

This can't be happening, thought Chris. "They can't," he said to the man seated next to him. The other man, the white one, had been searching in the closet, but now moved on to the desk. When he started taking pictures of the papers there, Chris blurted out, "You can't do that."

He tried to stand, but the man next to him grabbed his wrist and pulled him back down. He was stronger than he looked. It felt like he could break Chris's wrist if he wanted.

It was at that point that Chris became truly scared. These weren't cops.

"Look," said the man. "Look at this." He wanted to show Chris something on the laptop. Chris squinted and saw an article about some guy being arrested for child pornography.

Then he clicked through a few more articles about different men. "Look," said the man, clicking on a blue file. A spreadsheet opened. The man pointed out things with his cursor: "That's your IP address. That's the date, that's the time. That's the URL."

"That was DudePorn.com," Chris argued, his voice shaking. "Those are legal sites, none of this is illegal."

The man clicked back to the spreadsheet, and with the mouse, began pointing out URLs that were highlighted. He then opened another file, clicked on it, and a screen grab from a video popped up. "This is Brendan Francis Nelson," said the man, pointing at the naked boy's face. "He's fifteen; he lives in Austin."

Chris had never seen that boy, porno or not, but the man was already opening another file. "This is Kent Sampson, fourteen, Alameda, California." Chris did actually remember looking at that one. "Billy McCormick—what is this? Twinkworld—Littleton, Colorado, sixteen years old. Fourteen times in the last four weeks. We can go through them all if you want."

Chris protested that they weren't on his computer.

"They're on your computer," the man insisted.

Chris believed him. His mouth went dry. He wanted to ask the men to leave, but he couldn't come up with the words. *This is not fucking fair*, he thought. *This is total and complete bullshit. I will have your badge. I'll sue you to the moon and back, motherfucker.*

The man sitting next to him produced a cell phone and showed Chris a saved contact. "Okay, this number is for Ali Roth," he said. "She is the assistant U.S. attorney in the Eastern District. She'll prosecute your case. She's a boss in the courtroom, merciless. She works for us."

He scooted on his seat and leaned forward so he was facing Chris straight on. "Look at me," he said. His breath smelled like sour milk. "Look at me."

Chris did as he was told.

"You work for us now. This isn't law school." He studied Chris's face in a way that felt strangely intimate. "It's not court. You work for us."

The man leaned back on the couch. The other men had gone deeper into Chris's apartment, and Chris could no longer see them. The man on the couch angled the laptop toward Chris. It took a moment to understand that he was looking at a video of himself. It had been shot from the ceiling of his kitchen. The video showed Chris making coffee. It had been that morning. Chris was still wearing the same clothes.

The man closed the computer. "Do you understand what I'm telling you? We know everything about you. No, no, no," the man said, raising a hand, shifting in his seat and crossing one leg over the other. "I've been through this before. This is what we do. It seems big to you, but it's not. I've been through this a thousand times. I'll tell you one thing for certain—this is for real."

Chris—idiotically, in retrospect—protested about the camera.

The man raised a hand and silenced him. He reached out and put a hand on Chris's knee. "Your mother lives at 1709 Hunters Point Drive, in Boulder, Colorado," he said. "Your father lives at 3402 Suskind Road, Chapel Hill. Your sister lives at 693 Elmhurst Park Road, Palo Alto. Your grandmother lives in Ashland, Oregon. I only have to send a text message. It doesn't even bother me. It would be the easiest decision of my day. No, no, no"—he shushed Chris again—"stop making it so complicated."

By that point the two other men had returned to the living room. Chris thought it might be helpful to remember their faces, but he was too scared to look at them. Instead he stared at a space on the floor.

After a few seconds, the man with the laptop tapped him on the leg with the back of his hand. Chris looked at him and was surprised to see that his face had transformed; he didn't look angry anymore. He looked almost friendly. He held out a hand to shake and Chris shook it.

"You work for us."

Valencia Walker, when she got home that night, changed from her work clothes into sweatpants and a simple cotton T-shirt. She lived alone in an expensive, high-ceilinged, two-bedroom apartment on the Upper West Side that faced Central Park. Standing in her kitchen, she peeled Saran Wrap off her dinner bowl and looked at the salmon dinner her domestic assistant had prepared. Her attention was drawn to a grayish part of the filet. She put the bowl into the microwave and hit the button for ninety seconds. *Brain-colored*, she thought, while the microwave hummed.

Her thoughts shifted to the deliveryman and his ransom note. *Who the hell would have sent this guy?* She was just beginning to consider opening her bathroom blinds to signal a meeting when her thoughts were interrupted by an incoming call on her cell phone. She knew it was Elizabeth before she looked at it.

"Hello, my dear," answered Valencia, fitting her earpiece and muting the television news.

"I changed my mind," said Elizabeth.

"Tell me."

"What do you think of offering less, say a hundred thousand?"

Valencia took a sip of wine, set it down, and walked toward her living room. "I don't think that's a good option."

"Why not?" asked Elizabeth.

"Liz, this is not a lot of money." They'd already had this conversation back at the office. Valencia had explained the risk of not paying.

"It's not the price," said Elizabeth. "It's the partners—Gary? Jeff? Fuck, can you imagine? So guys, we're being blackmailed . . ."

"Tell them what I told you," said Valencia.

"That it boils down to—"

"That we have less than twenty-four hours," said Valencia, interrupting her. "That there is no reason to believe the threat lacks credibility; that the price is worth stopping the threat; and, finally, most important, that only in paying them—given the hand we've been dealt—can we identify them."

"So—"

"So, pay, identify, assess."

"And if the partners say, no?"

"Then you have a PR problem that costs a lot more than seven hundred and fifty thousand dollars to fix," said Valencia. She looked at herself reflected in the window and brushed at her eyebrows. Again, her mind returned to the question of who was blackmailing them. The truth was, she had no idea, and until she was told otherwise, she would treat it like one more problem that needed fixing.

After a long silence, Elizabeth spoke: "You know when I applied for my first job, fresh out of law school, they asked me what I saw myself doing in five years. You know what I told them?"

"Judge?"

"I said I wanted to run a midsized film studio."

Valencia smiled. The microwave beeped.

"I'll have a plan, on how we're going to pay, by tomorrow morning," said Valencia. "It'll be strong. My men are good, and I can bring in help for this. Experienced, professional, help."

"Okay," said Elizabeth. "I'll call you in the morning."

The line went dead.

Valencia walked back to her kitchen, took a dish towel and lifted the hot bowl out of the microwave. She pulled the plastic wrap off and watched the steam rise. A lemon seed in the quinoa caught her eye and she used her nails to pluck it out. She then spooned the food onto a plate, rinsed the bowl, and put it in the dishwasher.

Her mind, as she tidied up, stayed on Elizabeth. The woman was tough, there was no question about that. Valencia had seen her shout down a CEO in his own office. She'd seen her dismantle witnesses on the stand. Most important, she'd seen the way Elizabeth's colleagues and underlings acted around her. She demanded respect. So what would happen if she sat Elizabeth down for a dinner and mapped out exactly what forces were at play here?

She thought about a past dinner they'd had. It had been two or three years ago. They ate paella at a place in Chelsea, and they were on their second bottle of wine. Elizabeth was drunk and got emotional; she told a story about being molested by an uncle. The uncle—her mother's brother—had eventually been caught and charged with molesting his own children.

Elizabeth's mother demanded to know if he'd ever touched her. She told her mother no. "It was a simple choice," she said. "He'd already been caught. Why add more problems to everything else?"

Valencia un-muted the television; on it a baby-faced pundit carried on about congressional dysfunction. She glanced down at her food, isolated the gray bit of salmon, cut it off with her fork, and pushed it to the side of her plate.

At that exact moment, Chris Cowley, still tucked away in his office, sat clipping his fingernails. It was ten minutes past nine o'clock; a miserable thirteen hours had passed since the pickpocketing. He finished his left hand and swept all the white trimmings off his desk and into the trash. He wondered whether someone would come and collect the trimmings for DNA samples. Anything was possible.

After changing back into his street clothes, he patted his jacket pocket and confirmed that the thumb drive was still there. Then, keeping his back to the door, he took the drive out, wrapped it in a twenty-dollar bill, and tucked the whole thing back into his pocket.

When he was done, he closed his eyes, took a moment and tried to pray. *Just help*, he prayed. *Please, just help.*

He'd been given two tasks for the day. The first was to allow his cell phone to be stolen. That one—while technically criminal and certainly frightening—was relatively simple. The second task was more complicated. His handlers had given him a thumb drive and instructed him to plug it into his boss's computer.

He'd argued that he wouldn't be able to do that, that he didn't have access to her office.

The lead man, Jonathan, frowned, shook his head, and told Chris he would. "You have to think positively," he said.

And he did. After he confessed that his phone had been stolen, Elizabeth brought him to her office, told him to wait, and excused herself. Just like that, he was left all alone. Pretending to be completely unbothered, he looked around like he was admiring her decor. He yawned, turned, and searched for cameras. The only one he could see was attached to her computer.

I'll grab a pen, he told himself. *If they come, I'll say I was grabbing a pen; it's a pen*—he practiced in his mind—*I needed a pen.* Drymouthed, he pulled a yellow Post-it note off a stack on her desk and stuck it above the camera's lens. After that, he plugged the thumb drive into her computer and watched the screen. A prompt asked: *Are you sure you want to run program TX32H on this computer?* Chris looked at the door, looked back at the screen, clicked *Yes*.

The computer hummed; he waited in misery and watched the blue progress bar slowly fill. When it was done, he pulled the drive from the port, removed the Post-it note from the camera, pushed both into his right pants pocket, and moved back to the other side of the room. Less than a minute later, the door swung open, and Elizabeth and Michael D'Angelo entered the office.

After that—and after his trip back to Grand Central with Valencia and her men—Chris spent the rest of the day pretending to work.

He opened paper files and pretended to read them. He opened documents on his computer and pretended to work on them. He shredded the draft of a motion near the copy machines. He replied to personal emails. He clicked around online. He sat and stared at his screen.

Finally, at a little after four thirty Elizabeth called him back to her office. Valencia Walker, looking proud and relaxed, was already there. The phone had been found. Everyone was smiling. There was a moment where he felt almost happy. He'd had the thing stolen, and now it was back. Both sides won. He did his job, and it was done. The feeling was short lived. The deliveryman came.

Which is all to say it didn't matter if anyone came and collected his fingernails. He had enough problems.

On his way out, when he finally left for the day, Chris stopped by the bathroom, urinated, pulled on his penis—which seemed to have shrunk—washed his hands, and studied his face in the mirror. A new set of wrinkles had appeared near his eyes. During his walk from the bathroom to the elevator he passed four of his colleagues' offices; they sat slumped, typing away, utterly ignorant of what was happening around them. The elevator, when it arrived, smelled like cigarettes. He rode down alone.

Outside, he set off north by foot on Madison Avenue. His mind occupied itself with the question of whether he was currently being followed. Surely somebody from his own law firm would be watching. He could feel the eyes on him, but he resisted the urge to actually turn and look. It didn't matter. None of it did.

The street, at any rate, was strangely empty. A few tourists, shivering against the cold spring night, hurried back to their hotels after what appeared to be successful shopping trips. A homeless man begged for change from the doorway of a Brooks Brothers. Steam rose from a vent; taxis and Ubers passed by in steady streams on the street.

Maybe the lawyer's life isn't for me, thought Chris. What would it look like to work for a law firm for the next twenty years? Is that a life worth living? It was a depressing thought. If he could just navigate his way through this little situation, perhaps he'd be able to get out and have a genuine reset.

This was a wake-up call. He could go into public interest law. Get staffed at the ACLU. Get out of this white-collar hellhole. Maybe give up the law. Move to California. Write a novel. Write a thriller.

At East Forty-Ninth Street, he turned left and headed west toward Fifth Avenue. From there, he headed up to Fifty-Second Street, where there was a smoothie stand on the corner. After approaching it, he looked in and confirmed that the man he was supposed to meet was there.

Sitting alone inside the small trailer was one of Chris's tormentors, the shaved-headed Mexican-looking one with the scars on his face. He nodded when he saw Chris, looked at his watch, and pushed himself up. "What can I get you?" he asked, his eyes not looking directly at Chris, but above and beyond his shoulder at the street behind him.

Chris looked at the menu and realized he was actually quite hungry. "Strawberry-mango," he said. "Can you add protein?"

The man smiled and turned his back to Chris. He made the smoothie with a surprising level of attention, measuring the ingredients carefully. Chris watched him blend them together. He stared at his back while the man worked, and wondered what thoughts were running through his mind. There was something attractive about him, thought Chris. Maybe when it was all done and over, they could meet up, get a hotel, watch some Netflix. *Where do you live?* Chris thought about asking him, *Do you party?*

The man poured the smoothie into a plastic cup and scraped the blender until the cup was filled. He fitted a lid on the cup and brought it to the window.

"Six dollars," he said.

Chris pulled out the thumb drive—wrapped in the twenty-dollar bill—and passed it all through the window, just as he'd been instructed.

"Thanks," said the man, handing back fourteen dollars. "I'll see you later."

"Did I wake you?" asked Valencia.

"Nope, I'm up," said Billy Sharrock. He pulled the phone away from his ear and looked at the time. It was 4:45 a.m. He glanced at his bedroom window and saw that it was dark.

"I need you to go back to that little shop we were at," said Valencia. "The phone place. Talk to the owner."

"How much talking?"

"As much as he needs," said Valencia.

"Alone?"

"Is that a problem?"

"Nah, I'm just thinking out loud."

"Get there early, watch the door, make sure he comes in before you enter. We don't wanna give him any excuses."

"Come on, boss," said Billy. It was too early to insult his intelligence.

"Call me if you have any problems."

The line went dead.

Billy yawned and looked at his girlfriend, who was still sleeping next to him. They'd been using her for little jobs here and there. She was game and liked the money. For a second, while they'd been talking, Billy thought Valencia was going to ask him to bring her. He wished she had. It would be a lot more entertaining.

Billy had fractured a knee in Afghanistan, and it always felt tight in the morning. He went straight to the bathroom, shit, showered, and shaved. After getting dressed—he'd wear jeans, a hoodie, and a work jacket for this job—he went to his closet and grabbed a Mets hat.

In his office, he pulled up a chair near his safe, sat down, and twisted the dial until the safe opened. He looked at his guns and chose the 9 mm, put it in a soft case, and grabbed two spare magazines. From a different closet, he pulled out a large toolbox and fit the gun case into it. He grabbed a pair of heavy-duty pliers from a different box and a roll of duct tape, and put them in. He found his retractable baton, snapped it open, closed it, and put it in too.

He went back to his office and grabbed his lock-picking tools. From the back of the closet he pulled out a shoebox that held different license plates; he went through them and selected a set of New York ones, set them into the toolbox, and closed it all up.

From there he went to his kitchen, brewed coffee, and poured himself a bowl of healthy flakes. His girlfriend said he was getting fat, so he'd been torturing himself with this shit. While he ate, he looked at ESPN on his phone. The NBA playoffs had just begun. He'd grown up outside Indianapolis and liked to keep an eye on the Pacers.

When he got down to the garage below his apartment building, he pulled out his cell phone and, for billing purposes, took a screenshot of the time. Then he opened the back door of his van and set his toolbox inside. Moving efficiently, he switched out his license plates. He'd made the plates himself, copying numbers from other registered white vans, and using a tin press and enamel paint.

When he was done swapping plates, he pulled himself into the back of the van, took the toolbox, and placed it inside a larger lockbox. He then hopped out, got in the driver's seat, backed the van out of its spot, and headed toward Manhattan. He was happy to be up at this time; he liked to get an early start on his day.

It was 6:14 a.m. when he arrived at the location. He parked the van across from the building that housed the American iPhone Repair shop. Besides an old Chinese woman rooting around in some recyclables, and a few pedestrians walking west, nobody else was on the street. Billy opened his glove box and took out a laminated piece of paper with a New York City Department of Sanitation seal on it, and a phone number that went straight to voicemail at the department. As far as he knew, nobody had ever called. He'd never been issued a parking ticket.

Then he opened the partition between the front and the cargo area, stepped back, and opened the lockbox. He pulled his Mets hat on, got back into the driver's seat, and checked his appearance in the mirror. Then he got out of the van and walked west on Forty-Seventh Street. At this hour all the shops on the street were still closed, even the Starbucks on the corner. He circled the entire block looking for alternative service entrances but didn't see any.

When he got back into the van, he took the hat off, found a notepad on the floor, and set it on the seat next to him. He pulled out a small battery-operated radio from the glove compartment, turned it on, found some sports talk, and began watching the front door.

At fifteen minutes after ten, Billy began to suspect his target had stayed home that day. He put the hat back on and turned the radio off. In the back of the van he took the toolbox out, hopped out the back door, and crossed the street. The prospect of not getting results was already bringing on a kind of guilty feeling.

When he got close to the door, he pulled out his cell phone, and for the next five minutes pretended to have a conversation on it. If a person passed, he repeated phrases like, *I know, I know,* and *Yeah, sure, let me know, no problem.*

Finally, after five minutes, a young woman walked up to the door, rang, and was buzzed in. Still holding the phone to his ear and lugging his toolbox, Billy caught the door and followed her.

On the third floor, he found a piece of paper taped to the door of the American iPhone Repair shop. The note read *Temporarily closed. For phone pickup call (917) 258-4312.* Billy pulled the paper off the door, folded it, and put it in his pocket. He then looked at the lock, a dead bolt. It would take him less than three minutes to get in.

Elizabeth Carlyle's breakfast consisted of whole wheat toast with peanut butter and honey. She ate it alone standing at her kitchen island feeling a buzzing kind of dread. Still chewing, she poured coffee into a pint glass, added skim milk, dropped in three ice cubes, and then tapped her fingers on the counter while she waited for it to cool. She then drank the entire thing and set the glass in the sink.

Her husband was upstairs getting dressed. She hadn't told him anything about what was happening at work. She couldn't stand the idea of seeing any kind of amusement in his eyes. The man could find amusement in anything. A fine trait, except when it wasn't. Before leaving, she called up the stairs to him, "I've got to run, I'll see you later." He didn't respond.

Their marriage could be defined by these moments of one-way conversation. Elizabeth spoke, Tyler listened—at least he seemed to. The man was truly stuck inside his own head. Which wasn't to say he wasn't a great conversationalist. He could be—in fact, that's what initially drew her to him. The man could speak on any subject when he wanted to. Or he could be his perfectly unbothered silent self. *I'll see you later*, Elizabeth repeated in her mind as she backed down her driveway. He could have easily answered, *Yes, dear, I'll see you later.* Anything would have been better than silence.

They'd been together since Elizabeth was thirty years old. She still lived in the city back then, and one night on a whim she went to the birthday party of a colleague's friend. The party had been at the Odeon. The birthday boy had been Tyler. They got married in 1992, barely surviving Tyler's insistence on voting for the first Bush. She had a baby—a daughter, named Genevieve—while she was still at Heller, Bromwell, Burgess, Drake. Her second daughter, Mary, was born a year after Elizabeth joined Mooney, Driscoll, Hathaway, Evans, Miller. The two maternity leaves were the only times she'd ever taken off from work. She hated staying home. It didn't suit her.

It took ten minutes to drive to the Pleasantville Metro-North station. She arrived that morning six minutes before the 6:22 train. She walked past a group of bleary-eyed commuters and stared north up the tracks. The sky was gray and there was no wind.

Her plan, when she got to the office, was to corner Scott Driscoll—the most influential of the senior partners—and explain to him exactly what was happening. She'd then have him recruit two other partners—Iverson and Rosen seemed like the most likely candidates—and loop them in. With that small group, she could call an emergency meeting and have Scott ask the partners to sign off on a $750,000 discretionary investigation fund.

She could already see the twisted expressions that would appear on their faces: *Wait, what? What the hell kind of investigation fund? Nothing illegal*, she'd have Scott say, *but nothing you want to know about either.* Iverson and Rosen—on cue—would weigh in: *Yes*, they'd say. *Do it.* The other partners, God willing, would fall in line. Elizabeth thought the plan might just work.

When the train arrived, Elizabeth sat down next to a white-haired old woman who appeared to be headed off on a hike. The train rolled south. Elizabeth kept her eyes on the back of the seat in front of her. She had no desire to pull out her computer and work. She didn't want to read the news. She wanted to sit in silence.

While she sat, her mind bounced back and forth between the problem at hand and random, disconnected questions: Was her jaw more masculine than her daughter's? Did she currently have breast cancer? If the partners said no to the request for money, would she need to call Calcott immediately?

Then her thoughts shifted to Valencia. She pictured her getting dressed. Elizabeth had been to her apartment, but she'd never seen her closet. Now, she imagined it as large and airy. Her suits and dresses would be arranged by color. They would hang perfectly. There would be built-in lights. Her underwear and bras would be new and expensive. Smoothly sliding drawers would hold her jewelry. Elizabeth's own closet was nice, but not like that.

Right then, a man walking down the aisle interrupted her thoughts. The man looked similar to Michael D'Angelo; that was enough to start her mind racing. What had he learned? She took out her phone and called him.

"So?" she asked when he answered.

"He left the office a little after nine," said D'Angelo, referring to Chris Cowley. "He walked a few blocks to a juice stand, took a cab home, stayed there until at least one thirty, when I left."

"Did you check his emails?" Elizabeth asked.

"Not yet, Liz, I got home at two thirty this morning."

"Okay, do it when you get in. Thanks, Michael," she said, hanging up before he could respond. The man worked hard; she appreciated him for that, but he moved slowly.

She called Valencia next.

"Walker," said Valencia, sounding wide-awake when she answered.

"Tell me you have a plan."

"Did you talk to the partners?"

"Not yet," said Elizabeth. "Tell me the plan."

"Okay, presuming you get the money and decide to go that route, it isn't complicated. Our goal is to find out who is doing this. I'll make the payment. My men will be monitoring me. We'll sew GPS rats into the bag. We'll have drones in the sky watching the field."

"Are you out of your mind?" asked Elizabeth.

"I talked to my guy," said Valencia. "He's available tonight for whatever we need. I outlined the basic scenario, and he thinks two drones should be more than enough."

Elizabeth scooted in her seat, looked out the window at the dark trees. "This is absolutely absurd," she said.

"Liz, sweetie, this is war. We need to find out who they are and shut them down. If this sounds like too much, I think you should call John Braxton at the FBI. He's good, discreet; he'll keep it quiet."

"You've cleared your day, I assume?" asked Elizabeth.

"Honey, we are in full-fledge war mode," said Valencia.

"Good," said Elizabeth. "I'll call soon."

Elizabeth put her phone down and closed her eyes for a moment. She could feel panic in her chest: she felt it in her lungs, under her heart, above her stomach; it was in her brain, her temples, and her jaw. This was uncharted territory. *Steps*, she told herself. *There are steps that need to be taken. First, get the partners to sign off—*

"We've got a bird-watching group," said the old woman next to her. Elizabeth opened her eyes and turned her head toward the woman. "We meet once a month," she said, as if she were answering a question Elizabeth had asked.

Elizabeth pursed her lips and nodded.

"But not in the winter," said the woman. She appeared to have cataracts; her blue eyes were milky. "We're going to *good old* Central Park." The woman then scrunched her face up, as if a flood of beautiful memories were passing through her mind. "I'm trying to spot a hooded warbler," she said.

"It's good to have hobbies," said Elizabeth, squeezing her mouth into a smile, leaning her head back against the seat, and closing her eyes again.

The Rabinowitz brothers lived in a large four-bedroom house on Homecrest Avenue, in Sheepshead Bay, Brooklyn. Their uncle owned the house; they still had to pay nearly market rate to stay there.

That day, as noon approached, Yuri Rabinowitz, the older of the two brothers, had been awake for almost four hours. He'd been nervously watching MMA on TV, and he turned it off now. The fact that his brother was still sleeping annoyed him. This was not a day to sleep in. He shouldn't have to explain that. It should be self-evident.

Yuri got up from the couch and climbed the stairs, two at a time, to the second floor. Surely, some girl would be in Isaac's room; he could already imagine her, head turned away, long hair, shirtless. The idea of walking in on them caused an unwelcome feeling of shame to well up inside him.

Still, he knocked hard on the door, and called out, "*Wake up, fuck head.*" After not hearing anything, he turned the knob and looked in. He was surprised to see his brother sleeping alone. "*It's time to get up, bitch.*"

Isaac put a pillow over his head.

Yuri stepped to the bed and pulled the blanket back. "*You shit,*" he said.

"Fuck off," said Isaac, in English.

"*I told you not to get drunk,*" said Yuri.

"I didn't."

The air around the bed smelled like a homeless man; it smelled like vomit. Yuri wanted to slap him in the head. "*We have to go to the gym,*" he said. "*You have to snap out of this shit. Get your head right.*"

"It's my off day," said Isaac. He turned and tried to go back to sleep. "I did legs yesterday." He then turned back, looked at his brother, and said, "Besides, you should relax"—then, switching to Russian, added—"*Treat every Monday like a Monday and you'll be rich by Friday.*"

It was something their father used to say. Isaac was saying this to shame his brother. He was weaponizing the phrase to highlight Yuri's fear. A neutral observer probably wouldn't have read it that way, but both brothers understood it plainly. They had their own coded language. A shot had been fired.

Yuri walked over to his brother's closet and picked up a pair of his jeans that had fallen to the floor. An all-consuming anger filled him. His diaphragm felt pinched. Did his brother not understand what they were going to do that day? Did he have no fucking clue? They were about to blackmail a major New York law firm. What the hell was he thinking?

He pulled the leather belt out of the pants, let the pants fall back to the floor, and began looping the belt around his fist, tightening it with each turn. When he finished, he faced his brother, but Isaac had already hopped out of bed and was pulling on a shirt.

Yuri weighed whether or not he should still whip him. Sometimes it was the only way to get through. He hadn't hit his brother in a few weeks. Lately, he'd just been pinning his head to the ground. The last time he whipped him, he'd left pink welts on the younger man's back and made him cry. It had been a pitiful sight.

Their father, before he died, used to whip Yuri. It was what they'd always done. If things escalated beyond yelling, a whipping was in order. One couldn't allow anarchy to rule. Still, he couldn't strike his brother if he was actually getting ready. That would violate their unwritten rules. A mixture of relief and disappointment washed through him.

In the kitchen, he texted his friend Moishe Groysman: *Gym half hour.*

Yuri stood there for a moment, breathing and staring at the wood on the cabinet. *You need to get a hold of yourself,* he thought.

He pulled out the protein powder and began making smoothies. They couldn't be fighting today. A peace offering was in order. He was, after all, the older brother; he had to act more mature. Internal discipline. He scooped out the whey powder and dumped it into the blender. Treat every Monday like a Monday. *Fucking cocksucker.* He poured milk into the blender, cracked four eggs into it, peeled four bananas and put them in. After turning on the blender he stood there staring at it, watching the bananas swirl and disappear.

Upon waking that day, Chris Cowley experienced a tranquil few seconds of amnesia. A moment later his problems came barreling back. The prospect of being publicly charged with possession of child pornography wasn't even the worst of it. The worst was the injustice. He hadn't done anything wrong. He'd looked at pornography; that was it. Now his family was being threatened. Now he'd been pulled into a criminal conspiracy. He was ruined. A very specific and lonely kind of helplessness seeped into him and the only way he could think to fight it was to curse uselessly in his mind.

At work he spent most of the morning at his desk, wondering just who the hell he was dealing with. Besides giving their first names—and lord knows if those were even real—his handlers hadn't identified themselves. The skinny one, the leader, had said he was called Jonathan. He didn't catch the shaved-headed one's name. The small, ugly white guy was called JP or PJ.

Nothing more was given. No badges had been shown. He had no way of contacting them. On the two occasions they'd wanted to make contact, they'd simply approached him: once on the train, and once on the street outside his apartment.

Chris suspected they were working for some kind of intelligence agency; some kind of NSA-type group. They seemed too bold to be mere criminals. Besides, the Calcott case, with its Arabian Peninsula entanglements, was surely being monitored by some intelligence agency. Elizabeth hadn't filled the team in on exactly what that was about. She firewalled it, but Chris had heard enough to know that it involved Oman, shell corporations, and access to oil-licensing fees.

Elizabeth had made it clear that CDH wasn't going to address any of what the special opportunities fund was doing. "Don't worry about it," she said, when one of Chris's colleagues had asked. "It isn't relevant to *this* case." The few junior associates seated at the table exchanged glances, but nobody ever brought it up again.

Still, Chris found it hard to believe that any U.S. government agency would act so unlawfully. For God's sake, he was a member of the New York State Bar; he worked at one of the most powerful law firms in the country. Would they do that? Was that even possible? He didn't know.

At noon, on his way to the restroom he was approached by one of his coworkers, David Moss, a mid-level associate who was two years his senior. "You're off the case?" Moss asked, grabbing his arm while they walked.

"Yep," said Chris.

"Why?"

"Conflict," said Chris, politely freeing his arm. "I have a cousin who works at Emerson."

"Why didn't you tell us earlier?"

"I didn't know."

That was the script Elizabeth had given him last night: Conflict. A cousin. I didn't know.

"Lucky bastard," said Moss. "I'd give up my firstborn son to be off this case."

"So quit," said Chris, ducking into the bathroom.

At the urinal an obvious question occurred to him: Why hadn't Elizabeth fired him yet? Why wasn't he fired yesterday? Why not today? More questions: What would happen if he was fired? What would those men do if he lost his job? He'd be useless to them. They wouldn't need anything else from him. He'd be free.

That thought provided comfort for less than two seconds. The men who were running him wouldn't want some useless lawyer walking around knowing they were involved in this case. In fact, he remembered the ugly guy saying: "You gotta stay in the game, though. Once we sub you out, we can't sub you back in."

He hadn't understood what that meant at the time. Everything they'd said had washed over him; now it was beginning to make sense.

A few hours after his hallway conversation, he had another disturbing encounter. Michael D'Angelo, CDH's investigator, stopped by his office to ask more questions.

"Hey, knock, knock," said D'Angelo, opening the door and poking his head in. "Let me ask you a question?"

"Yeah," said Chris, turning from his computer. He hoped the expression on his face would suggest he was busy, but the man seemed blind to hints.

"Had you ever *seen* that pickpocket before?" asked D'Angelo.

"Why would I have seen him?"

The investigator stepped in farther, closed the door behind him. "Look, Chris, I'm sure you know what's going on here. This is big. This is a really big problem." He lowered his voice, like he was letting Chris in on a secret plot: "We think you may have been targeted."

A silence hung between them for a moment.

"Maybe you would have *seen* someone hanging around?"

Chris's mind flashed to the idea of the surveillance footage from his own apartment building. Would someone eventually look at that and see his unwelcome visitors? Had they taken care of the video? Surely, they would have thought of that. "No." He shook his head. "I don't think so."

"Any strange emails?" asked D'Angelo.

Chris's eyes went back to his monitor. He let his head drop to the side a little, pursed his lips, pretended to think. "Not that I know of." He shook his head, looked at the investigator, pushed himself back in his seat a little. "Do you think I'm going to get fired?" he whispered.

"I think that's the least of your worries."

Chris rubbed around his eyes. "I'm so fucked," he said.

It was only partly an act; he was fucked, but he wanted the investigator to have a certain impression of him. He wanted to seem naive and scared. "I'm so fucked," he whispered, again.

D'Angelo stared at him with a flat expression. "Anyway," said the investigator, shrugging with his face. He then turned and left.

The door closed. Chris Cowley was alone.

* * *

During his unexpected visit the day before, the deliveryman, Juahar, had laid out what they should expect. "You'll get an email," he told them. "They'll tell you what to do." He recited that part from memory. Then he turned the piece of paper around.

"See," he said. An email address had been scrawled in the center of the page: *newyork186241@yahoo.com*. Below the address, *Password: abracadabra321.*

He shook his head as though everything he relayed caused him as much pain as it did the others in the room. "They'll tell you what to do," he said. "They'll email you. They say, 'Write it down'—I write it down. That's all I did."

So it wasn't a surprise when at 3:21 p.m., Elizabeth received a text message from Valencia: *Message*, it said. That was all. Elizabeth excused herself from a meeting and walked down the hallway to her office. Standing outside the door, typing something on her phone, was Valencia.

"Danny got it," said Valencia, referring to her own assistant, Danny, who had been monitoring the account.

"Did he read it?"

"Just the subject," said Valencia. "It says: 'Welcome.'"

Elizabeth walked past her, opened the door to her office, headed straight to her computer, and sat down. The Yahoo tab was already open on her screen. "'Welcome,'" she said, reading the subject line. "What is this? It's sent from the same account?"

"Slightly different," said Valencia, bending down and pointing at the screen. "186242, off by a digit."

"Well," said Elizabeth, clicking on the message. She read it for Valencia: "Seven hundred and fifty thousand dollars in one-hundred-dollar bills. No dye. No GPS." She leaned back from her desk, looked up at Valencia. "That's it?"

"For now," said Valencia.

Elizabeth suddenly felt a bit more confident. The whole thing seemed like total bullshit. It seemed amateurish, the work of somebody who had been watching too many Hollywood movies. *No dye!* "What is this?"

"We'll find out," said Valencia.

Elizabeth looked at Valencia's face even closer. There seemed to be a bad mood brewing behind the woman's eyes. "I mean, they're amateurs, right?" Elizabeth asked.

Eyes still on the monitor, Valencia didn't answer; she just shook her head.

Elizabeth leaned closer to the screen. "What is this 186242 business?"

"Danny ran the original address through his databases. He broke it up into parts, ran just the numbers to see if they'd been associated with any other email accounts," said Valencia, looking down at her phone, apparently reading a message from her assistant. "He'll run the new one, too, same thing, break it down . . ."

While Valencia was speaking, Elizabeth's mind drifted. She indulged a short fantasy about being kicked off the case, pushed out of the firm, and publicly humiliated. She saw herself getting divorced, moving to France, to the Loire Valley, learning to cook, taking long bicycle rides. In the winter she could make fires and read books—a more civilized life.

Meanwhile, Valencia had moved on to a different subject: "My guy at Yahoo says the account was created yesterday at 20:16 UTC—that's 4:16 our time. The IP address tracks to Kazakhstan. It's a network known for anonymizing proxy service."

"So what's that mean?" asked Elizabeth.

"Nothing special. Anyone could do it."

As Elizabeth looked at the screen, a new email came in. Both women bent down to read it. Elizabeth could smell Valencia's shampoo. It smelled like gardenias.

Elizabeth read it out loud: "'You have two hours to get money.'" She looked at her watch, looked back at the screen. "'Then we send further instructions.'"

Even before she got the okay from the partners, Elizabeth had sent an associate to get the money from their bank. The money was bagged up and locked away in one of Michael D'Angelo's evidence lockers.

Elizabeth leaned back, crossed her arms in front of her chest, and closed her eyes. "You don't think we should go to the FBI?" she asked.

"I thought we already charted that out." said Valencia. She used a soothing kind of voice, which annoyed Elizabeth.

"We did. I'm second-guessing our conclusion."

"A few years ago, I handled a kidnapping negotiation in Mexico," Valencia explained. "A movie producer down there, a Mexican guy, his son was kidnapped in the middle of Mexico City. I don't even speak Spanish, but they called me down; I analyzed the situation—as best I could—and advised the guy to pay the money. Just pay it. Different circumstances, but—just like here—it made sense. In the end he didn't pay, he went to the police."

"And?" asked Elizabeth.

"The kid got beheaded."

You are one of the most arrogant women I've ever met, thought Elizabeth. She took a deep breath, closed her eyes for a moment, centered herself, and then looked at Valencia. "You know what I like most about you?"

"Tell me."

"Your decisiveness."

"I'm a Taurus," Valencia said. "We're decisive."

That evening, at the appointed time Valencia pulled her car into a spot across the street from Dyker Beach Golf Course in Brooklyn, not far from the Verrazzano Bridge. She was out of practice: it had been months since she'd last driven, and the drive from Manhattan had left her tense.

She backed up, pulled forward, turned the wheel, and put the car in park; it would have to do. With the car off, she took a deep breath, exhaled, looked in the mirror, fixed her hair behind her ears, and told herself to calm down. Then she popped the trunk and got out.

The money had been placed in a large gym bag borrowed from a young attorney at the firm. The instructions had specifically demanded that Elizabeth Carlyle make the delivery, but Valencia had insisted on taking her place. "They'll have no idea," she said. "A woman's a woman. I'll wear a hat."

When she lifted the bag, it felt heavier than when she had put it in. She closed the trunk and began carrying the bag—leaning with the weight of it—toward the corner of Twelfth Avenue. The neighborhood had a slightly rundown suburban feel. "Do you see me?" she whispered into her earpiece.

"Affirmative, I have you westbound, north side Eighty-Sixth," answered her drone man, Colter Jacobson, through the earpiece in her right ear. Two drones watched from above. Valencia resisted the urge to look up. She listened for it, but—apart from the sound of nearby traffic, city noises in general, and a distant barking dog—she didn't hear anything.

"Milton? Are you set?" she whispered, barely moving her lips.

Milton's voice came through her earpiece: "Yes, ma'am." He and Billy were parked on Twelfth Avenue, between Eighty-Fourth and Eighty-Fifth Streets.

"Danny?"

"Yes, ma'am, same—moving . . . west on eight six," said Danny Tsui. He was at their office in Manhattan tracking the GPS device that had been placed in the bag.

"Knock it off with all this ma'am shit," whispered Valencia.

Danny said, "Yes—" and then cut himself off.

Cars passed in clusters on Eighty-Sixth Street, and Valencia flinched when a truck's horn blared. For a moment, her mind went back to her CIA training at The Farm. Her team leader had been an old hand named Roland Faraon. During her first week there, she'd been told she had to do a solo night trek, humping a fifty-pound bag in the woods of Northern Virginia. Roland pulled her aside, told her not to worry, that it was perfectly reasonable to feel fear. He reminded her that they weren't training her to be an assassin. "We just want you to be able to walk your ass out of a hostile country."

After filling her in on the details—fourteen miles, no trail, no moon, rainy night—he pointed at a few of her male classmates who were standing near a fence. "Those guys think you're going to be too scared to do this," he said. "Are you?" She told him she wasn't, and it was true.

Right then, an old man walking toward her on the sidewalk interrupted her memory of the hike. He wore blue pants and a long-sleeved navy blue polo shirt. He walked with a slight swing of the hips, like he'd been injured in the past. He had wide cheekbones and looked Russian. The idea that this man might just ask for the bag brought with it the feeling that everything was speeding up.

"Man approaching," she whispered.

"I have him," said her drone man.

As they got close to each other, the man kept his eyes firmly on Valencia; he offered a small smile as their paths crossed. Valencia turned and watched him walk away. Then on her right, she noticed an old woman staring at her from a porch. Valencia stared back, and waited for the old woman to look away; but she held steady, and it was Valencia who finally gave in.

She continued walking west. At the corner she set the bag down on the ground, and opened and closed her hand to get her circulation going. She waited for the light to change. When it did, she picked up the bag and crossed the street. Every person in every car seemed to be watching her. On the other side of the street, she looped back in the direction she'd just come. The fenced-off golf course was now directly next to her.

There were other people walking on this side of the street. An old woman walking a tiny white dog with brown smears around its eyes sauntered past. Next, two teenage Chinese boys, wearing glasses. The sound of passing cars rose and fell with the flow of traffic.

On her right, the chain-link fence separated the sidewalk from the wooded area that bordered the golf course. The instructions had said to enter at the middle of the block, and then walk through the woods to the edge of the course. She would receive further instructions there.

Valencia's team had scouted the area beforehand. They told her there was an entrance in the middle, a simple cut in the chain-link fence. Coming upon it now, Valencia found it even more primitive than she had imagined. A cut ran from five feet straight down to foot level, where it split in both directions. Beyond the fence was a dark wooded area. She wondered whether the drones would be able to see through the trees.

For a moment she thought again about her training at The Farm. They'd spent a week simulating customs and immigration stops in a fake airport. The place came complete with the right carpet, fluorescent lights, and intercom system making announcements. She remembered one occasion where the person playing the immigration official yelled at her and called her a liar. They brought out a dog, a German shepherd, who sat within biting distance, barking.

Valencia repeated her cover story. Afterward Roland Faraon told her she'd rushed it. "You're jumping the gun," he said. "Just sit back and let the game come to you. Don't rush it. React to what's happening, not what you think needs to happen."

Valencia looked at the cut fence and thought about that. The situation she now found herself in was way more complicated than simple blackmail. She needed to sit back and practice a little bit of patience. It was all about making the right choice in the right moment.

"I'm at the cut," she whispered.

"There is nobody near you," said the drone man. "Closest body inside the fence is four hundred yards east."

"Copy," she whispered. Her mouth was dry now. She pushed the fence apart, leaned her leg against it, and then pushed the bag through. After that, she looked left, then right, and then, awkwardly, struggled through herself.

On the other side of the fence she noticed that she was breathing loudly; she reached up and covered the mic on her earpiece. She breathed in and out through her nose and tried to put herself into the mind of whoever was making her do this—but she couldn't.

The woods, in a canopy, stretched farther in front of her than she'd imagined. Trash lay scattered on the ground in all directions. It disgusted her. She took her hand off the mic, and whispered, "Okay."

"You good?" came Milton's voice.

"Yeah," she said.

Bag in hand, she entered the wooded area, stepping carefully and trying to avoid any hidden holes. She cursed herself for not having brought a weapon. In the office, that choice had felt wise; here in the woods, it felt foolish.

"Talk to us," said Milton.

"It's clear," said Valencia. She turned and looked back toward the street. "It's fine."

Thirty paces farther, she saw an opening that indicated the end of the woods. When she reached the golf course proper, she set the bag down, exhaled, and looked around. The sky was still not quite dark. The grass field opened wide in front of her. It was a beautiful sight. Her eyes tacked from left to right, and she felt herself become calm.

"Do you see any movement?" she whispered into her earpiece. The instructions had said to walk straight to the golf course, but they hadn't said what to do after that. She presumed they were going to ask her to leave the money, but she didn't know how they planned on conveying that message.

"All clear," the drone man said. "Nothing moving."

Valencia was calculating how long until dark when her thoughts were interrupted by a cell phone ringing. Moving her head around like a dog, she tried to locate the sound. She stepped out farther into the grass. The ringing stopped.

After a moment it started back up. Glancing back at the bag of money behind her, she kept walking toward the sound. Finally she found a black Nokia flip phone. It stopped ringing.

"They left a phone," she whispered into her earpiece. She picked it up and then looked around to see if anyone was watching her, before walking back toward the bag.

The phone rang again. She answered it. "Hello?"

A beeping sound, something like a fax noise. Valencia took the phone away from her ear for a moment, looked at it. "Hello?" she repeated.

"Very good," said someone at the other end. The voice sounded like it had been electronically pitch-shifted. Valencia squinted and tried to place the accent. "You win," they said. "Bring bag to Batchelder Street, B-as-in-boy-A-T-C-H-E-L-D-like-dog-E-R, Batchelder Street, between Avenue Y and Avenue Z. Still Brooklyn. Batchelder, got it?"

Valencia put her free hand to her head. "Batchelder," she said.

"Come alone."

"I want to talk face-to-face," said Valencia, but the phone went dead.

Yuri Rabinowitz's phone vibrated in his hand. He answered it.

"*I told her,*" said his brother Isaac.

"*Okay, go back,*" said Yuri. "*Smash the phone.*"

He waited for his brother to affirm that he'd heard his instructions, but Isaac stayed silent. "*Do you hear me?*"

"Yeah, yeah," said Isaac, switching to English. "I hear you."

"*Smash the phone, dump it, and meet at the spot,*" said Yuri. "*Don't speed. Don't run any lights. Hey! Wait!*"

"What?" asked Isaac.

"Did you see anything?" asked Yuri.

"Nothing."

Yuri's little brother had been parked down Eighty-Sixth Street. It had been his job to watch the area around Thirteenth Avenue, and make sure there was no activity from that end. Yuri had told him to dress in gym clothes and to keep his gym bag on the passenger seat.

Yuri, for his part, was tucked away in a friend's mother's apartment on Eighty-Sixth Street, at the corner of Twelfth Avenue. The friend was in Miami, but his friend's mother had let him in. "*I need to watch something,*" he'd said, pointing at her window.

"*You boys never stop with this monkey business,*" the mother had said, speaking with the same accent as Yuri's own mother. "*Why always sneaking here, sneaking there? Go to law school. Become a lawyer if you want to sneak around.*"

"*I know,*" he had told her. "*I will, I want to, but first . . .*"

Yuri had watched the woman park, and now he saw her walk right underneath the window. He'd seen her carrying the bag and then turn and look at the old man when they passed each other. Everything was going as planned, but he still felt very uneasy.

The other window in the living room looked up Twelfth Avenue. Yuri paced between the two windows, looking first this way, then that way. There were no signs of activity coming from either direction. No cars circling, no plumber's vans; no men walking dogs; no FBI women pretending to push strollers.

Yuri had placed one of his associates, a young man called Felix, one block to the north on Twelfth Avenue. Felix had parked his car and now—accompanied by a teenage girl he'd brought to help him blend in—sat on the front stoop of a vacant house that was for sale. Yuri had told him exactly what to do. It would feel more natural. He told him to sit and watch the block. Watch every person—look for anybody trying to blend in.

So they had all three sides under surveillance. The fourth side was the golf course itself, which didn't need to be watched.

"So we can see what we are dealing with," Yuri had said. There had been no signs of trouble, no cops, no tails, no FBI. Still, he wasn't at ease. His guts felt pulled. He took out his phone and called Felix.

"Yes?" said Felix.

"*What do you have?*" asked Yuri.

"*There was a van, it stopped, nobody got out. Then someone got out of it and went into an apartment. That's it.*"

"*Nothing else? No other people?*"

"Nothing."

Yuri told him to wait for fifteen minutes before leaving and to remember to make noise when he did. He ended the call.

"*I don't like this,*" said their friend's mother. She was sitting on the couch in the same room, dressed in a long white nightgown, something a grandmother might wear. Her glasses reflected the television screen, which played the local news without sound. Yuri saw sirens on the television screen and watched for a moment.

"*It's a game, auntie,*" he said.

"*Do I look stupid?*" she asked.

"*Stupid?*" he said. "*You look like a professor.*"

She had, in fact, been a professor of economics in Moscow, but the comment only made her shake her head and smirk. She took her remote control and changed the channel; then she smacked her lips and shook her head again. She seemed genuinely annoyed at Yuri.

He went back to the window and stared at the area where the woman had entered the park. When she finally came out, he stepped a foot back from the window and raised his binoculars to look at her. He couldn't see her face, but her body language suggested she was scared, and he took some measure of comfort in that.

"*You boys will end up in an American prison*," his friend's mother said. "*Think about that for a minute.*"

Valencia parked next to a fire hydrant on Batchelder Street, shut the car off, and studied the area in front of her. It was a residential block. The kind of unadorned, large brick buildings that dominated New York City stood on each side of the street. She counted eight stories on her left, and six on her right. The buildings on her right had paths cutting through them. The one on her left had a large courtyard in the middle, so the front door was set back almost two hundred feet from the street. Ideal landscape for a sniper, she thought.

A few people hunched against the evening chill seemed to be making their way home for the night. Valencia watched a delivery driver on an electric bike speed past. From there, her attention shifted to a man fussing with his dog's leash. She watched him until he turned and walked away. Then she looked back at the building across the street from her. *Brooklyn*—she thought, attempting to ground herself—*New York, America, Earth.*

Then, trying to put herself in the right mood, she repeated the phrase, *Let me help these people*, three times in her mind. She breathed deeply, exhaled, opened her eyes, and spoke. "I'm parked."

"We have you," said the drone man. "Still, do me a favor and tap your brake once."

She tapped it.

"We have you," he repeated.

"Milton?" asked Valencia.

"Parked one block south," said Milton. "Billy's out. You should see him behind you."

Valencia looked in her rearview and then side mirrors, but didn't see him. "Danny, where are we on the Emporis floor plans?" she asked. She wanted a three-dimensional image of the buildings on either side of her.

"Working on it, boss," said Danny.

Thinking that one of her men could lift a fingerprint or DNA, she refrained from touching the phone as much as she could. While she waited for it to ring, she opened the glove compartment, found two pens, and—using them like sewing needles—flipped the phone open. She then pressed the talk button and looked at the call history. Besides the calls that had come in at the golf course, there had been another series of blocked calls earlier, at 4:45 p.m. It occurred to her that they'd been practicing. There was something pathetic about that.

Using the pen, she punched in her own number, and hit the green talk button. Her iPhone lit up with a 718 number.

She spoke into her earpiece: "Danny, run this number—718-936-5156, tell me what you see."

"Yes, boss."

"After you're done, give Dale Burkhart a call and have him do the same thing. Tell him this is *real*. Danny, you gotta say it like that: '*Real*.'" Dale Burkhart was an FBI agent in Newark. He'd have more access and could possibly tell her where the phone had been sold.

The drone man's voice came into her earpiece: "Okay, Valencia, the building across the street from your location, the tall one, we have five warm bodies in windows, one on the second floor, one on the third floor, one on the seventh, and two on the eighth, at the same window."

"Copy," said Valencia. She bent down in her seat and craned her neck to look up at the tower, but she couldn't see any signs of warm bodies. She looked at the phone, and breathed deeply through her nose.

"Do you want the other buildings?"

"Not now," said Valencia. "Just the street."

"You have two warm bodies near the front door of that same building, and a group of three bodies, moving in your direction, from one block north on Avenue Y."

"Copy," she said. Her eyes went back and forth between the people at the door and the area where the three people would be coming from. They still hadn't come into her view.

"You should see Billy," said Milton. His voice sounded like an AM radioman.

She lowered her head and looked in the side mirror. She still couldn't see Billy. He'd be dressed like a homeless man, complete with a long-haired wig and an authentic smell. Out collecting cans, he'd be strapped with a gun, handcuffs, and his fake badge. Wally Philpott, Valencia's NYPD detective, was standing by at a bar on Nostrand Avenue, just in case they needed him.

She pulled down the visor and checked in the mirror for food or lipstick on her teeth. Then she shut the mirror, leaned back in her seat, touched two fingers to her wrist and felt her pulse; slowly breathing in and out, she tried to get it to settle. *Snug as a bug in a rug*, she told herself.

"The three inbound just turned back on Batchelder and are now headed away from you—northbound," said the drone man. "A cluster of six new bodies inbound from the south."

"Hold the updates, for a minute," said Valencia.

"Copy," said the drone man.

Valencia's earpiece went silent.

She closed her eyes for a few seconds and waited for her mind to steady. When she opened her eyes, she looked again in her side mirror. This time she spotted Billy on the other side of the street. He was drinking a beer and examining a large pile of trash bags. He looked the part. He'd speak Polish if anybody questioned him.

Right then the phone rang on the seat next to her. It sounded louder than it had in the field, and its ringtone, a vintage jangle, took her back ten years. Touching the phone as little as she could, she answered it.

"Welcome, friend," said the same pitch-shifted voice.

"Thank you," said Valencia, scanning the street in front of her.

"You are parked?"

"Yes."

"You are parked across from 2520?"

He was referring to the tower with the courtyard. "Yes," she said, looking over at the front door.

"Hold, please," said the voice.

Valencia sat there blinking. *Hold, please?* She looked at the area in front of her, but didn't see any movement. She glanced in the side-view mirror and saw Billy walking away from her.

Her iPhone lit up with a text from Danny. It was the floor plans. She clicked on the 2520 building and gave the layout a quick look, making note of all the stairways. Then she looked back at the street. A car had pulled up in front of the building, and an older woman was slowly pushing herself out of the backseat. The man on the phone was presumably waiting for the area to clear.

Before making her way to the door, the old woman had to speak to the driver for a bit. Valencia almost smiled; all eyes—including two drones—were on this old woman. The world had stopped for her.

"Exit the car, bring the money in the bag, and walk to the doorway of 2520," said the voice on the phone. "There are benches there. Sit down on one of them. Keep the phone on you. We'll call back."

"Okay," said Valencia. The call ended.

She reached for the trunk release lever. "Showtime," she said.

"Copy," said the drone man.

"Copy," said Milton.

She opened the door and set her feet on the ground. As she exited the car, she became dizzy and momentarily experienced something like stage fright; she felt watched.

The feeling passed. She pulled the trunk open, lifted the bag out, put the strap over her right shoulder, and began lugging the bag across the street. She walked at a measured pace, not too fast or slow. *If anyone out there doesn't want me to do this, now is the time to speak up*, she thought.

Right then, a black Monte Carlo pulled up behind her. It was blaring hip-hop, and the bass vibrated through her body. She turned and looked at it, but she couldn't see anything through the blackened windows. Still, she could sense men leering at her from inside. She took a moment and mentally prepared herself to fight. *Go for the knees*, she told herself. *Knees, throats, balls, and noses.* But the car roared off, its muffler adding to the noise. Valencia was left alone on the block again.

She walked into the courtyard and toward the door of 2520 Batchelder.

"Two men standing at the door," said the drone man. "You still have the same warm bodies in windows on floors two, three, seven, and eight."

She didn't answer. The two men in the doorway were thirty yards from her; they wore puffy coats and smoked. She couldn't see their faces because they were lit from behind. She kept moving toward the bench, and then sat on it, slipping her hands under her butt to warm them.

The phone in her pocket rang. "Okay, Elizabeth"—they still thought she was Elizabeth, which was somehow comforting—"cross back over Batchelder," said the voice. It sounded to Valencia like he was reading from a script. "Walk between the two buildings directly across the street from where you are. Before you get to the side door of the building on your left, you will see a trash can. It is the only one there. It's fifty meters from the sidewalk. Put the bag in the trash can and then return to your car and leave the area."

"Put the bag in a trash can across the street from me?" she asked, so her men could hear what she was being instructed to do.

"Yes," said the voice. The pitch-shifting couldn't disguise his nervousness.

"Do we have your word that you won't come back to us again?" asked Valencia, saying what she thought Elizabeth Carlyle might say.

"Yes," said the voice. "Put the money in the trash can and leave. Thank you."

The line went dead.

She crossed Batchelder Street again and looked for Billy, but couldn't see him. The space between the buildings was lined with park benches. There was a little plot of grass on her right. The streetlights cast the area in pinkish orange and hummed unnaturally. There was nobody else in her line of vision. *Put the bag in the trash*, she thought. *This is ridiculous.*

She found the trash can. It looked like any New York City trash can. There was a lid on top, the kind meant to discourage people from dumping their own bags of trash. It wasn't locked, and she pulled it open. She looked in and saw a black plastic garbage bag and no trash. She placed the gym bag in the trash can and then put the lid back down. She turned and raised her hands to signal that it was done.

Feeling like men in every window were watching her, she straightened her shoulders and began her walk back to the car. *Now we wait*, she thought.

As soon as she was in the car, she asked her drone man what he had. "Nothing yet."

Valencia, pumped up on adrenaline, pulled her seatbelt on, pushed her hair back, started the car, turned her lights on, checked her mirrors, and drove away.

Billy watched Valencia's car disappear down the road. He'd found a carton of halal chicken and rice in the trash, and, fully committed to his role, ate from it like a man who'd skipped a few meals. It wasn't bad. Still chewing, Billy stepped into the doorway of an abandoned building. He set his food and drink down and then lowered himself to a seated position. From there, he could watch the trash can. He sipped his beer, adjusted his earpiece, and leaned back against the door.

While he watched, he switched to autopilot; fragments of sentences passed through his mind: *Wait and watch . . . walk the block . . . filled up . . . tossed out . . . he said duck . . . .*

A little over two hours later, Valencia came on his radio and told him to take a walk. "Billy, time for your lunch break."

He was happy to go for a walk; his back and knees had stiffened up, and he was getting cold too. He might have to buy another beer to keep up his cover.

He walked three blocks west—didn't turn to look behind himself once—and found a bodega on Nostrand Avenue. Colter, meanwhile, sent regular updates through his earpiece: "Holiday," he'd say, meaning the field was clear. Then ninety seconds later he'd repeat it, "Holiday."

"Wassup, player?" Billy said to the store clerk when he walked in.

The clerk, a young Arab, raised his eyebrows, shrugged, shook his head.

Billy walked to the back, scanned the beer, grabbed a can of Olde English, and stepped to the register. "Let me get two loosies," he said. The clerk looked at him for a moment, like he was wondering if Billy was a cop; but then he reached under the counter, grabbed a pack of Newports, and shook out two cigarettes.

"Three fifty," said the clerk.

Billy gave him five, took the change, picked up a lighter that was tied to a string, and lit one of the cigarettes.

"Billy, we're gonna need you to take a look in the box," said Valencia in his earpiece.

Billy stepped back outside. "Take a look? Or grab?" he said into his earpiece.

"Take a look," she said. "Confirm it's there."

"Copy," said Billy.

He walked back down Batchelder across from the tower. He first went to the trash can on the far side of the street, looked into it, dug around, pulled some paper bags out, pretended to look through them.

"Holiday," said Colter.

If Allah wills it, it will be done, thought Billy, trying to talk himself calm. Truth was, he was feeling nervous. He couldn't help it.

He walked toward the target, following a drunken line from the sidewalk onto the dead lawn and back. Twenty feet from the can, he stopped walking and made a show of finishing his beer. He tossed his head back and guzzled with his elbow out like a college kid. Then he dropped the can to the ground, crushed it under his boot, and belched loudly. He took a second, turned, and scanned the entire area. He didn't see anyone.

"Stay there for a minute," said Valencia. Billy became aware that she was watching him from Colter's van.

Today is not my day to go, thought Billy. He leaned up and turned a circle, scanning all the windows for scope shines. A white SUV drove down the block and Billy watched it. After that the street became silent again. Billy tried to relax his shoulders; then he stomped on the beer can twice more, and picked it up.

"Okay, Billy," said Valencia.

He turned and walked toward the trash can. For the first time that night, he noticed the sky above him, with the clouds lit by the moon, and beyond the clouds, two stars. After tossing the can into the trash, he took a step away, then pretended to have second thoughts, and turned back to it.

He stepped up and tried to peer in, but he couldn't see anything. He grabbed the top of the receptacle and pulled it open. When he looked in, it took a moment to understand what he was seeing. There was a black plastic trash bag, but it had been cut. Underneath that, at the bottom of the receptacle, was the can he'd just thrown in.

He looked in deeper. "Bag's gone," he said.

Colter Jacobson's van was outfitted with boxes of computer hardware stacked and belted against the walls; neatly bundled cables extended from those stacks to a larger black trunk behind the driver's seat; above the trunk, attached to a wall behind the driver and passenger's seat, were eight small monitors. Sitting on a bench facing that wall was Valencia. She could see the white glow of Billy's body on the screen, the dusted landscape of the lawn, the concrete street that played gray on the monitor. For a moment, the idea that Billy was at the wrong trash can passed through her mind.

She turned toward Colter, who was seated next to her. "That's the right can?" she asked, knowing full well it was.

Colter pushed his glasses up, frowned, and nodded.

"Fuck." She spoke into her earpiece: "Milton, come pick me up."

Colter busied himself talking to his pilots, who were flying the drones from his office in White Plains. At that moment he was reading an indecipherable list of coordinates from a notepad.

Valencia dropped her head and closed her eyes for a second. She touched her ear and spoke: "Billy, drop back, cross the street, and wait for us. We're coming."

She turned back to Colter and asked, "You have a quarter-mile view on the field?"

He nodded, pointed toward one of the monitors.

"And you've grabbed every license plate that has come and gone since we've been here?"

"That's right," he said.

"Okay, sit tight," she said.

She hopped out of the van and watched Milton's SUV speed down the block to get her.

"Shit's bad," she said, when she got in. "Real bad."

Milton, silent, whipped a U-turn.

Less than half a minute later they saw Billy walking toward them on Batchelder. They stopped and he got in the back.

"You fucking stink," said Valencia. Billy knew better than to respond. The car bumped over a pothole; sirens could be heard responding to some other incident in the vicinity. An older African American woman stopped and stared at them as they sped past.

Milton stopped on the street, near the sidewalk that led to the trash can. The three of them sat there looking toward the drop spot.

Valencia was the first to speak. "Fucking shit," she said. "Back in and drive down that way."

Milton was already moving. He pulled forward and lurched the car in reverse. Bumping over the curb, he drove backward toward the trash can.

"Hold on," said Valencia. He stopped. She touched her earpiece. "Colter, is the area clear of police cars?"

"No cars in the area. You have one body, a block over on Voorhies, but he's moving away from you."

"Hit it," said Valencia.

"Hard?" asked Milton.

"Yes."

When Milton stepped on the gas the three of them turned in their seats and watched out the back window as they headed for the can. The noise, when he rammed it, was quieter than Valencia expected.

"Pull up," she said.

He pulled forward.

"Let's go."

They got out and walked to where the trash can had been. In its place was a two-foot-wide hole. "Son of a bitch," said Valencia. She shined the light into the hole. It appeared that the trash can had been placed over some kind of sewage tunnel.

Valencia handed Billy the flashlight. He took his jacket off, stepped to the hole and then put his head over it, then pulled back, like a gunfighter looking around a corner. He then leaned over and shined his light into it. Convinced it was clear, he lowered himself in. Valencia moved closer and watched him. There was an iron ladder attached to the wall of the tunnel.

Valencia then went to examine the trash can. The New York City Department of Sanitation logo seemed to mock her. She reached down and touched the bottom of the can. It looked as if it had actually been fixed to the path with cement. A false bottom had been attached to the can with screws. It was either a very smart job or she was an idiot.

She stepped back to the hole. "What is it?" she called down.

"It's a sewer," Billy answered. "A sewer," he repeated. "You're gonna wanna see this, though."

Valencia stepped to the hole, looked down, and stretched her foot to the first rung of the ladder. Billy lit her way from below. When she reached the bottom of the ladder, she had to hop about four feet down. Billy offered his hand, and she accepted it. When she was down, he shined the light on the gym bag, which sagged empty in a puddle. The two small GPS devices they'd placed in the bag sat next to it on some dry concrete.

Billy then directed her attention to one of the walls. A crude devil with a tail and a huge erect phallus had been spray-painted in white. He swung his light for Milton, who was lowering himself down.

Valencia stared and blinked at the dark black space where the painted devil had been.

3

A BEAUTIFUL PLACE

The sewer—from the point where the money was dropped—passed directly below the Coney Island Wastewater Treatment Plant, continued east, and finally let out onto the muddy beach of the Shell Bank Creek. The Russians hadn't dug the hole, or placed the trash can over it; it had been there for years. In fact, many of the teenage residents of the Kings Bay Houses knew about it.

Moishe Groysman had been waiting in the sewer underneath the trash can. As soon as he took possession of the bag, he began removing the money straps, fanning through each stack, and searching for GPS devices and dye packs. One by one, he searched, re-banded, and placed each stack into the bag he'd brought with him. Since there were seventy-five stacks, it took him a little more than twenty minutes to finish the job. Yuri had assured him he'd have time to do this, and indeed he did.

From the drop point Moishe carried the money a third of a mile to where the sewer let out at the creek. The round door at the end of the tunnel was barred and locked, but the bars on top had been cut, leaving a space of about three feet by two feet. When he got there, Moishe took a moment and watched from behind the bars. Then he pushed the money over the top, placed a piece of cardboard over the bars, and climbed through the hole.

He had a cell phone signal now; he stayed in the shadows and checked the text messages on his prepaid. Yuri hadn't sent any updates. Apparently their victims still had no idea what had happened. It almost made him want to laugh, but he was too nervous for that. He took the cardboard down and set it on the ground and watched the area around him. There were fishing boats in the creek, but no other signs of movement. He looked at his watch: thirty-two minutes had passed since the drop.

A stolen delivery scooter sat waiting in a parking lot adjacent to the tunnel. He walked to it now and began securing the bag to the scooter's back rack with two bungee cords. He was amped up and everything he did stood out with unusual clarity. At one point, while he was work- ing, he heard the distant sounds of sirens—which made him pause until he realized they were coming from a different neighborhood.

Instead of exiting directly onto Knapp Street, he got on the bike and headed deeper into the dirt parking lot, which eventually became a dirt alley that skirted past the tunnel in the direction of the fishing boats. He had to hop off at one point and push the scooter through some sand, but he finally emerged onto Knapp Street just south of Avenue Z. From there, he turned his headlight on and headed south at a reasonable speed.

He took Emmons until it turned into Neptune Avenue in Brighton Beach. There were people on the streets here, which helped Moishe relax. He parked the bike a few blocks from Ossip's Locksmith Shop, untied his load, and walked the rest of the way carrying the bag of money over his shoulder.

When he arrived at the locksmith shop, he reached through the metal gate and knocked on the glass door behind it. Ten seconds later the door opened, and Ossip—a Rabinowitz family friend—opened the gate and ushered him into the shop. It was dark inside and smelled like cigarettes.

"*I had tea for dinner—you know what that means?*" asked Ossip. Moishe didn't know, and he didn't say anything, he just followed the older man—who was flipping lights on as they went—to the back of the shop. Ossip must've been seventy years old. He was squat, sturdy, and had a big belly. The flesh under his eyes sagged, and the eyes themselves seemed red.

He pointed toward a safe in the corner, which sat open and ready. *"He said he'd pay tonight,"* said Ossip. *"That's between him and me, I know, but I think we would both prefer to get it out of the way."*

"Don't worry about it, uncle," said Moishe, making a face as though he sympathized, but motioning with both hands that he was not to talk about such things.

Ossip poured two glasses of vodka, told Moishe he needed to calm down, and then took the bag from him and set it on a small card table. The older man then counted each stack out loud, setting the stacks down in neat rows as he went. *"What kind of shit is this?"* he asked, turning toward Moishe when he finished. *"You know what this is? More money, more problems. That's not bullshit! I get it, we have to live, we have to eat, but this is too much money for one night's work."*

His eyes shifted over Moishe's face like a man with some kind of brain condition.

Moishe stepped to the table, pulled four of the stacks from the pile. *"For the bank,"* he said, tossing one of the stacks to Ossip. He then tucked the other three into the front of his waistband, pulled the ties of his sweatpants tight, and tied them. "Gangster paradise," he said in English. The two men regarded each other for a few seconds.

"Pour us another," said Moishe. After they drank, they put the rest of the money back into the bag and set it in Ossip's safe.

"Seventy-five minus four," said Ossip, holding up four fingers. *"Seventy-one."* He pointed at Moishe, as if to say, *You're my witness,* and then walked him back to the front door.

From there Moishe took a black car to the Roxy Club, a few blocks away under the train tracks. The doorman, a huge Russian called Cyprus—a name he'd earned in Chechnya—greeted Moishe with a handshake, pulled him in for a half hug, and whispered in his ear, *"Two new girls, one of them is a redhead."*

He then motioned for Moishe to go in. Two other bouncers waited inside. They both shook his hand. A cashier sitting near the next door blew him a kiss when he walked past.

The club itself wasn't crowded. Moishe felt the girl onstage notice him when he walked in. The whole energy of the room shifted. Keeping his left hand on the money at his waist, he walked to their normal table, shaking hands with an associate on his way. Then he sat down and began waiting for the Rabinowitz brothers to show up. They were going to get extremely drunk tonight.

Sitting in her home office, finishing a bottle of Chablis, Elizabeth Carlyle's patience was wearing thin. In an effort to stop thinking about what was happening in Brooklyn, she'd reviewed over a thousand pages of discovery for one of her other cases, done a week's worth of online shopping, and eaten her dinner at her desk. Her eyes went from the clock on her computer back to her phone. She checked the little button on the side: the ringer was still on.

A guilty feeling began loosening in her stomach; she felt like she'd done something horribly wrong. Her eyes went back to the computer, and she clicked on a Valentino dress, zoomed in on it, and became convinced it would make her look ridiculous, an old lady trying to look young. She hit the back button on her browser and continued scrolling through all the dresses. *Fuck. Fuck. Fuck. Fuck. Fuck.*

Finally, at 11:46 p.m., Valencia called.

"What happened?" Elizabeth asked.

"They're better than we imagined."

"What is that supposed to mean?" asked Elizabeth, aware of the slight drunken slur in her voice.

"They managed to collect without showing themselves."

Elizabeth closed her computer. "Tell me exactly what happened."

"It's too complicated for the phone," said Valencia.

Elizabeth tried to understand what she was hearing.

Valencia continued, "We'll identify them by the end of the day tomorrow. It's easy from here. You have my personal guarantee on that."

Elizabeth rubbed her eyes. *What is this?* she thought. A mix between a yawn and a silent cry stretched her mouth. She forced her mouth shut, then said, "I swear to God."

"I'll update you first thing in the morning," said Valencia.

Elizabeth found herself saying goodbye, hanging up, and ending the call. A rush of unasked questions flowed through her mind: First and foremost, what happened? What the hell had happened? What was she possibly going to tell the partners tomorrow? She'd given away three-quarters of a million dollars, with nothing to show for it. She would have to resign.

She looked at her cell phone; no point in calling back. She'd only get deflections. Nothing was going to happen tonight. She left her office and walked downstairs to the kitchen. The place looked sterile, lifeless. The refrigerator hummed, and she pulled it open.

Inside, she pushed things around drunkenly until she found a rotisserie chicken. She pulled that out and began tearing meat off the breast and putting it into her mouth. She tore a wing off, chewed it, crunched the end of the bones. She ate more meat from the other breast. Then she put the plastic lid back on, put the chicken back in the refrigerator, and moved a bottle of mayonnaise to hide the mess she'd made.

In the freezer she found her husband's unopened ice cream; she put it in the microwave and heated it for thirty seconds. She ate the entire thing standing and staring into the dark dining room. When she finished, she put the empty container and the spoon into the sink and washed her hands and rinsed her mouth and spit into the drain.

From the kitchen, she walked back up the stairs, touching the wall at one point and leaving a wet handprint. She headed down the hallway to her bedroom. She pulled off her clothes, dropped them on the floor, then flopped onto the bed. Her husband sighed and shifted away. She lay there for a moment, feeling the bed spin.

Her mind shuffled through a series of trifling thoughts: she had to call her tax man. Bob, a partner at the firm, was growing increasingly arrogant. She got up on her elbow and looked at her husband. His back was to her. Then clumsily, she shifted over to him and hugged him from behind and propped herself up on her elbow and began rubbing her groin against his hip. He turned, scooted still farther away, and leaned up like he'd been startled awake.

"What the fuck are you doing?" he asked.

Danny Tsui's head was on his pillow, his eyes were closed, and his mind was just beginning to shift from nagging thoughts to a wordless dream, when his phone buzzed and chimed. He picked it up off his nightstand. Valencia Walker, 1:12 a.m.

"Are you sleeping?" she asked, when he answered.

"No, boss."

"Do you have your computer open?"

He pushed himself up. "Yeah," he said, opening it.

"I need you to find the owner's name," Valencia said, sounding strangely calm. "You have all the information on the place, right?"

"Yeah, yeah," said Danny. He clicked on an email draft where he was keeping notes on this project. He read aloud to her: "'American iPhone Repair at 29 West Forty-Seventh Street, third floor, office eighteen.'"

"Did he give you a description of the guy?"

Danny scrolled down, read from his notes: "'Boss—thirty-five- to forty-five-year-old. Jewish, pale skinned, five feet ten inches, one hundred ninety pounds, bald-headed, brown on sides, wears a yarmulke, glasses. American, New York accent, no scar on face, no tattoos visible, soft lip'—I don't know what he means by that—'walk normal, no limp, no wedding ring.'"

"He said, 'If he looks like a celebrity that would be the actor who plays the, um, plays the lawyer on *The Wire*, bald guy, lawyer for Barksdale, but less handsome.' I have to look that one up, boss."

There was silence on the other end of the phone. Valencia finally asked, "So what do we have so far?"

"No UCC filings on American iPhone in Manhattan at that address. New York Department of State doesn't have anything, either. Names on all American iPhone variations in the city record sound more Chinese or Indian. I don't think he registered the business under that name, maybe a different name, but the address doesn't pop up, either. I checked the civil court records in Manhattan, no hits for that business name. There are some for American Phone Repair, but a different address.

"Building manager called me back last night and said he's not on site, but the rent is paid by wire transfer every month. Wouldn't tell me the name on the account, he's nice, but he said they need a subpoena for that. Says they have a super named, Javier, who I've left two messages for."

"Can you find the guy's name by the morning?" asked Valencia.

Danny stared at his computer screen for a moment, licked his lip. "Yeah, boss, if data exists online, I'll find it for you."

"Do it by nine a.m., and I'll give you a ten-thousand-dollar bonus," said Valencia.

"Boss, you don't need to do that—this is my normal job," said Danny, pushing the blanket off, and swinging his legs off the bed.

"It will be my pleasure," said Valencia.

They ended the call.

Danny lived alone in a one-bedroom apartment in Hell's Kitchen. His parents, who lived in Queens, were proud of the money he made. He told them he did data management for a law firm. He hadn't gone to college. He was introduced to Valencia by another lawyer he had worked for. He'd been with her for two years.

In the bathroom he urinated. He then washed his hands and splashed water on his face. From there, he went to his kitchen, opened the refrigerator, and pulled out two energy drinks. He went back to his bed, picked up his laptop, carried it to his couch, turned on the television, changed the station to ESPN, and began searching. He was a talented hacker, but this job wouldn't involve any hacking.

It was a manual labor job that would involve searching every corner of the web until he found a trail that led back to his man. He had access to Valencia's private investigator databases, and he began there. He opened two of those and ran simple business searches. He'd already done this, but he did it more thoroughly now.

He ran searches on 29 West Forty-Seventh and scrolled through all the records looking for anything that caught his eye. Meanwhile, other tabs popped open on his browser, and he began running down various rabbit holes. He skimmed message boards about iPhone repairs; searched articles that mentioned 29 West Forty-Seventh; looked at other businesses in the building. He searched Facebook, Twitter, Instagram, LinkedIn, and YouTube.

On LinkedIn he searched for anyone who had worked at American iPhone. There were no hits. He then searched for all cell phone technicians in New York. There were 816 hits. He began clicking through those, and eventually came across someone named David Weiner, who had listed "American Phone" on his resume. It wasn't quite right, but it was something. He went back to Facebook and searched through all the David Weiners in New York until he found the same person.

From there, he went through all of David's friends, looking for anyone who matched his target's physical description: thirty-five to forty-five, bald, white. David Weiner had eighteen friends who matched that description. About half of those eighteen friends' accounts were set to private. He created a table and put each of the names in their own box.

He began searching the databases and social media for all of those individual friends, going through each one until he could find some way to rule them out. He'd jump back to the database and run basic searches on family members, then he'd skip back to Facebook and look through the family members' photos for any hints.

Eventually, after a few hours of pinging around the web this way, he came across an Instagram account of a guy who was friends with David Weiner, someone named Michael Moskowitz—Instagram handle: PsychoboyMosko212. Among his photos was one that caught Danny's eye: A bald man in a club, holding up five cell phones like a hand of cards. The caption read *Cell phone KingsNYC Nizzzzzz.*

Danny cracked open his third Red Bull and then looked through the twelve people who had liked that picture; one of them appeared to be the same bald man who was in the picture. That person had an Instagram account called QueenzGodF. The account was set to private.

Danny googled: "QueenzGodF" and found a message board where QueenzGodF had weighed in on a debate about whether Nas was the best rapper from New York. Danny then jumped back to the databases and ran an email search for QueenzGodF@gmail.com. There were no hits. He tried QueenzGodF@hotmail.com and found a hit. The email address had been associated with an individual named Avram Lessing, date of birth 12/3/74.

Danny considered sending a phishing attack to the Hotmail account from a spoofed Instagram; he'd try to get him to log into the fake site and capture his password. But he didn't think Avi would fall for that, and he didn't want to wait to find out.

He sat there for a moment and then something clicked in his mind. He went back to David Weiner's Facebook page and searched through his friends for people named Avram. There was a hit for an Avi Doncic. The profile picture showed the basketball player Luka Dončić.

Danny tapped his forehead with the heel of his hand. He tried to look at Avi's photos, but they were set to private. He went back to the database and ran a basic person locator search for "Avi Lessing," with the DOB, and got a hit for an Avram Lessing. There were six addresses listed. The first was in Queens. The second was 29 West Forty-Seventh Street.

Danny was sure this was the guy, but he needed a photo and he wasn't going to get it from his Facebook page. He ran a quick image search, spent about thirty seconds going through the photos, and then decided he needed it faster than that. He thumbed through his contacts and found the number of a sergeant at the 18th Precinct—someone Wally Philpott had set them up with. The contact read *Edgar.Rodriguez.NYPD.NIGHT.WP*. Danny had never spoken with him, but he called him now.

"Rodriguez," said Edgar Rodriguez, picking up after the third ring.

"Hi, sergeant, my name is Danny. Wally Philpott told us to call you if we ever needed anything during the night shift."

"Who?"

"Wally Philpott."

"Oh, yeah, right. What can I do for you, kid?" he sounded tired and unimpressed.

"I need a DMV photo for someone named Avram Lessing, DOB 12/3/74."

"Fax it?"

"Can you email it?" asked Danny.

Sixteen minutes later the photo arrived on Danny's computer. He looked at it. He then googled, "Lawyer for Barksdale in *The Wire*." He looked at the picture that popped up for the actor Michael Kostroff. The two men looked similar.

Danny emailed the DMV photo to Valencia. The subject line read: *IS THIS HIM???*

It was 5:41 a.m.

Twenty seconds later, Valencia responded: *$10,000.*

*   *   *

Chris Cowley was standing in court arguing a motion in front of a sour-faced judge he'd never met before. A few of Chris's high school classmates were spread out in the gallery behind him. They weren't his friends: the truth was he couldn't remember their names, and he had no idea why they were there. He looked at the jury box and saw that individual houseplants—the same kind that were in his mother's house—had been placed in each seat. Suddenly, it all made sense: he was taking part in a mock trial, but he hadn't prepared at all for it. He looked down at his notes and saw that they'd gotten wet and were now smeared and illegible. The ink had gotten all over his hands and he was just wiping them on his jacket when he woke up and understood he'd been dreaming.

The clock on his bedside table said it was 5:41 a.m.

After pulling the blankets over his head, so he could hide from any cameras, he masturbated. When he was done, he went straight to the shower, scrubbed his body, and washed his hair. He shaved at the sink, doing the job slowly, with focus.

In the kitchen, he made a smoothie using pretrimmed kale, yogurt, frozen blueberries, oats, orange juice, a banana, and a heaped scoop of protein powder. While he assembled and dumped the ingredients, he stayed partly aware of the camera in his kitchen. It was in the fan duct; he had crawled up and seen it. He wasn't sure if there were other cameras in the apartment, but he assumed there were. It made him feel depressed; but he'd somehow grown used to the feeling.

He took his smoothie to the couch and began ruminating on the idea of revenge. He'd shoot the men that had made him do this. The skinny one that invaded his house—he would literally shoot him if he could. *Yeah, what's that bitch? How's that? What? You don't like guns in your mouth?* Chris could see it all so clearly.

But that kind of thinking wouldn't do. It served no purpose. He had to reframe the problem. *This is an opportunity*, he told himself, while he changed into his work clothes. *You're happy to spy for them. You'll do whatever it takes. You will work for them, and you'll do it in a cheerful manner.*

He buttoned up his shirt, pulled on his sweater, and then closed his eyes and tried to convince himself that what he was saying was true.

Before leaving his apartment, he snuck up to the living room window and peered down at the street below. There was a white van parked on the corner in a no-parking zone. Its hazards were blinking. It seemed too obvious. Still, he stared at it.

After stepping out of his building, he went in the opposite direction from his normal route. He'd take the F train today. *Fuck them*, he thought. It was a small change, but it made him feel rebellious. *I mean, who do they think they are?*

He'd only gotten two blocks when he heard footsteps coming from behind. The speed of the steps caught his attention, and he turned his head to look over his shoulder. The man coming toward him appeared to be in his fifties. He was white and dressed like he was headed to a low-paying office job. Chris had never seen him before.

As he got closer, Chris noticed that there was something unsettling about his face; his expression was flat, but his eyes looked angry. He was waving his hand down, a gesture that to Chris, looked like, *Keep going.*

Chris was confused; still, he let the man catch up to him.

"Which way is the A train?" asked the man. He was over six feet tall, somewhere around two hundred and twenty pounds.

"Excuse me?" asked Chris, reflexively taking a step backward.

"The A train?" asked the man. He looked Chris up and down in a way that felt accusatory.

Chris pointed vaguely toward Cadman Plaza. "Up that way a few blocks."

The man leaned in close. "And which way is the F train?" he asked, making it sound like a threat. Chris could smell cigarettes on his breath.

"This way," said Chris. "That's where I'm going."

"Then I guess we'll go together," said the man.

A wave of nausea passed through Chris. *What the fuck is this guy's problem?* He turned and began walking again.

The man caught up to him. "My routine is to take the A train," said the man. "But what the hell. Live a little, right?" The man was clearly one of his tormentors.

Chris ducked his chin, lowered his voice. "The A is running with delays," he said.

"No, it isn't," said the man, shaking his head and clenching his jaw.

For the first time, Chris noticed that the rims around the man's eyes were red, like he had bad allergies. They both stopped walking again, and Chris suddenly worried that the man might try to fight him: there was that kind of tension in the air. Chris felt his own eyes fill with tears.

"Fucking bullshit morning," said the man, turning and looking at all the buildings around him with a grimace on his face. "Thanks, pal," he said, and then he continued toward the York Street station.

Chris stood there and watched the man walk away. Then he changed his mind about how he was going to get to work. He had no desire to see that guy again, so he turned around and headed for the A Train.

"You need to tell her," said Valencia, looking at the receptionist, "that I can come and go as I want. I can't stop and wait for you every time I get off the elevator."

Andy, Elizabeth Carlyle's assistant, nodded and stepped to the woman; he leaned down and whispered the message in her ear. She then stood, turned, and looked at Valencia. "I'm sorry Mrs. Walker, they trained me to stop everyone, but it won't happen again."

"Sweetheart, it's not your fault, but I bill by the hour," said Valencia, turning and walking toward Elizabeth's office.

Andy caught up with her. "I'm sorry," he said.

"Don't be," said Valencia.

When they got to Elizabeth's office, Andy bowed his head, opened the door for her, and then closed it behind her.

Elizabeth was sitting at her desk. Her bad mood lingered in the air like a foul smell. "What the hell happened?" she asked, leaning back in her chair.

"They're good," said Valencia. "Better than—"

"So you said last night," said Elizabeth, interrupting her. "I need to know exactly what happened so I can tell the other partners." She crossed her arms in front of her chest, as if the room were cold.

Valencia sat down on the chair facing Elizabeth's desk. She took a moment to look at her own red fingernails. Breathing into her diaphragm, she loosened her shoulders, and made sure her posture was straight. She gathered herself up fully and, in a soft voice, sketched out the events as they'd happened: Dyker Heights, the golf course, the phone, Sheepshead Bay, the towers, the trash can, and the sewer.

When she finished the story, she shook her head, gave a tiny shrug of her shoulders, and then settled back into herself.

"So what is your plan?" asked Elizabeth.

Valencia opened the file in her hands, took out a piece of paper, and slid it across the desk. "Avi Lessing," she said. "He's the man who had the phone. There is a nine-in-ten chance that he's involved in the blackmailing."

"Nine in ten?" asked Elizabeth, sounding incredulous.

"Liz, this is what we have. I'm not working for them. This is crisis management; it doesn't always go exactly how we plan."

Elizabeth raised her hand to stop the lecture, then set her hand back down on the desk. "I thought that's why we brought you in? I thought that was your thing—to know exactly what is going to happen and plan accordingly."

For a moment, Valencia's mind went to a couple of the tasks she'd taken care of the previous week. On Monday, she'd paid hush money to a pregnant hairdresser in Staten Island. On Tuesday, she helped kill a negative story about the CEO of a bank that was set to run in the *Times*. She'd had to get creative for that one.

She had Danny work up a background on the editor of the story. It turned out the man's daughter had recently been rejected by Yale. Valencia knew the editor well. She'd been feeding him stories for years. She pressed him for a same-day lunch. Before the food arrived, Valencia managed to name-drop the dean of Yale College.

Over coffee, Valencia finally brought up the story about the banker. She said he was a friend and he'd asked her for advice. "It's a very weak story," she said. Right then her cell phone rang. She picked it up, looked at it, and laughed when she saw the New Haven number.

"Will you look at that," she said, showing the editor the phone. "Dean Schraeger," she said, answering right there at the table. "I was just talking about you. Listen, let me call you back, I'm having lunch with a friend." She hung up.

"Anyway," she said, "Dean Schraeger and I are very close. I call her my soul mate." She looked the editor in the eye. "She would do anything for me. But that story does seem weak, doesn't it?"

The man sat there blinking at his decaf cappuccino. "You know," he said finally. "It is kind of weak, isn't it?"

On Thursday, Valencia flew to Jackson, Wyoming, sat down with the COO of a large oil company, and convinced him it was time to retire. She hadn't even needed to blackmail him. She just talked it through. That was just last week. So yes, taking care of these little problems was her *thing*.

Valencia looked at the woman sitting across from her. "Elizabeth."

"What?"

"We'll take care of this. We'll clean it up. It might take a few moves, it might take more than a few moves, but we'll have them soon. These problems are temporary." She made her voice as soothing as she could. "Sweetie, this is what I do. Honestly, this hasn't even gotten complicated yet."

They sat in silence, Elizabeth staring at a spot on the ground to her right, Valencia staring at her.

"So this is where we are," said Valencia. "Avi Lessing, forty-three years old. Lives with his parents in Queens. No criminal background. The guy is a nobody, but he has friends."

"And?"

"And we believe he's involved. He passed the files on to someone he knows. He'll tell us."

"How do we know it was him?"

"His shop's abandoned. He literally moved out after we visited. Packed up and disappeared. I said 'nine in ten' cautiously. It's higher than that. He's involved."

Elizabeth made a show of brushing her hair behind her ears. "I'm not—" She stopped and thought for a second. "Why didn't you take care of this when you were face-to-face with him?"

"Because we were trying to keep our footprints small. We got the phone and—"

"And they blackmailed us."

"And *now* it's time to hit back."

"How?"

"We're going to apply pressure."

"This is turning into such a royal pain in my ass."

Valencia watched the woman's chest rise and fall with each breath.

"I am so over this place," whispered Elizabeth, looking around her office.

They sat in silence for a bit.

"It's a beautiful place," Valencia finally said.

*   *   *

Billy Sharrock spent the morning parked down the block from Avi Lessing's parents' house on 122nd Street, in Kew Gardens, Queens. The neighborhood had a suburban feel, more like Long Island than New York. The houses were stand-alone; they had pitched roofs and aluminum siding.

Billy had parked himself thirty yards north of the target house with the back of his van facing the door. His windows were blacked out with silvered polycarbonate; you could see out, but not in. He had a folding chair with a cushion on it. He sat on it now and watched the front door of the house.

His notes had three entries: at 6:49 a.m. he started his watch; at 9:14 a.m., an older man—Avi Lessing's father—had exited the house and walked south toward the JZ stop on Jamaica Avenue; the third entry—*GEL 5861*—was the license plate number of a silver SUV parked in the driveway. Billy had sent the tag to Danny Tsui and it came back as registered to their target.

He'd been instructed to sit in that spot until he had visual confirmation that Avi Lessing was inside the house. He'd packed enough white bread, peanut butter and jelly, apples, corn chips, bottled ice coffee, and water. He kept the food in a large red camping cooler pushed up against a wall of the van. He also had a Hassock Portable Toilet, which he kept inside a second large plastic box. He could stay in the van without leaving for days.

When he'd arrived at the site that morning, he'd taken two 10 mg pills of Adderall to help him stay up. He took another one mid-morning. They worked just like the old orange Dexedrines they used to pop in Afghanistan, and now his mind was humming right along. He chewed tobacco, and spit into a Gatorade bottle.

It didn't take long to confirm that Avi Lessing was there. At 1:14 p.m., the man walked out of the house, wearing a brown sweater.

He walked right past the van—within ten feet of Billy himself—and didn't even glance at it. From the expression on his face it looked like he was trying to solve a complicated problem. Billy's heart raced like a beagle's on seeing a pheasant.

Yep, we got this son of a bitch, he thought. Right after the man passed, he texted Valencia: *He's here.*

He then popped up out of his chair and moved to the front of the cargo area so he could peek out the front of the van. Ten seconds later he returned to the back window and watched the street that way long enough to confirm he was alone. In his mind, he repeated the meaningless phrase, *shit-ma,* just like he used to do in combat. He took the chewing tobacco out of his mouth and pushed it into the Gatorade bottle and rinsed his mouth with water.

Valencia texted back: *We're on our way.*

Billy opened the door and popped out of the back of the van. Before he closed the doors, he fussed with a box and pulled out a big pair of headphones so he would look like everyone else. He stood there and plugged them into his phone, then quietly closed the van's back door and began walking in the opposite direction from Avi. He passed the target house but didn't even glance at it.

He walked another twenty yards down to Hillside Avenue, then crossed to the opposite side of 122nd Street and doubled back so he was walking in the same direction as his man. He couldn't see the dude from where he was, but he knew he'd catch up to him. When he passed the house for the second time, he stole a look at it. All was quiet: the blinds were drawn, and there were AC units in the windows upstairs and down. By the time he passed his van again he could see Avi ahead of him about a hundred and fifty yards away.

Billy nodded along to some imaginary hip-hop, but the headphones were silent, and he was just thinking about how he'd like to choke this dude out. He'd put his head in his arm, wrap up his neck, and just squeeze. But not yet—just tag along and watch right now.

"Good boy," Billy muttered to himself. "Good boy."

By the next corner he'd closed the gap and he had to work to stay back. The sky was blue, and Billy was high from the pills. He pulled out his phone to make sure he hadn't missed any calls, and when he looked back up, he saw a young woman walking a pit bull right toward him. She looked Puerto Rican or something, and she had hoop earrings, and she smiled when they passed each other.

Avi Lessing made a dogleg right onto Breevort Street, and Billy followed him. An old dude raking leaves from his lawn stared at Billy as he passed, and Billy threw up a two-fingered peace sign like someone bidding at an auction. The man looked down and kept raking.

Billy watched Avi Lessing enter a little bodega on the corner of Metropolitan Avenue. Without breaking stride, Billy walked right past it and sat on a bench near a bus stop with his shoulders slumped like a man who'd been waiting all day. He checked his phone, breathed in deeply from the pills he'd taken, leaned to look for the bus, tapped a little drum solo on his knees, and then glanced back at the bodega. Nothing. He shook his head, closed his eyes, and cursed.

His phone vibrated; it was Valencia, and after glancing again at the bodega, he answered.

"Where are you?"

"He went to the store," said Billy, speaking into the microphone on the wire of his headphones.

"Okay, stay back, don't get made."

"Yes, ma'am," said Billy.

"You ready to pull him?"

"Yes, ma'am," said Billy.

"We'll be there in twenty minutes."

Billy looked over his shoulder just in time to see the man come out of the store. "Gotta go, call you back," he whispered.

Avi Lessing was carrying a plastic bag and seemed to be walking faster now. Billy let him disappear around the corner and then sat there looking down Metropolitan like he was deciding on whether to take the bus or walk. In his mind he counted back—*five, four, three, two, one, zero*—then stood up and followed him.

The guy raking the lawn was gone this time. Up ahead, Billy could see the brown of Avi's sweater swinging back and forth with his walk, like the backside of a horse. Billy crossed to the other side of 122nd Street, so he wouldn't be directly behind him if he turned. He stayed about fifty yards back, and in an effort to look less suspicious, pretended to be texting on his phone.

After watching Avi enter his house, Billy got back in his van. He went to the large toolbox at the front of the hold, spun the combo lock, and opened it. He pulled out a black duffle bag and started filling it with tools. He put in some heavy-duty bolt cutters, a Maglite, a fifty-thousand-volt stun gun, duct tape, a spool of Kevlar wire, a pack of plastic double flex restraints, a ski mask, a pair of plastic gloves, a cinching hood, a Leatherman, and a crowbar.

Next, he pulled out a pair of black polyester pants, shook them out, and changed into them. He took the belt off his jeans and put it on the new pants and cinched them tight. He pulled his shoes back on, and then put on a shoulder holster and tightened the strap at his underarm. He checked the clip on his handgun and put it in the holster. He then pulled out a black jacket and put that on over everything.

To keep his face off any cameras, he put on a black baseball cap. Finally, just in case, he hooked his fake FBI badge onto his belt and covered it with his shirt.

When he was done with all that, he sat back down on his folding chair and watched out the back window, taking deep breaths to try to calm down. He was so amped up, he noticed he was sweating around his hairline and on his back. *Shit-ma*, he said in his mind—*shit-ma*.

Fifteen minutes later Valencia called back and said they were five minutes away. "Did you check the yard?" she asked.

"Yes, ma'am. House to the south—to the left if you're facing the front door from the street—has four windows that face our dude's house. The windows have blinds drawn, Danny said that house is occupied by a Mexican family. The house to the north doesn't have any windows facing the lawn. There's a large apartment building directly behind the target, but the trees block that pretty good."

"And you can get in?"

"Yes, ma'am."

"Get set up. We'll text you when we're moving. It will be a thirty-second count from text to knock."

"Got it," said Billy.

The call ended. Billy stood up near the back window and watched for a minute. The butterflies in his stomach felt like small birds. All was quiet. He then hopped out the back doors, pulled the duffle bag out, and got in the front of the van. He started it up, checked his side mirror, pulled away from the curb, and then made a quick U-turn. He cursed Avi's house when he passed it, and drove toward Hillside Avenue.

At the red light, he stopped and put on his right turn signal and watched three separate people walking in different directions. When the light changed, he made his turn and drove one block down to 121st Street, and then turned right. He parked just past the apartment complex.

After hopping out, he turned and pulled his bag out, set the strap on his shoulder, and walked toward the side of the apartment building. An older man standing and smoking near the door of the apartment didn't pay any attention to him.

Billy kept to the side of the apartment, down below the windows, and moved toward the back. There was trash on the ground and the trees were thick with green leaves, putting everything into shadow. He came out on a little alley that cut between the streets and found the fenced-in backyard of the Lessing house. He turned his back to the fence—which was chain-linked and ribboned with privacy tape—and stood there for a minute looking and listening to the area around him. Down the block, some reggaeton played on a sound system, but otherwise it was quiet.

Earlier that morning, he'd hopped the fence and scouted the location, but now he took out his bolt cutters, clipped the padlock on the gate, and then put the cutters back into the bag. He stayed there for a minute, making sure nobody had seen what he'd done. Then he took the cut lock, set it on the ground, and slowly pushed the gate open against some tall weeds on the other side.

The center of the yard was concrete with two little paths of overgrown grass running down its middle. There was a rusted-out barbecue grill, a few flat-tired bicycles, a barrel filled with trash, and two sagging clotheslines with nothing on them except clothes pins. Empty buckets, tangled hoses, and stacks of bricks filled the rest of the yard.

Watching the windows of the house, Billy walked next to the fence on his left. When he got about ten feet away from the nearest wall, he set his bag down and pulled out the spool of Kevlar wire. Then he crossed the yard, walking tall, like a man who had every right to be there.

On the other side, he bent down and tied a quick clove hitch, attaching the wire to the fence. When he was done, he walked back to the north side, clipped the wire, and, leaning into it, pulled it tight. He then hitched it to that fence about twelve inches off the ground. When he was done he plucked it like a guitar string.

Billy picked up the bag, walked right up next to the Lessing house, set the bag on the ground and pulled out his stun gun. Then he leaned with his back against the wall of the house and tried to listen for noise coming from inside.

All he could hear was his heart racing and the reggaeton playing down the block and a plane coming in to land at LaGuardia. Billy kept telling himself that nobody was going to come out that back door. *They aren't coming out.* His phone vibrated and he looked at it and saw a text from Valencia: *Set.*

He texted back: *Set.*

Then he closed his eyes and began counting back from thirty to zero. When he was at twelve, the back door of the house flew open and Avi Lessing came barreling out and hit the wire and went crashing down hard like he'd been shot. The impact knocked the air from the man's chest.

Billy picked up his bag, walked over to the fallen man, looked all around for spying eyes, but didn't see any. Avi was just starting to push himself up when Billy touched his shoulder with the stun gun and delivered fifty thousand volts, sending his body shaking like a hooked fish. When Billy was done, he looked back at the house and didn't see any people or movement.

He looked at both houses around him and didn't see anyone watching. Billy took out the flex-cuff and tied the unconscious man's hands behind his back. Then he took the black hood and pulled it over the bald man's head, cinching it tight. He grabbed Avi Lessing—hooded now—by the sweater and pulled him back toward his house and out of sight of the neighbors.

Billy kneeled down, put a hand on the man's shoulder, watched the backyard and the surrounding area, and listened. Everything was quiet.

A sailboat somewhere on Long Island Sound.

The water was as still as a lake, not a single ripple, and Avi Lessing, squinting at the water, was trying to make sense of that. Why wasn't it moving? How could it possibly be this still? There was a saying that addressed that kind of question, but he couldn't remember it.

Anyway, it was a bright sunny day, and he turned and looked toward the bow of the ship and saw his mother and father standing there with paper plates in their hands. A small circle of strangers, also holding paper plates and talking quietly, stood around them. Avi was just starting to step toward the group when everything in his vicinity—the boat, the water, his parents, the strangers, the blue sky—got sucked up like a napkin and pulled through a tiny hole below his feet until all that remained was blackness.

When Avi opened his eyes, he found himself looking at the parquet floor in his living room. His ears were ringing. He could see dust motes and individual hairs on the floor. His mind was fogged, and his chin and knees hurt. There was a mineral taste in his mouth—blood; he moved his tongue around to check his teeth. He tried to raise his hand to his mouth, but it was stuck. He realized his hands were bound behind him.

What the hell was he doing on the floor? He turned on his side, looked up and saw a woman seated about five feet away. She had dark hair and she was dressed like a businesswoman, wearing a black pantsuit with a white shirt. She wore bright red lipstick. She was staring down at him with a flat expression on her face, and Avi, for a moment, had the distinct impression that she was a doctor.

A car honked outside, and everything clicked into place. He recognized her as the woman who'd come by the phone shop. *Oh shit*, he thought. He rocked back and forth and tried to pull his hands free, but they were strapped tight. "I gave you the phone!" he finally said.

The woman's legs were crossed; she had on high heels. Her hands were folded in her lap. Her head moved about an inch and her eyes narrowed. She leaned toward him like she hadn't heard what he'd said.

"I gave you the phone," he repeated. In his mind, he ran through a list of people to blame, landing eventually on Yuri Rabinowitz.

He was just beginning to shift the blame to the Africans when a fresh wave of pain in his chin distracted him. "I didn't do anything," he said. "They brought it to me. What? I'll tell you who it was. The guys that sold me the phone, I'll show you them. I'll take you to them."

Right then two things occurred to Avi Lessing: First, he noticed that he was missing his glasses. The second thought came on the heels of the first—*Mommy is going to fucking kill me for this one.*

He looked around the room. "Where is my mother?" he asked. He rocked on the ground, struggled against the binds until his wrists hurt. "Where is my mother?"

Then he yelled out "Mommy!"

The woman sitting across from him raised a finger to her mouth and shushed him.

"What did you fucking do with her?" he asked. "Where are my nieces? This is not—you can't—you can't just come into someone's home. For what? For a phone? What is this? Where is she?"

"She's downstairs with my men," said the woman.

Avi's eyes began blinking uncontrollably. *Downstairs? Downstairs is an unfinished basement*, he thought. *It's filled with cobwebs, it's dirty— even I don't go down there.* He felt himself begin to sob. He couldn't stop.

"What do you want? What the fuck do you want?" he asked. He craned his head up at her, aware that his face was now covered with snot. "What do you want?"

The woman leaned forward, squinted again, and scratched her neck. The house itself was silent. Beyond the house, Avi could hear the Dominicans down the block blasting their music. He pulled on his wrists again, but they pinched like they were being cut with a knife.

"Did you take something from that phone?" the woman asked.

"No!"

She stared at him in silence. "Did you take anything from that phone?"

"No!" he said, again. "Mommy?" he called out to the quiet house. Another shorter wave of crying passed through him.

"Those men who are with me, the ones who tied you up," said the woman, standing up and walking to look out the window, "are downstairs with your mother and nieces."

Avi watched her take out her cell phone and look at it.

"I've convinced them to give me five minutes. I wanted to see if talking worked. It seemed like the best way. I want you to think carefully about the next question I ask you," she said. "Did you take anything off of that phone?"

"I copy all of the phones that pass through my business," said Avi. "I back them all up, it's normal, everyone does it. It's called *being careful*. What the fuck?" He banged the side of his head against the floor in frustration.

"And after you copied it. Let me ask you this: did you give someone a copy of anything from that phone?" The woman sat down on the chair again.

"You'll let us go?"

"I'll let you all go."

"My mother's okay?"

"I think so," said the woman.

"I sold it to an associate, a guy I know named Yuri."

"Yuri what?"

"Yuri Rabinowitz," he said. "It's fucking Yuri Rabinowitz."

The next morning, Yuri Rabinowitz stood at his living room window, holding the curtain back, staring out at the block outside his house. He took special interest in a white van parked forty yards to the north. "*What's with that van?*" he asked his brother.

Slumped down with both hands in his underwear, Isaac turned from the MMA men fighting on the television, looked blankly at his brother, and asked him what he was talking about.

"*Come here, asshole,*" said Yuri.

The television blared: "Martinez going for the rear naked, he just needs to get that leg hooked around."

"What?" asked Isaac.

"Turn that shit off—come here."

Isaac cursed under his breath, muted the television, and pushed himself up off the couch. He looked even more hungover than Yuri felt.

"That one," Yuri said, pointing when his brother joined him at the window.

"That's Narek's," said Isaac, nodding at the house across the street from them. "Narek's son, you know dude—what's his name—Lil Dap, the weight lifter."

Yuri was confused, because he'd understood that Lil Dap had moved to Florida.

"He's a plumber," Isaac continued.

"You're sure it's the same?" asked Yuri.

"It's always there."

Yuri watched his younger brother's eyes go from Narek's house to the van; there was something in his face that suggested he wasn't sure.

"Do you know, or don't you?" Yuri asked.

"What the fuck's your problem?" said Isaac.

Yuri put a hand on his brother's shoulder, but Isaac shrugged it off. For a moment it felt like they were screaming at each other without speaking. It felt like they might get into a physical fight, but Isaac turned and walked away.

On the television a man lifted a naked underarm and sprayed it with deodorant. Yuri's gaze went back out the window and his mind sped through two memories. The first occurred over twenty years ago: he'd shot his brother in the face with a rubber band. His father was still alive then, and Isaac ran to him and tattled. As punishment his father tried to make Yuri sit still while Isaac shot him in the face with a rubber band, but both brothers had cried hysterically and the whole episode fell apart with spankings for both of them.

The second memory, from just a few weeks ago, involved an episode in an Uber. Isaac was drinking 7Up with cough syrup, and he'd spilled it in the back of the car. Something had snapped in Yuri, and he'd pummeled his brother in the head and neck and shoulders until their African driver screamed at them to get out.

Yuri turned toward the kitchen. "Do you know, or don't you?" he yelled out, again.

The only answer was the sound of the refrigerator slamming shut.

At the front door, raging, Yuri stepped into his running shoes, opened the closet, pushed aside some coats, found his golf bag, and pulled out a five iron. He cleaned dirt from the head of the club with his sweatshirt. *Motherfucker*, he thought to himself. *Motherfucker*. He stepped outside into the morning sun, holding the club in his hand and keeping his eyes on the van.

He approached the van holding the club in both hands, loosening his wrists with little half circles like a batter. The van was a Chevy, over ten years old, rusted on the top near the windshield. Yuri felt sure he'd never seen it before.

His pulse thumped in his right temple and an angry feeling throbbed in his chest. When he got to the van, he peered in through the passenger window. A crumpled McDonald's bag lay on the floor, along with two paper soda cups and a free magazine. The passenger seatbelt, oddly, was buckled.

Because of a partition behind the seat, Yuri couldn't see into the back cargo area. He walked around the van, but there were no windows, not even in the back. No writing, no phone numbers. He put his ear to the back door and tried to listen. Then he tapped on the back door with his club, three times, politely, like he was afraid of waking a possible resident. The rear bumper had been dented at some point and cobwebs ran along its near edge.

Yuri's stomach filled with dread. He felt like he wanted to cry. When he looked back at his house, he saw Isaac's head disappear behind a curtain in the living room window.

Yuri turned and crossed the street to Narek's house. When he pressed the doorbell it buzzed sharply, and a moment later the door swung open. Narek, an Armenian, stood there in sweatpants and a Knicks jersey, a gold chain hanging from his neck. Gray chest and back hair curled out from the shirt. Yuri watched the expression on the man's face morph from concern to a kind of fake friendliness.

"Hey, wassup Mr. Yuri?" said Narek, drying his hands on his jersey. "Come in, come in."

"It's okay," said Yuri. "I'm just wondering: is that your son's van?" He pointed at the van with the handle of his golf club.

"Yeah, why? You don't want it there?"

"No, it's fine, I saw someone looking into it."

"Oh shit"—Narek turned toward the interior of his house and yelled—"Yo Dap!"

"The guy left—just to make sure, you know."

"Dap!" yelled Narek. "I told him not to park on the street," he said to Yuri.

A moment later Lil Dap came down the stairs dressed like he'd just rolled out of bed. He was a large man, over two hundred and thirty pounds. He looked tired and slightly confused to see Yuri standing there. "What's good, homey?" he asked, walking to the door and bumping fists with Yuri.

"Mr. Yuri saw a man looking in your van," said Narek.

"A black dude?" asked Dap.

"I didn't see his face," said Yuri.

"You know, what's-his-name?" asked Dap. "What's-his-face, over there on Beaumont, your homey the fat dude?"

"Alex?" asked Yuri.

"Yeah, yeah, he told me his whole toolbox was taken out of the back of his van," said Dap, stepping closer to Yuri and putting an oversized hand on his shoulder as he peered out toward his van with a concerned look on his face. Yuri smelled marijuana on him. "They had the motion lights and everything. What's good with you though, man?"

"I'm good," said Yuri, stepping back from Lil Dap.

"What was you gonna do, fuck this dude up with your golf club?" asked Lil Dap, laughing and looking at his father.

The older man crossed his arms, shook his head. "The whole neighborhood's gone to shit," said Narek. "It used to be neighbors watched out for each other."

"They still do, Pop, look at him," said Lil Dap, nodding at Yuri.

"Okay," said Yuri. He felt sweat on his forehead. He stepped back again, finally freeing himself of Dap's hand.

"Hey, tell your bro to get his ass over here for some *Call of Duty*," said Lil Dap.

"I will, I will," said Yuri, backing away and returning to his house.

What the fuck has come over me, wondered Yuri. *Why am I so nervous?*

Right then he heard the revving sound of a motorcycle and he knew it was Moishe Groysman.

His friend rolled up to him in the middle of the street, put the bike in neutral, pulled up his visor. "Grigory came this morning," he said. "He asked when Uncle can expect to hear from you."

"Fuck," said Yuri. "Park over there, we'll take a car."

"Do I look okay?" asked Valencia, batting her eyelids. She was in the passenger seat of Milton Frazier's SUV; they were parked in a no-parking zone on Lafayette Street, just off Foley Square, across the street from the U.S. District Courthouse. Valencia watched Milton's eyes go from her face to her shirt, and back up.

He nodded his head, looked out the front. "Yeah, you do."

She held up ten freshly painted fingernails and wiggled them at him. "Hair? Makeup?"

"It's all good," said Milton. "You look perfect."

Valencia checked her teeth in the visor mirror and then bent her head and looked across the square at the courthouse. "Have you ever met this guy, Sandemose?" she asked.

Milton shook his head.

"He's a pervert." She opened the door, stepped out, and then leaned back in the window. "Stay close, this shouldn't take more than half an hour."

After passing through the security line, she made her way toward Judge Palmetto's courtroom. Utah Sandemose's secretary had said the lawyer would be there all morning. Valencia needed a face-to-face for this; a phone call wouldn't do.

Before entering the courtroom, she paused and imagined herself being bathed in a shower of white light, a warm beautiful bath that would make her posture perfect and her skin shine. Cleansed. When she finished, she took a deep breath, felt her chest expand, and pulled the door open.

The attorneys, the judge, and the two marshals ignored Valencia when she entered. The judge's clerk—who tracked her with her eyes—was the only person who seemed to notice her.

Valencia sat in the back row, folded her hands in her lap, and listened as the assistant U.S. attorney—a man she'd never seen before—argued against a reduction of bail. While the man droned on and on about the defendant's prior history, Valencia watched Utah Sandemose, who sat with another attorney at the defendant's table. The defendant himself, for some reason, didn't appear to be in the courtroom.

After ten minutes of argument, the judge made her ruling—bail reduction denied—and the lawyers, making small talk, gathered their papers and began moving toward the door. Sandemose didn't notice Valencia until she stood. When he saw her, he flinched in mock surprise.

"Ms. Valencia Walker, to what do we owe the honor of your appearance?" He looked like a bigheaded cowboy dressed in a suit.

Valencia looked at the other man and noticed that he didn't have any ears. It looked as though they'd been cut off.

"My paralegal, Vic," said Utah, smiling.

Valencia shook hands with the paralegal. She wondered whether Utah was drunk. There was something about the volume of his voice that suggested inebriation. "I need to speak to you about something," she whispered.

"Hear that?" He put his face in front of the paralegal and, moving his lips to allow for lip reading, loudly said, "I'll meet you out front."

"I'll be there," said the paralegal. He smiled at Valencia and left the two of them standing there inside the courtroom.

"Genius of a mind," whispered Utah, nodding after the man. "Served six years in Allenwood, knows the law better than you and me. So, what the hell can I do for you?" he asked, stepping back and shamelessly looking at her chest.

"Yakov Rabinowitz," said Valencia.

Utah exhaled audibly, looked away, licked his lips. "What about him?"

"We need to meet."

"Oh, boy," said Utah, lifting a hand to wave goodbye to the marshals. Then he ushered Valencia out into the hallway. "Now what the hell do you want to meet an old coot like him for?"

Valencia stopped walking and squared up to the lawyer. She let her head drop to the left a few degrees and softened her expression. "I need help from him," she said in her smoothest voice.

"With what?"

"You don't want to know."

"I probably don't—you are right about that. So let me ask: is this for someone else?"

"The less you know the better," said Valencia.

Utah's eyes went over her shoulders. He watched some lawyers from another courtroom disappear down the hallway. "You know I don't represent him anymore?"

"But I'm sure you're still friendly with him."

"Hell yeah, I am," said Utah. "I kept him out, didn't I?"

"I need to meet him," she repeated.

They began moving toward the elevator.

"Tell me this: is your showing up going to make his day worse?" asked Utah. "He's a nice fella, don't look mean or anything, but he's not the kind of guy you want to make mad. You understand what I'm talking about?

"I think so," said Valencia.

"He gonna be unhappy to meet you?" asked Utah.

"Is anyone ever unhappy to meet me?"

The lawyer smiled, raised his eyebrows. "And you'll agree to have dinner with me?"

"Of course I will. You know that."

"And you're not going to bring any of your old friends from over there"—he nodded east, toward Foley Square, toward the FBI offices —"into our little friend's orbit."

"I don't have friends over there," said Valencia, forcing herself to smile.

"Okay, here's the deal," said Utah. "I'll give him a call, tell him you want to meet. I'll tell him I have *no idea* what the hell you want to meet about. I'll advise *against* it. Cover my ass that way. I'll say, 'If I were you, I wouldn't even take this meeting.' I'll have to tell him who you are." Here he leaned in and whispered: "Langley, all of it." Utah straightened up, spoke in a normal volume: "He's gonna find out anyway. Don't worry, I know that old boy, probably make him want to meet you even more."

"You should come work with me," said Valencia. She grabbed his wrist and gave it a squeeze. "We would make a hell of a team, wouldn't we?"

"First a non-sexualized dinner," said Utah. He pointed a big cowboy finger at her. "And you're buying."

* * *

"*Take out a hundred, plus twenty,*" said Yuri.

"*A hundred?*" asked Moishe. "*I thought we said seventy-five?*"

"*The idea is to get more work, a calling card, not just the minimum.*"

"Right here?" asked the Uber driver.

"Right there," said Yuri, leaning forward and pointing at Ossip's Locksmith Shop. "Right here, right here."

Moishe took a moment folding the paper sack he'd brought with him and then got out of the car, leaving Yuri, Isaac, and the driver waiting.

When he got to Ossip's door, he found it locked. He knocked and then cursed when he saw that Ossip wasn't alone in the shop. A man stood near the counter with him. It was early in the day, but both men looked drunk. Ossip, smiling, came to the door and unlocked it.

"*You have someone here?*" whispered Moishe.

Ossip's face reacted like he'd heard something obscene. "*Him? He's my cousin, you know Dimitri!*"

Moishe leaned his head to look into the shop. Dimitri, the cousin, stood with both hands on the counter, like he was at a bar. He was skinny, had greasy hair, and wore a loose gray suit. He had a drug-weathered face and for the time being kept his eyes on the floor. Moishe didn't recognize him.

Moishe turned back to the locksmith. "*Wait right here, don't fucking close that door.*"

When he got back to the Uber, Moishe stepped to the front passenger window, leaned down, and spoke into it. "*He has someone else.*"

"What?" said Yuri, leaning forward to see. "*I thought you told him we were coming?*"

"*I did.*"

"*Who is it?*"

"*He says it's his cousin, Dimitri.*"

From the back of the car, Isaac said, "Dima? Nah, he's hella cool. He just got out. Hold on." Isaac started to open the door, but Yuri turned and told him to stay where he was. He told Moishe to hold on, then pulled out his phone and sent a text message.

Moishe felt uneasy. He glanced at the driver, who was fussing with his own iPhone and pretending not to pay any attention to them. Moishe leaned away from the car and looked at the block around him. Everything was normal. An old woman carrying sagging bags walked past them on the sidewalk. A car honked at another car and pigeons flew into the air.

"I'll come with you," said Yuri, putting his phone in his pocket and getting out of the car. *"We don't hang out, we don't drink, we just get what we came for."*

When they got to the door, it was closed but unlocked. Inside the shop, Ossip, seeming more sober now, introduced Dimitri. *"He just got out,"* said Ossip, speaking quietly to Yuri. *"Sing Sing. A friend of your uncle."*

"Dima," said the man, bowing his head formally and holding his hand out to Yuri. They shook. "Dima," he said to Moishe, limping over to him and bowing his head again. He held his left hand on his chest like he was apologizing and shook hands with his right. The hand that Moishe grasped was both clammy and rough. There was something repulsive about it. Moishe himself had rough hands from lifting weights, but they weren't anything close to this.

He pictured the man obsessively scraping his hands on rock walls until they bled and then cauterizing them over a candle. Moishe rubbed his own hands on his shirt and tried to catch Yuri's eye, but his friend was staring blankly toward the front door. Moishe stepped to Ossip, grabbed his arm, and led him toward the back.

"Yeah, yeah," said Ossip. Moishe followed, leaving Yuri and Dima in the front of the store. The hallway to the back was dark. Ossip said something about a bulb needing to be replaced.

"Why do you have someone here?" whispered Moishe.

"*He stopped by,*" said Ossip. "*What am I going to do? He's my aunt's son. He's a good boy.*" Ossip went to the safe, bent over, and began spinning the dial. The windowless room was bright with fluorescent light. In addition to the safe, it contained a few file cabinets and a table covered with random tools and trash. Papers, receipt books, binders. A pornographic picture of a woman was taped to the far wall. The room smelled of cigarettes and dust.

Moishe could hear the low tones of Dimitri's voice coming from down the hallway, but he couldn't make out the words. He turned back just as Ossip was lifting the bag of money out of the safe and setting it on the worktable.

After unzipping the bag, Moishe counted out twelve ten-thousand-dollar stacks. Besides the hundred thousand for Yuri's uncle, they were going to split another twenty for spending money.

When he finished, he turned toward Ossip and noticed that the man appeared to be nervous. "What's a matter with you?" whispered Moishe. He then went back to the bag and silently counted the rest of the stacks. It was all there.

"*Nothing,*" said Ossip. "*My heart hurts,*" he added, tapping his chest. "I tell you, my friend—every day in this place," he said, briefly switching to English. "*How many did you take?*"

"Twelve," said Moishe. He put the money into the paper sack and rolled it shut. "Twelve," he repeated.

The older man then moved the rest of the money over to the safe, put it in, and locked it. "*Seventy-one minus twelve: fifty-nine,*" said Ossip.

"*Don't say anything,*" said Moishe, nodding toward the front of the shop.

"Don't treat me like a fucking idiot," said Ossip. "I wasn't born yesterday." He shook his head and led the way to the front of the store.

Moishe found Yuri—arms crossed, eyes cast down—listening to the end of some kind of war story. The only part that Moishe caught was something like "*and that's why Russian, white, black, Latin, it doesn't matter.*"

When Dima finished the story, his eyes went straight to the sack in Moishe's hands. It was only a split second, and then his eyes ticked away, but Moishe felt the glance in his nervous system like he'd seen a snake on the ground. It jolted him.

Right then, Ossip—pulling Moishe by his free arm—said, "*And now we have a drink.*" He grabbed four small glasses and filled them with vodka. "*For our cousin coming home.*" He raised his glass. "*A good boy.*"

They toasted and drank. "*One more,*" he said, pouring another.

Yuri tried to protest but was ignored. A car's horn blared outside.

"*To Ossip,*" said Dima, lifting his glass. "*The best locksmith in Brooklyn.*" The men lifted their drinks and drank.

The bell on the front door chimed just as they were finishing their drinks. All four men swung their heads and saw Isaac walk in.

"I told you to wait," said Yuri.

"You should keep the door locked," said Isaac, speaking to Ossip.

"We should go," said Moishe, rolling the top of the paper sack tighter.

"Gotta pay my respects to the big homey," said Isaac, stepping to Dima. "What's good with you, man?" he asked.

Moishe watched in disbelief as Dimitri wrapped Isaac up in a bear hug and lifted the younger man off the ground. He then watched as the two of them had a back-and-forth, each complimenting how good the other man looked, squeezing each other's arms and making promises to go out and party soon.

After another round of drinks, they finally headed for the door, but before they got there, Dima called out one more thing to Yuri: "Make sure you give my regards to your uncle."

* * *

Earlier that morning, on the subway ride to work, Chris Cowley was approached by another man he'd never seen before. Chris had been standing near the door of the car holding on to the handrail when the stranger appeared in his peripheral vision. The train was three-quarters full; standing so close felt intentional. Chris didn't turn and look, but he could tell the man was white and that he had brown hair.

For a moment, Chris experienced the unmistakable lifting feeling of attraction; his insides pulled up. His go-to phrase, *Wanna fuck*, passed through his mind. He became nervous. His problems momentarily disappeared, and as the train began to move, he was swept along, feeling the energizing sense of romantic possibility.

The fantasy was short lived. Moments after the train cleared the station, the man turned his head slightly and spoke into Chris's ear. "Listen to me," he said. "They want me to tell you to stop acting so depressed."

Chris turned and looked. The attraction vanished. The man was ugly. His eyes were set close together, he had a large Adam's apple, and he'd missed a spot shaving that morning, which gave the side of his chin a gross pubic quality.

"Excuse me?" said Chris.

"Don't be so"—the man pantomimed a depressed person—"all the time."

Chris looked at him and then dropped his eyes to the floor of the subway.

"Try to act normal," said the man. "You're pissing off the wrong people."

The man then stepped to a nearby seat, sat, and stared at Chris. Chris turned back to the window and watched the dark tunnel speed past. *What the fuck?* A sick feeling moved in his guts.

His mother had taught him to name these feelings but all he could come up with was—*a glacier, a gross, dirty glacier*. He turned back to the man and tried to glare at him, but the man's face looked angry, as if he wanted to fight; and just like that Chris got scared and looked away.

Pathetic, Chris thought. *I am truly pathetic.* He licked his lips. Had there been any witnesses to this interaction? A glassy-eyed old woman stared at him, but in a vacant way. Nobody else seemed to be paying any attention.

The train pulled into the East Broadway stop and Chris patted his pocket to make sure his phone was there. He found it inside his jacket. Then he closed his eyes and tried to breathe deeply. *Calm down, you piece of shit.*

Thankfully, the man didn't follow him off the train. In fact, he even appeared to keep his eyes closed while Chris made his exit. That didn't stop Chris from looking over his shoulder three times on his way out of the station. As he walked, he repeated *Act normal* to himself, like some kind of mantra.

Chris spent the morning seated at his desk, taking shallow breaths and trying to will the toxicity out of his guts. He couldn't help wondering whether that man was even part of the other group—but of course he was.

After lunch he attended a meeting and did his best to appear alert and eager. He played his role, sat straight, and didn't say anything except *hello* and *goodbye*. As soon as he left the meeting the conversations in his head picked back up: *All I did was look at pornography, you fucking sickos. You backward-ass mother-fucking thugs.*

His problems continued. Shortly after the meeting, walking to the bathroom, he crossed paths with Elizabeth Carlyle. He couldn't avoid her this time. There was nothing he could do. The sight of her caused his blood pressure to shoot up; his bowels tightened.

Still, he maintained his stride, kept his eyes on her, and even managed to nod. They were alone in the hallway. They didn't speak, they just passed each other, and the look on Elizabeth's face left Chris feeling bothered for the rest of the afternoon. He played the scene over and over in his mind and tried to analyze exactly what had been so disturbing about her expression. It wasn't the displeasure; beneath that he sensed something worse: sadness. Anger was one thing, sadness another. She was sad for him. She pitied him. *Fuck*, Chris thought. *I really am fucked.*

At 3:47 p.m. he checked his cell phone and saw that he'd missed a call from his mother. Standing by the window in his office he called her back. They had just gotten through their normal routine of insipid greetings when she said something truly disturbing: "So remind me who that friend was that stopped by last night?"

"What friend?" asked Chris. He tried to make his voice sound calm and not betray any of the fear he was feeling.

"Didn't you listen to my message?"

"No, Mom—I just called you back," he said, chopping at the air with his hand. "What friend are you talking about?"

"Hold on."

Chris looked out the window and imagined throwing himself from it. He'd feel the rush of air and see the ground racing to meet him; the traffic noise would grow louder as he flew down, and the gray pavement would turn black.

"Where is it?" said his mother. "Oh, here, yes, I wrote it down: John. He said to tell you he happened to be passing through town and he thought you'd be here. What?"

"I didn't say anything," said Chris.

"Honey, I told him—wait, I had something else I needed to tell you. What did I—"

"Mom, what did he say? Who was he?"

"He said he was your friend."

"What did he look like?"

"Honey, he looked like your friend Drew, but older. I thought he was one of Drew's brothers for a minute but—"

"What exactly did he say?" asked Chris, taking the phone away from his ear and speaking into it like a handheld radio.

"He said, 'Hi, Ms. Cowley.' I said, 'Ms. *Peterson* now,' and he said, 'Is Chris around?' He said you told him you'd be here."

"That's it?"

"You're in New York. You're not coming home, are you?"

Chris rubbed his eyes and thought about how much he should tell her. "No, Mom, unfortunately, I'm not. I think we just got our signals crossed."

"Our what?"

"We got our signals crossed. Mom, listen, let me call you back a little bit later, okay?"

"Okay, honey, Bill and I will be at Murphy's with Linda and Tim, but after that—"

After ending the call, Chris stood there staring out the window. *How bad*, he wondered. *How bad is this?* It was clearly a threat. The man on the train came back to him: "Stop acting so depressed."

Chris turned from the window and was startled to see Michael D'Angelo, the investigator, standing in his doorway. "Jesus," Chris said. "Don't you knock?" He couldn't hide his anger.

"Sorry, I didn't want to interrupt you," said D'Angelo, stepping into the office, holding his hands in front of his crotch. "It sounded . . ."

"It's my mother," said Chris. "She's having a really hard time."

"It sounded urgent."

"No," said Chris. The two men stood there staring at each other for a moment until Chris asked what he could do for him.

"Just checking in. You seemed kind of shaken up the other day. Again, I just . . ."

Chris stood there blinking. How the hell was he going to get rid of this imbecile? He tried to smile, but it only made him feel sadder. He turned toward the window, then back to D'Angelo, and said, "I'm having a really hard time with my boyfriend. He just, like, doesn't get me."

D'Angelo nodded, pursed his lips, and said, "Well, like I said, any time you need to talk, just let me know." He took a step back toward the door.

Chris saw his advantage and pressed on. "It's just, like, relationships aren't easy, you know?"

"I do," said D'Angelo, but instead of retreating the way Chris had hoped he would, he stopped and stood there, looking at the ground and shaking his head.

"Anyway," said Chris.

"Yeah," said D'Angelo, looking up. "I'll let you get back to it."

At his desk, Chris put his head in his hands and hummed a song to himself. Then he straightened up and checked the time; it was 3:51 p.m.

The expression on Elizabeth Carlyle's face wasn't the kind of pitying look that Chris had presumed. It was simply depression; an etched-on, deep depression. Which isn't to say she'd forgotten about Chris, just that she was done thinking about him. Her energy was not well spent on such a small character. Her problems were much larger than Chris Cowley. Her problems were legion.

At four p.m., Edwin Kerins, one of the Calcott Corporation's in-house counsel was calling for his regular weekly update. Elizabeth had already told him Chris Cowley's phone had been stolen, and that it had documents from the case on it. She hadn't yet told him they were being blackmailed, and she didn't intend to.

"Edwin in five," said Andy, when she passed his desk.

"I know," she said, entering her office and closing the door behind her. She went to her mirror and applied a new coat of lipstick. She checked her skin and brushed off a little bit of visible powder on her jawline. She checked her roots for gray. *Stand straight*, she told herself, pulling her shoulders back, and adjusting her bra. She went to her desk and sat down.

For the hundredth time that day, she reviewed the state of the case as she waited for the call to come in. After the failed merger, Emerson Trust Bank sued the Calcott Corporation for breach of contract and other claims. Calcott, in turn—under Elizabeth's guidance—counter-sued with forty-six claims of their own.

Embedded inside one of these claims was an allegation that Emerson Trust had colluded in bond-price manipulation. The fact of the matter was both banks had colluded in this way. They'd been fixing the price of unsecured bonds for years. Elizabeth was essentially playing a billion-dollar game of chicken. She was daring Emerson to go through with their suit, telling them she would expose both of their bond-rigging practices if they went forward. It was the nuclear option, and she was playing it in the opening hand.

All of it—because of the money to the shell company in Oman. Elizabeth thought about the conversation she'd had with the fund manager who made that transaction. He told her it had been vetted by someone named Maurice Denny, another in-house attorney for the Calcott Corporation. When Elizabeth tried to talk to Denny, she was told that he had retired eight months earlier.

When she called him on his home phone, Denny apologized. He told her he wouldn't be able to speak with her, and that she should call his attorney. She'd brought this information to Charles Bloom, the CEO of Calcott.

He'd stood up from his desk, stepped to the door and closed it. He motioned for her to sit at the table near the window. He then told her that the money had been sent to encourage a licensing deal on an oil field in Saudi Arabia.

"It was a sloppy move. I shut it down," he said. "Maurice Denny is a good man. He's a family man. He worked for me for sixteen years. I asked him to retire when this came to my attention."

It had taken Elizabeth great effort not to show any sign of incredulity. "I asked him to retire," repeated Charles Bloom. "And he did. As far as I'm concerned that little chapter is closed."

Chiming over her intercom, Elizabeth's assistant interrupted her thinking: Edwin Kerins was on line three.

"Edwin, how are you?" said Elizabeth, leaning back in her chair as she answered the phone.

"I've had better days," he said. "You saw the judge's ruling on our motion to preclude?"

"Yes," she lied, opening her email and scanning it to see if she'd missed anything. There was nothing about a ruling. "Unbelievable. But predictable."

"Exactly," said Edwin. "Bloom's gonna have a real shit fit over this." The man was famous for his shit fits. "But what is he going to do? Fire us all?"

"Tell him bad rulings are good for the record, and Judge Sandoval is leaving a—"

"Honestly, Liz, I think in this situation it would make more sense if you could inform him. I mean it was your gang that argued it, and it seems like you might have a better handle on the—"

"Okay, let me talk to Sujung. I'll schedule a call for tomorrow," said Elizabeth, tapping her hand impatiently on her desk.

"Perfect," he said. "And just so we're on the same page, narrative-wise, Jimmy Hipps says the best approach, press-wise, is absolute silence. No stories. I know you know that, but Jimmy, well—you know."

"Of course," said Elizabeth. She checked her cell phone for any missed messages from Valencia. There were none.

"So, from our end we'll have Eric, Miles, Ken, and Doug J. work on the discovery requests, and on your end, you and Sujung and her team will continue with document review and evidence prep."

Edwin Kerins droned on for another thirty-five minutes. Elizabeth pictured him sitting back in his chair with his feet crossed on his desk. That's what kind of lawyer he was. He was twelve years her junior, with extremely limited trial experience. Nevertheless, when he paused, or, even better, asked if she agreed with what he was saying, she told him she did. The man wasn't worth arguing with. He was a non-player, but she couldn't just ignore him; she had to humor him.

When the call finally ended, she dialed Valencia on her mobile. She needed good news, but the call went straight to voicemail.

Fourteen miles to the south, in Brighton Beach, Yuri, Isaac, and Moishe were just arriving at Agniya's Laundry Service. After entering and seeing that there were no customers, Yuri thought about turning the dead bolt and flipping the sign to *Closed*. Instead, he made a little show of looking out the front window like he was afraid of being followed. In the middle of this he realized how tense his face was.

He tried to make it relax by opening his mouth, then decided this might look even more strange, so he turned back into the room and made a fuss of brushing at some lint on his pants.

Agniya, a doughy woman in her seventies, was a distant cousin of the brothers and had grown up with the older Rabinowitz family outside Moscow. Now, standing behind the counter, with her hands in her sweatshirt pockets, she greeted the boys by shaking her head like they were late.

Yuri watched Isaac step to the counter. He leaned over it and kissed the old woman on both cheeks in a way that made her smile. As this was happening, Moishe placed the bag of money on the counter, dusted his hands off, and patted his pockets.

"*Boys,*" said Agniya, "*it's been over a year since you've come to my house. We're old now, how much longer do you think we have?*" She looked at each one of them, pleading. "*The only pictures we've taken were at Leonid's wedding. You were children then. I have beautiful picture frames at home that are hanging on the walls empty.*" She stopped talking long enough to take a breath. "*Nothing inside. Empty frames. Do you know how horrible that is?*"

Just then a fire truck raced past the store, sirens blaring. Yuri pulled at his jacket sleeves. Agniya had a special talent for making him feel guilty.

The woman moved to the bag of money, put both hands on the paper sack, as if she were estimating its girth, and then called out, "*Yulia!*"

A moment later a young laundress wearing a head scarf appeared from the back of the store and without looking at the visitors, picked up the bag of money and disappeared behind the garment conveyor.

Yuri watched her go, then looked back at Agniya.

"*I'm telling you this not for my own benefit,*" said the old woman. "*I'm saying it for your well-being. You never know how much you miss your relatives*"—here she tapped her bosom, frowned—"*until they are gone.*" She knitted her meaty fingers together in front of her chest. "*Think of your father.*"

"*Auntie, please,*" said Yuri. "*We'll visit. We promise. We'll even bring Moishe.*" He put his hand on his friend's back.

"*Please?*" said Agniya.

Yuri nodded. "We will," he said, switching to English.

"*You're going to see your uncle now?*" she asked.

When they said yes, she went to the conveyor and pulled out four plastic-covered dress shirts. "*Drop these to him,*" she said. The men kissed her goodbye, opened the door, and left.

"Fuck," said Isaac, when they got outside. "She's worse than Mom."

From there, they walked under the Q tracks toward Yakov's office. Isaac carried the clean shirts slung over his shoulder. While not all the shopkeepers in the area knew specifically who these young men were, they had a sense of *what* they were, and they watched them without making a fuss.

The office was on the third floor of a corner brick building on Brighton Beach Avenue. The ground floor of the building housed a discount clothing store. The men walked past the store—flirting with a young saleswoman on their way—and rounded the corner to a side door that led up to the office. Yuri pressed a small black doorbell and all three men stood straight for the camera until the metal door buzzed open.

Yuri led the way up the stairs. The second floor of the building housed a real estate firm Uncle Yakov had helped set up. Yuri glanced in the window but didn't see anyone and kept climbing the stairs. When they got to the third floor, they rang a second doorbell, and again stood with their faces toward a small camera.

Yuri looked at the floor and saw a tangle of light brown hair. A moment later, their uncle's bodyguard, Grigory Levchin, opened the door. The big man greeted each of them, shaking their hands, giving Yuri a half hug, and then leaned and looked down the stairs to make sure nobody had followed them into the building. He put his arm around Isaac, squeezed his biceps, and led the group toward their uncle's office.

While he walked, he spoke in Russian about an associate of theirs who had been arrested in Germany.

The hallway was carpeted, and there were posters of vacation destinations on the wall, making it look like they'd walked into a travel agency. *Jamaica, Puerto Vallarta, Costa Rica, Málaga.*

Yuri could hear the sound of a baby crying somewhere on the other side of the office, and, from the other direction, the pounding noise of a jackhammer. He could smell Grigory's cologne. It smelled like sandalwood.

Their uncle's door was closed. Grigory took his arm off Yuri's shoulder, turned toward the three of them, and held his hands up like he was trying to calm an impatient crowd. *"He's just finishing something,"* said Grigory.

"We saw Dimitri," said Isaac.

Grigory made a pained face, as though this news bothered him. *"Six years, but he kept it"*—Grigory made a zipped-mouth gesture— *"the man is a crazy son of a bitch, you have to respect him. What did he say about us?"*

"*He said to say hello,*" said Isaac.

"*To pay our respects,*" said Yuri.

"Whatever," said Isaac, switching to English. "Dima's the man. I love that guy."

Grigory shook his head, pointed at Isaac. "*Dimitri is not the man. He can be a good person for keeping his mouth shut, but you say hello, you greet him, you shake his hand, you pay your respects, and you move on. You don't go drinking with him. You don't go to your clubs with him. The man is tainted, you know what I mean?*"

Yuri turned toward his younger brother. "I told you," he said. He grabbed the laundry out of his brother's hand. "You'll wrinkle it, stupid."

Isaac made a face; Yuri's behavior was embarrassing him. Yuri's cheeks got warm and he pretended to attend to the shirts. *Fucking little shit*, he thought. *Arrogant prick.*

After a moment the door opened and they heard the sound of goodbyes being exchanged. Three men Yuri had never seen before stepped out of the room. They looked Russian, but there was something different about them. For a moment, Yuri wondered if they'd come from over there.

"*Mr. Rabinowitz's nephews,*" said Grigory, lowering his chin and holding his hand toward Yuri.

The man closest to Yuri was tanned and had deep wrinkles on his forehead; the comb-marked sides of his white hair were slicked back behind his ears. All three of the strangers wore neatly ironed pants, silky sweaters, and expensive shoes. One of them had a gold chain visible underneath his sweater. One carried a soft briefcase. The wrinkle-faced one shook Yuri's hand, lifted his eyebrows to the laundry and said, "*Good boy.*"

Grigory shook hands with all three of the men, and then they were led out. "Los Angeles," said Grigory, under his breath when they were gone.

"Hollywood," said Isaac. "MTV, fucking Vanderpump, all of it. Send me to work for them. I'll be their protection."

Grigory shushed him, and they entered their uncle's office. The place was large and had high ceilings, but it wasn't fancy. The lights were fluorescent. About a dozen cardboard boxes, stacked three high, leaned against the far wall. A never-ending supply of merchandise seemed to accumulate in this building.

Yuri's eyes passed from the cardboard boxes to a pile of new purses in the far corner. A tall, dust-covered fan stood near the purses and blew a soft breeze back over the room. Yakov Rabinowitz—wearing a light tan sweater and looking wealthy—sat behind his desk and smiled when he saw the group. He seemed well rested and pleased with the meeting he'd just had.

Grigory took the laundry out of Yuri's hands and hung it in a closet. The place smelled of cigarettes even though a window had been cracked.

Uncle Yakov got up from his seat and crossed the room. He grabbed Yuri's hands, pulled him in, and kissed him on both cheeks. He then repeated this greeting with Isaac and Moishe. "*Good boys*," said their uncle, gesturing toward the closet. "*You visited your sweet aunt.*"

He tapped his chest: "*Agniya—poor light from the sun—you wouldn't know it now, but she used to be the most beautiful girl.*"

"*She's still beautiful*," said Isaac.

Uncle Yakov stepped to him and rubbed his cheek. "*That's right*," he said. He raised his hand toward a couch, and the boys sat down.

"*So?*" asked their uncle, sitting across from them.

"*We dropped something for you at Auntie's*," said Yuri.

"*You dropped laundry*," said Grigory, looking up from his phone.

"*Dropped your laundry*," said Yuri.

Uncle Yakov made a troubled face and waved his hand up and down as if saying, *Be quiet, there is no need to speak of such things.*

"*Now,*" he said, leaning toward the boys. "*They used to say, 'If you don't have a river to jump in, then don't pick a fight with a wasp.' Have you ever heard this?*"

Yuri shifted in his seat and shook his head.

The older man lowered his voice: "*It means if you pick a fight with a law firm, don't mail them letters first saying exactly what your plan is.*"

Yuri didn't know what his uncle was trying to say. When he glanced at his brother, he saw him nodding along like he understood exactly what the old man meant.

Uncle Yakov decided to get to the point. "*Does anybody know what you did?*" His face became serious, almost sad-looking. Nobody answered.

"*I had a call from a friend. He says a woman has been asking about me and wants to meet. You know what I said? I said this seems very unusual.*" He turned toward Grigory and said, "*Right?*"

Grigory clenched his jaw, nodded his head.

"*My friend says this woman is a very high-class kind of person; she works for important people. Rich people. Americans. She wants to meet with me. I think to myself, I have no business with this woman. Why would she want to meet with me? I'm thinking, lawyers, lawyers, lawyers—you know—law firms, Manhattan lawyers, law firms, lawyers, it hits me: You boys. Your little plan,*" said Yakov, rubbing his forehead like he had a headache.

"*Uncle,*" said Yuri.

"*No,*" said Yakov, holding up his hand and silencing his audience. "*I wouldn't have said okay to you boys if I didn't want you to do it. That's my fault. Still, here we are.*" He looked at each of the younger men in turn. "*Listen to me: we are businessmen; we take chances.*" He turned toward Grigory. "*Right?*"

Grigory frowned and shook his head: he didn't know if the statement was right or wrong.

"*I need to know something, though,*" said Yakov. "*I need to know exactly how many other people know about it. No*"—he raised his hand

and again shushed the men on the couch—"*I need the facts so I can be well informed when I speak with this woman. I don't want to say the wrong thing.*"

Yuri pictured Avi Lessing's face—soft and smiling—and it occurred to him that he'd made a great mistake. "*The only person who knows is the man who brought us into it.*"

"*And who is this?*" asked Yakov.

"*He's a friend, he's a, um, he's—*"

"*A Russian?*"

"*He's an American Jew.*" Yuri glanced at his brother next to him to see if he was planning on joining the conversation at any point, but Isaac sat there silently. The expression on his face seemed to suggest he'd been against the plan the entire time. "*He's harmless.*"

"*Well, harmless or not, I would consider talking to him, reasoning with him. Just make sure he never speaks to anyone,*" said their uncle.

Yuri looked down at the floor and tried to understand exactly what his uncle was suggesting. "*Talk to him?*"

"*Talk to him,*" said the older man.

Yuri looked at Grigory for help, but the large man just sat there shaking his head.

Billy Sharrock sat in the back of his white van. Parked just down the block from Yakov Rabinowitz's office, he had a good angle on the boys when they emerged from their meeting. He used his remote control and snapped a burst of pictures. After looking at the images on his computer monitor, he went over to his blacked-out back window so he could observe them with his own eyes.

Billy hadn't been following them that morning; he'd been watching their uncle. He started the day at 4:09 a.m., parked a block away from the old man's house. Nothing happened until 9:22 a.m., when a black SUV pulled into the driveway. The driver got out and entered the house. Billy texted the plate number to Danny Tsui, who told him the car was registered to a limousine service in Queens.

At 10:48 a.m., Billy watched the driver come back out of the house. This time he was accompanied by Yakov Rabinowitz. Billy snapped away with his camera and got pumped up on adrenaline just from the sight of the man. He trailed them to Park Slope, where Yakov Rabinowitz appeared to visit a doctor's office. At one point, his driver stepped out and entered a café—presumably to use the restroom—and Billy was able to attach a small GPS device to the SUV's chassis.

It was 1:48 p.m. when the boys came out from meeting with their uncle. Billy had already identified Yuri Rabinowitz and his little brother Isaac when they entered the building. He'd been given a packet of information that included their pictures. A third unidentified man had accompanied them in and out.

Billy had already told Valencia that the younger Rabinowitz boys were in the building. She had told him to call her when they came out.

"I'm looking at them right now," he told her.

"How are they acting?" asked Valencia.

"Well," said Billy, "they aren't hiding their faces, let's say that. No hoodies, no hats."

"Little shits," said Valencia.

"I put a rat on the old man's vehicle. You want me to stay with the boys, see what they're up to?"

"You read my mind," said Valencia. "But don't—I repeat—*don't* let them see you. I don't care if they lose you. Stay way the hell back."

Something about the way she was speaking annoyed Billy, but he didn't say anything.

"Got it?" she asked.

"Yeah, I got it," said Billy. They ended their call.

The boys stood on the corner talking. The older one seemed to be speaking heatedly to the younger one. He tapped his brother on the chest and shook his head. The unidentified man stayed out of it and just stared down the street with his arms crossed. A woman walking past gave them a wide berth.

Then a car pulled up, and the men walked toward it. Billy watched Yuri Rabinowitz walk around to the front passenger door. Right before he got in, Yuri took a moment and stared across and down the block, directly at Billy's van.

Reflexively, Billy held his breath and leaned back from the window. He didn't follow them when they left.

Instead, he called Valencia and told her he thought they took a look at his van when they drove past.

"Go home," she said.

"Yes, ma'am," said Billy. He cursed himself up and down. An ugly and foul mood came over him that seemed like it would last the rest of the day.

Later, Valencia's phone buzzed again. This time, it was Yakov Rabinowitz's old lawyer.

"Just got off with our friend," said Utah Sandemose.

"And what did he say?" asked Valencia. She was sitting in her living room, wearing a bathrobe. Her hair was wet.

"You're gonna owe me more than dinner," said Utah.

"Ooh la la," said Valencia.

"He said he'd meet with you tonight. You're free, right?"

Valencia felt a tightening around her shoulders and chest. She looked out her window at the storm clouds that had moved in over the city; but it hadn't started raining yet. She pulled her robe closed. "Will you be there?"

"Hell, no, I'm staying out of this shit," said Utah. "I made it very clear that I didn't think he should sit down with you, although I did tell him you possess your own charms."

"Well, then I definitely owe you more than dinner," said Valencia. She leaned over and peered through her bedroom door just in time to see Milton Frazier—wearing nothing but a white towel—walk past.

"First things first, though," said Utah. "There's a spot he likes to go to—don't ask me why—it's in the Garment District, a little kosher spot, Uzbek. It's nothing fancy. It's at 358 West Thirty-Seventh Street. You got it?"

Valencia repeated the address.

"Eight p.m. Get the stuffed cabbage. It's actually pretty damn good."

"And when are we going to have our own date?" asked Valencia.

"Shit," said Utah. "I'm about to be in trial, but don't think I'm not gonna be thinking about you every single night."

"I'm sure you'll call me when you're ready," said Valencia.

"Guilty as charged," said Utah.

After ending the call, Valencia sat there for a moment, biting her thumbnail. Her mind jumped to the question of why Rabinowitz had chosen a location within walking distance of the law firm. *I'm not afraid*, he seemed to be saying. *This man is a little son of a bitch*, she thought. *A cheeky little bastard.*

Right then, Milton walked into the living room, tying his tie.

"Have you ever had stuffed cabbage?" asked Valencia.

"We used to eat that over there sometimes," said Milton, referring to his time overseas.

Valencia stood up from the couch, tightened her robe around herself. "Mr. Rabinowitz has agreed to meet me tonight," she said, trying to make it sound like bragging. But she felt her spirits plunge as she spoke.

"So I heard," said Milton.

"What do you think I should wear?"

"He'd probably like to see you in that little white suit that you wore to that one thing."

"No," said Valencia, walking to her bedroom. "This is an evening date, I'll wear my navy blue suit, the tight one, and put on lipstick and wear gold."

"We call that your bad-boy suit."

"Who's 'we'?" asked Valencia, turning from the doorway.

"Me and Billy."

"You guys sit around and talk about my clothes?"

"Only like, 'Watch out—she's got her bad-boy suit on—don't say nothing out of turn.'"

Valencia walked to her closet, pulled the suit out, and laid it on her unmade bed. In her dresser she found her favorite underpants. She took her robe off and pulled those on, and then fit herself into a matching bra. Something about Milton's tone had annoyed her. He was being overly familiar. Even if they had just shared a bed, she was still his boss. "I'm going to need you to drive me there and wait for me," she called out over her shoulder.

"Yeah," he said. "No problem."

She stepped to the mirror in the bathroom and wiped fog from it. Then she examined her face in the reflection and gently patted in toner. In her mind, she played with ideas of hurtful things she could say to Milton, but all her options seemed too obvious.

"Billy's a naughty boy, and he needs to be spanked," she whispered to herself. Then, practicing what she might say to Milton, she whispered, "Get out."

She rubbed some cream into her face and puckered her lips at her reflection. Her mother had given her porcelain skin; she was thankful for that. She'd look perfect for the meeting, glowing. Yakov Rabinowitz wouldn't be able to resist her charms. *Thank you, Mother*, she thought.

After getting dressed, she came into the living room, where Milton was sitting up straight on the couch, as if waiting for a job interview. It was too much. She looked at the clock; it was only a quarter past six. She didn't have to leave for another hour and fifteen minutes.

"You know what," she said flatly. "Why don't you go and get some fresh air. I need to make some calls. Just text me at seven thirty, when you're downstairs."

After she said them, the words hung in the air for a moment. Milton's lower lip pushed out and covered his upper one. He lifted himself up off the couch and pulled on his coat. "Sure thing, boss," he said, unable to hide his annoyance.

When the door closed, Valencia flopped herself down on the couch in the spot he'd just left, checked her cell phone, and then put her fingers on her wrist and felt her pulse. "Call your fucking wife," she whispered, speaking to an imaginary Milton. She closed her eyes, and in her mind she saw the clouds outside her window covering the sky completely. Then she saw her mother, who had passed away many years ago.

Chris Cowley stood in the lobby of his office building waiting for his Uber. He held his phone in his left hand and used his right finger to race through the headlines. The news did nothing to calm his nerves. The world was falling apart. The president was a joke—a racist laughingstock; there seemed to be a new climate disaster every day. There were mass shootings and terrorist attacks. And his Uber driver—as he tracked him on the app—was moving like he had four flat tires. *Fuck me*, thought Chris.

Across the lobby someone barked out a demonic laugh. Chris squinted that way but all he saw was a group of security guards, and none of them were laughing. He looked back down at his phone: his Uber was two minutes away.

"Don't be so depressed"—he couldn't stop thinking about that. *Don't be so depressed?* Who were these people? Literally who were they? Nothing about the situation he found himself in made sense, but there was something particularly maddening about being told not to be depressed.

When his ride arrived, Chris walked out to it and spent a second comparing the plate number to the number on his phone. "For Chris?" he asked, opening the back door. The driver was white, which made Chris pause, until the man spoke with a Slavic accent of some kind and confirmed that Chris was at the right car.

They looped around and headed downtown on Park Avenue, where they hit a red light. Outside Chris's window, an old white-haired woman bent down and looked in at him. She was only a few feet from the window. She didn't appear to be homeless, but there was something off about her. She squinted and gestured with her hands like she was asking, *What?*

Chris had no idea what the woman wanted; to avoid looking at her, he pulled out his phone. A moment later, she banged on the window right next to his head; she tried to open the door, but it was locked.

It made Chris flinch; he scooted to the other side of the car.

The driver rolled down his own window to talk to her, but then the light changed and he took off.

"What was that?" asked Chris. He turned in his seat to look for the old woman, but he couldn't see her.

"I think she thought I was her ride," said the driver.

Chris busied himself buckling his seatbelt, hoping to cover up how scared he'd gotten when she tried to open the door. He thought about saying something but stayed silent.

"People are crazy here," said the driver, gesturing out at the street in front of him. "Everyone is crazy, you know that?" He reached out and grabbed the rearview mirror and adjusted it at an odd angle so he could look right at Chris.

Chris shook his head. He didn't want to be stared at.

"They're all depressed," said the man.

Chris's mouth dried up. "Excuse me?"

"Everyone so depressed. My country poor, but not so many people crazy."

Chris leaned and looked at the little identification placard on the dashboard. The name read Abdulmalik Juraev, which didn't seem to match the accent. "Where are you from?" asked Chris.

"Florida," said the man, smiling at the lie. "I was born and raised in Florida."

Chris looked at his Uber app to make sure he was in the right car. He felt nauseous. There was no end to his problems. "Where are you really from?"

"I'm from Tajikistan," he said.

"Nobody's depressed there?" asked Chris.

"Depressed? I tell you what, people there are depressed because they're poor. People here—what do they—people get depressed if they're not being followed."

Chris leaned forward in his seat. He couldn't tell if the man was trying to deliver some kind of message. "What are you trying to say to me?"

"What?" Right then a truck veered into their lane and the driver jerked the steering wheel and hit the horn. The driver's eyes went back to the mirror.

"I'm sorry—please," said Chris, gesturing at the road.

"I'm saying here people are depressed when they're not being followed by the paparazzi—when they're not on camera all the time."

"Seriously, if you have something you want to tell me, just—"

The man—suddenly seeming angry—interrupted him. "I'm telling you it's not all about money—you don't just take, take, take. Try helping someone."

"Me?"

"America," said the man.

Chris bit his thumbnail and looked out at the street. People were leaving work to meet their friends. They were going out to have drinks.

He used to be one of those people. He used to go out to clubs and hook up with random dudes, make out with them. He used to send text messages to his friends and go out for brunch. He used to listen to podcasts and watch movies and cook food and go out to dinner. What happened to all that? What happened to exercising, yoga classes, bicycle riding, farmers' markets? Was that life completely over?

The driver adjusted his mirror; moved it back to its normal place. Chris watched him shake his head, like he couldn't believe how stupid his passenger was. The stupidest passenger he'd ever had.

They rode the rest of the way in silence.

Valencia arrived at the restaurant at two minutes before eight p.m. The windows of the place had butcher paper taped to the insides, making it impossible for her to see in. She took a moment to quiet her mind and then pulled open the door.

Standing there waiting for her was an old man with a mustache. He wore a navy suit, no tie, and he looked startled to see her. Apparently expecting someone else, he raised a hand and spoke, "No, I'm sorry, ma'am, we—"

Before he could finish, another man interrupted him in a language that sounded, to Valencia's ear, more like Turkmen than Uzbek. The man came from the back. There were ladders leaning against the near wall, and the room smelled like paint. Valencia shifted on the balls of her feet so her back was to the wall on her right instead of to the door. The second man had joined them by now, and he was making a fuss of looking her up and down.

He was large, and rough-looking. He wore a suit coat over a turtle-neck, and Valencia assumed there was a gun under his coat on the left side of his torso. He reminded her of a few of the Russian agents she'd run into in Turkey.

"Ms. Walker?" he asked, with a thick accent.

"Yes," said Valencia, lifting her hand to shake his, and taking a step forward. "Valencia Walker, pleased to meet you." Her heart thumped away in her chest. She looked him in the eyes and could sense, from the tension in his face, that he was nervous too.

"Please." He held his hand out for her, indicating that she should walk in front of him. "Painting, construction—sorry."

They walked past eight tables, all with plastic sheets thrown over them. As they crossed the room, the large man spoke harshly over his shoulder to the suited man. Valencia didn't understand the words, but the tone suggested something like, *Lock the door, you idiot, and don't bother us.*

They pushed through some swinging doors and then stepped into a dark, fake-wood-paneled hallway. Framed portraits of unsmiling men wearing suits and sitting around tables hung on both sides of the hall.

After passing through another set of doors, they entered a second dining room. This room was plain, with cheap black-and-white tiled linoleum floors. Spotlights on the ceiling cast an odd glow. Four empty tables occupied the near side. Farther back in the corner were two round tables. Three men sat around the furthest one.

Valencia ignored the man next to her and the other two men at the table. She locked her full attention onto Yakov Rabinowitz and walked directly toward him. Her training kicked in, and immediately she started thinking of him as an old friend. She wanted to set him at ease; the fastest route to that goal was to set herself at ease.

"Valencia Walker," she said, smiling and extending her hand across the table. Yakov Rabinowitz took hold of it. Valencia felt something like a wave of energy travel up her arm.

My God, she thought, *you are a powerful little man.* She'd seen pictures of him, but none of them captured the strength of his presence. He was bald on top, but the hair on the sides of his head was pure white and cropped short. The most striking thing was how smooth his skin was, like a baby's—but tan. His eyes were milky blue, and they stayed glued on her.

"How do you do?" he asked, with his Russian accent. He squeezed her hand one more time, and then seemed to raise his eyebrows to her as if he were acknowledging a kind of kinship. It occurred to Valencia that he was trying to make her relax too.

"Pleased to meet you," she said. With their hands still touching, she thought, *I'm here to help.*

He smiled again, and their hands came apart.

Rabinowitz turned to the man on his right and spoke quietly in Russian. He then turned to the other one and repeated the message. The man on his right raised his palm to Valencia and said, "Excuse me." He was an old man, and he wore a beautifully tailored suit. She smiled and nodded.

The other man seemed annoyed at being asked to leave. Rabinowitz said something else to the two of them, and they walked away. Rabinowitz then spoke to the large man who had walked her in.

When he had finished, he raised his hand toward the man and said, "You met Grigory? He's my closest partner. He looks mean, but he's a gentle soul. Look at him; he writes love poems. Beautiful poems. He's a published poet. Admired."

Valencia looked at him.

"No, no," said Grigory lowering his eyes bashfully and shaking his head.

"Please," said her host, turning back to Valencia, "take a seat. Make yourself at home."

Valencia pulled back her shoulders, breathed in deeply, and flipped her hair as they both sat. The large man, Grigory, sat at a table behind them.

"You speak Russian?"

"Not well," she said. "I speak Turkish."

He lifted his eyebrows. "You're hungry?"

"Oh, no," she crinkled her nose for him. "Thank you."

"Fine, we'll have a drink, and we'll have a little bit of dessert." He raised himself up in his seat and spoke in Russian to the waiter. "They aren't normally open today. For you, for us . . ." A glass appeared in front of her and vodka was poured into it.

"Mr. Sandemose suggested I get the stuffed cabbage," said Valencia. "But I had an early dinner."

"Ah yes, Utah Sandemose," answered Rabinowitz, speaking each word with precision. He laid both his hands flat on the table. "A good actor in the courtroom." He closed his eyes. "His voice—He has a deep voice that carries. I am told judges, particularly female ones, respond to it."

Rabinowitz touched his chest, opened his eyes, and looked at Valencia. "I don't know about the jury, because I've never seen him in front of one." He looked at her as if checking whether she'd challenge him. "I'm not sure if he has a brilliant legal mind. He never showed it to me. Sometimes though, you want your lawyer to be an actor, not a genius. And you? You are a lawyer too?"

"I spent five years at The Bronx Defenders. I haven't practiced law in quite some time. I'm more in communications now."

He smiled. "I see, and I'm told that you also work in intelligence."

Valencia returned his smile. "Used to."

"In Russia, there is no 'used to.' Maybe it is the same here." Then, peering over Valencia's shoulder, he spoke in Russian, and waved his hand as if discouraging a nuisance. Valencia turned and saw the back of the retreating waiter.

When she faced Rabinowitz again, she noticed that his face had become rather serious. "You know, I have many good friends who work at your organization," he said, leaning forward. "Chris Meisner, Berlin station chief."

"I had dinner with him about two months ago," said Valencia. She smiled and sat up straighter.

"A charming man," said Rabinowitz.

"Wonderful," said Valencia. She hated Meisner and hadn't seen him for years, but for the moment, she wanted to agree with everything Rabinowitz said. This stage of the negotiation was a dance, so stepping on toes was bad form. She wanted to find some kind of flow.

Right then, the waiter reappeared and placed a plate of baklava on the table.

"*Za vashe zdorovie*," said Valencia, ignoring the dessert, and raising her glass.

"To your health," said Rabinowitz, looking into her eyes in a way that, for a moment, seemed to suggest a kind of displeasure.

They drank. Valencia felt her stomach and chest warm up. As soon as she placed her glass on the table, it was filled again.

"Tell me: how long were you an official member of the CIA?"

"Ten years," said Valencia. "But they used me just like this, just meeting people, talking."

"That's not what I hear," said Rabinowitz, leaning forward. "Why did you leave?"

Valencia's mind went to a black site in Bosnia—a place where detainees were tortured with electricity. "Between you and me, I wanted to make more money."

"I see," said Rabinowitz. "And for whom do you make your money these days?"

"It's funny you should ask." She watched Rabinowitz's eyebrows squeeze together. "I work for the Calcott Corporation. Have you ever heard of them?"

"I'm afraid not," said Rabinowitz.

Valencia breathed in deeply. "I think it would probably make the most sense if we could be honest," she said, offering a sympathetic smile. "I'm not going to beat around the bush. I know you're a busy man, and I want to be respectful of your time."

"Please," said Rabinowitz, turning his hand for her to continue.

"We're having a problem with your nephews."

"I'm sorry," he said. "Which nephews? I have"—he looked up at the ceiling—"sixteen, excuse me, seventeen nieces and nephews. Some here"—he counted off on his fingers—"some in Russia of course, two in Israel, one in Kazakhstan, one in Syria, and one in China."

He knew exactly who she was talking about, and playing dumb was diminishing his charm. "Your nephews here in Brooklyn, Yuri and Isaac."

She watched his mouth open, and his chest deflate as he exhaled.

"Not them," he said, shaking his head. He raised his fingers from the table, as if telling her to slow down. "You must be confused; these are very good boys. They are young. I'm afraid you've been given false information."

Valencia lowered her chin and looked right into the old man's eyes. "Your nephews"—she paused for a moment, made sure she had his attention—"came across some files that belong to the Calcott Corporation. Sensitive files from an active court case, a federal case. They used those files and blackmailed the law firm that represents Calcott. The law firm paid your nephews. I advised them to do that. It was a one-time act of generosity. It won't be repeated."

Rabinowitz tented his fingers on the table. A dark expression settled on his face. "I'm going to say it again. My nephews had nothing to do with whatever it is you're talking about. To be polite, I will ask you a hypothetical question. If the boys did do that—these boys would never do anything like that—but if they did do something, what is it you would have me do?"

Valencia mirrored the man's hands and posture. She then turned her wrist toward her nose and sniffed her perfume. She leaned forward, picked up a piece of baklava and took a bite of it. She sat there chewing for a moment, enjoying its taste, then took a sip of vodka.

"We made the payment. Now we need the problem to go away. I'm going to be clear with you, so please don't think I'm trying to threaten you. If it doesn't go away, if for some reason we hear something else about these files, I will be forced to call Albert Dunning. Do you know who that is?"

"I'm afraid not," said Rabinowitz.

"He's the special agent in charge of the Newark FBI. He is a very dear friend of mine. We worked together for two years. I've been to his house. I've swam in his swimming pool. If I called him and told him to have customs agents take a look at containers coming from Shenzhen, if I told him specifically to examine all shipments from the Piang Won Company, what would he find?"

"I don't know," said Rabinowitz, shaking his head. "What would you find if you looked in there?"

"If I looked?" asked Valencia, glancing at the ceiling, smiling. "I would probably find shipments of different chemical substances. Maybe methylone. Depending on what time of month, pentedrone, maybe crystal meth. All kinds of things."

She held up her left hand while she spoke and showed him her perfect red fingernails. "But I don't look in shipping containers. I'm not a customs agent."

"You are in communications."

"Exactly."

He closed his eyes and appeared to give her words some thought. He stayed silent for almost ten seconds. Valencia kept her eyes on him the whole time.

"It is impossible that my nephews would engage in such behavior," said Yakov Rabinowitz, his voice softer now. "They are good boys, but since you have come here, and because we have mutual friends, I will suggest to them that they should never even think about anything like that in the future."

She raised her glass, locked eyes with him. "Can we drink to that?"

4

IT FELT
WONDERFUL

Two nights later, Elizabeth Carlyle attended a party at the home of one of her husband's colleagues. It was a Friday night, a few minutes after eight. Party guests stood around the living room in groups of two or three. They leaned in with their heads, and held their drinks in front of their chests as if they were cradling baby birds. They spoke civilly; occasionally a joke was told, and the sound of male laughter could be heard over the general murmur of conversation. The place teemed with fifty-year-old brokers and traders. It was, to put it plainly, Elizabeth's idea of hell.

She didn't want to be there; she planned on quietly drinking her way through the evening. "Fill it to the top this time, please," she said, handing her glass to the rented bartender. He pulled his lips into a tight smile, nodded, and filled the glass three-quarters full. Drink in hand, she turned to face the party and wondered who was the least boring person she could talk to.

Her husband didn't appear to be in the room. She took a sip of sauvignon blanc, cleaned her teeth with her tongue, and fantasized about climbing into the bed of her husband's colleague. Not for sex, just for sleep. Her eyes went to the television on the far wall and she wondered what would happen if she turned it on and sat down to watch the news.

A man could do that, she thought. A man could watch sports as much as he wanted.

Right then, one of her husband's coworker's wives, a woman named Louisa, a corporate lawyer with a distinguished reputation, appeared at her side.

"There you are," said Louisa, sounding nasal, like a dame from an old Hollywood movie. She looked drunk. "I've been searching *everywhere* for you. You're the only person who *I'm sure* agrees how *boring* this party is."

Elizabeth's eyes went from the woman's face to her chest. She couldn't help wondering if the woman had gotten implants. "You're looking marvelous," said Elizabeth, keeping her eyes there.

"Don't make fun of me," said Louisa, studying Elizabeth's face like she was appraising a fine piece of art. "And you? What's your exercise routine?"

"Klonopin," said Elizabeth.

"Darling, now you're speaking my language," said Louisa.

They locked eyes. "So? Work?"

"Please, my blood pressure," said Elizabeth.

For a moment, the issue of the three-quarters of a million dollars she'd given away bobbed up into Elizabeth's consciousness. Her armpits dampened. Valencia had promised to find a way to fold the money into her bill. Her mother's voice popped into her head: *Fold it into a bill?* She gulped her wine, looked around the party, shifted her weight.

Louisa pivoted so they both faced the crowd. "Are you guys really going to trial?" she asked out of the side of her mouth.

"On what?" answered Elizabeth, pivoting back so she could face her.

"Calcott, Liz, what else?"

Any number of people could have sent her as a spy. There were probably half a dozen hedge fund managers at the party right then who would pay an obscene amount of money for that information.

"We're preparing," said Elizabeth. Then, lowering her voice, she added, "Honestly, between me and you, I hope we do. I'm starving for it. The board's starving too. They want to go nuclear. Scorched earth. End this thing once and for all." She dropped her voice lower still: "Can't think of a better scenario, better even than a settlement."

The truth—of course—was the exact opposite of everything she was saying. She wanted the case to disappear. Wanted nothing more. She was exhausted. But she could never admit that. After allowing her mouth to form into a lustful little smile, Elizabeth faced her friend full on. "And you?" she asked. "What are you up to?"

For the next few minutes, Louisa droned on about some trial her firm had just won. Elizabeth squinted, listened, smiled when it seemed appropriate, raised her eyebrows, nodded, and finished her wine.

Conversation still going, Elizabeth moved toward the bar, passed her glass to the barman, and had him fill it again. Louisa, meanwhile, had transitioned to blathering on about some charity or other whose board she'd recently joined.

My God, thought Elizabeth. It was all so boring.

Her mind shifted back to Valencia. She wouldn't just stand there listening to this kind of inane conversation. She wouldn't be caught dead at a party like this. Valencia and her fancy clothes—she was probably off having sex with someone.

Elizabeth checked the level of her drink against her companion's. She then drank half her glass and looked around the room for her husband. Someone, not the host, had begun to make a toast, but it didn't stop Louisa's monologue; it only lowered its volume. Elizabeth had successfully tuned her out, until she heard her say something about "protected discovery."

"Excuse me?" said Elizabeth.

"I said the stock fell."

"When what?" asked Elizabeth.

"When Judge Shapiro unsealed the discovery."

"I'm sorry, sweetie," said Elizabeth, sobering up, and brushing her hair off her forehead. "My mind wandered. I was looking for my husband. What case are we talking about?"

"LongWeather," said Louisa, squinting at Elizabeth like she was suddenly curious to know just how drunk she was. LongWeather was one of Louisa's firm's clients—it had nothing to do with any of Elizabeth's cases. The crowd around them gave a polite round of applause to the man who made the toast.

A bad feeling gripped Elizabeth's guts. It felt like one of her organs had finally failed and was currently spewing waste inside her abdomen. Her forehead became moist. Dizziness set in. She put her empty glass onto the bar. Louisa asked her if she was okay.

"Ate something," whispered Elizabeth, squeezing Louisa's arm and walking away. To get to the bathroom she had to cross the living room floor. As she began her journey, the party guests all seemed to turn and watch her as she went. She noticed a man with a square of toilet paper stuck to his shoe. She didn't recognize anyone, and she moved through the crowd with her lips clamped together involuntarily, like a dried-up clam.

In the bathroom she vomited wine and shrimp violently. She hadn't done that in years. Afterward, she rinsed her mouth at the sink, spit, fixed her hair, pinned it back, and took a moment to collect herself. The vomiting had relieved her discomfort, but she still felt weak.

The door handle rattled. Short of breath, Elizabeth called out, "Just a minute!" It occurred to her that she might actually be unwell. She turned her face from side to side in the mirror, then bent down and searched under the sink; she found some air freshener and sprayed a little cloud into the air.

Stepping out, she nearly ran into a short man with gray hair and glasses. She put a hand on his shoulder, apologized vaguely, and stepped past him. He smelled of curry. She moved away from the living room in search of her husband. The lights in the hallway were bright, and she walked with her left hand held up like she was telling someone to stay away from her. She'd been in this house quite a few times; still, she felt oddly disoriented.

Finally—around a corner and down the hall—she found the doorway to the backyard and the pool. Breathing through her mouth and grimacing, she stepped to the glass door and gripped its handle.

Outside, the first thing she saw, of course, was her husband. He was talking to a skinny, short-haired, short-skirted woman who couldn't have been more than forty years old. With his eyebrows raised wisely, and his arms crossed in front of his chest, he seemed to be doing all the talking. As she moved toward him, Elizabeth felt her body temperature rise. She vowed not to seem angry.

"Darling, there you are," said Tyler, sounding strangely like an Englishman. "I want you to meet Jeb's daughter. She's a lawyer." Elizabeth stepped toward them, doing her best impression of a smile.

"Are you all right?" asked Tyler. "You look ill."

"Ate something," whispered Elizabeth, pulling her smile tighter. No hands were shaken. The daughter, whoever she was, angled her head, made a sympathetic face, and pulled her martini glass a bit closer to her chest, like she was scared Elizabeth was going to smack it out of her hands.

Just then, as if on cue, Elizabeth's cell phone vibrated in her pocket. She pulled it out and read a text message from Jimmy Hipps, head in-house counsel for the Calcott Corporation. Elizabeth had never received a text message from the man before.

She squinted to read it: *Tommy Sanzone WSJ just called and asked for comment on an anonymous source story. Says source has documents speaking to very allegations of fraud.*

Elizabeth tried to make sense of the message and another one came in, this one a correction of the first: *Speaking to very *serious* allegations of fraud.*

Another message popped up: *Can you get on a conference call with me, Mark, Ben, Paul, Zach, and your Scott in five minutes?*

Suddenly sober, Elizabeth looked from her husband to the young lawyer. "I'm sorry, excuse me," she said. "Work issue."

She stepped toward the pool and started walking around its edge. It was lit up and perfect. Somewhere inside the party a man laughed like Santa Claus.

Nobody was standing on the far side of the pool, and there was a padded reclining seat. Elizabeth moved toward it and texted a one-word answer: *Yes.*

That same night, to avoid going home, Chris Cowley stayed late at the office and forced himself to do actual work. His apartment was making him a nervous wreck. The constant surveillance had taken a toll on his psyche. He felt unhinged. Less than three weeks ago his problems didn't exist—now they were everywhere.

At a quarter to nine, he stood, put on his coat, and took a moment to stare at the iPhone sitting on his desk. How much trouble, he wondered, would leaving it right there bring? The question caused his internal temperature to rise, but the decision had already been made. He was leaving it. He wanted a night to himself. That would be step one. He reached out, turned it facedown, and walked out of his office.

In the lobby downstairs, two guards stood alone behind the front desk. Their eyes stayed on Chris as he made his way to the exit, but they didn't say anything.

As soon as Chris stepped outside, he saw a forty-year-old man standing on the sidewalk about eight car lengths from the door. This man, like the others he'd spotted following him, wore a business casual outfit. He held a phone to his ear, and his lips moved as if he was in the middle of a conversation. Chris silently cursed him and began walking to the Bryant Park subway stop. It was cold outside. He wanted his night to begin.

Just as Chris got down to the subway platform, a downtown-bound F train came roaring into the station. He couldn't help interpreting that as a good sign. On the train, he pushed his way to a seat and sat down aggressively between an old woman and a young kid in a puffy coat. They both scooted over to make room.

Chris looked around the car and wondered who else might be following him. It could be anyone, he thought. But none of the people in his vicinity seemed likely. He leaned back and dried his hands on his pants. The train bumped along and Chris counted the stops as they passed: 34th, 23rd, 14th.

At West Fourth Street, he counted how long the doors stayed open: nine seconds. He closed his eyes and reminded himself that it wasn't a crime to get off the subway. The train started up again and made its slow turn east, heading toward the Broadway-Lafayette stop. A few passengers began drifting toward the door. Chris stayed seated.

The train jolted to a stop, and the doors opened. Chris counted back—nine, eight, seven, six; the exiting passengers by that point had disembarked. A few people boarded and settled into their seats or stood with their hands on the bars. Chris kept counting; it seemed impossible that the doors would remain open for another three seconds.

When he got to two, he stood up from his seat and rushed off the train, just as the doors closed.

He appeared to have been the last person off. Still, he spent a frenzied few seconds looking back and forth across the platform. Then he began moving toward the exit, along with everyone else.

The train left the station. Across the tracks, a black guy in a puffy coat stood staring at him. The man averted his gaze as soon as Chris looked in his direction. Farther down the platform, Chris noticed a white girl in a tight skirt and a short fur coat. *A hipster*, Chris thought. He stared at her, blinking. Wasn't she a little old for that outfit?

He told himself he was being ridiculous, turned his back to the tracks, and pretended to examine a movie poster.

Exiting passengers gone, Chris took the stairs up to the mezzanine level. A crowd of about ten people passed him on their way down.

They all shuffled by without so much as looking at him. He turned his collar up and took the last few stairs two at a time.

Outside, in the cool air, he headed east on Houston with no exact destination in mind. Eventually, on Elizabeth Street, he found a bar that looked quiet. He went in, sat at the bar, and—feeling giddy—ordered a gin martini.

Valencia Walker, meanwhile, was in her apartment watching a romantic comedy on her laptop. The movie was about two friends who had opened a bakery together and fallen in love. Valencia had eaten a bowl of ice cream. She was in her sweatpants, and, if asked, she would have placed her general mood somewhere around a 7.5 out of 10. Her phone rang, and she frowned when she saw it was Elizabeth calling; her mood dropped down to a 6.

When she answered, Elizabeth told her that a story about the Calcott Corporation would appear on the front page of tomorrow's *Wall Street Journal*. She said the reporter had received copies of internal Calcott emails. "C-suite shit, absolutely radioactive," said Elizabeth.

Valencia, phone to ear, closed her computer, swung her legs out of bed, picked up the bowl, walked to the kitchen, set the bowl in the sink and filled it with water. "Shit," she said.

"It's hard to state how bad this is," said Elizabeth. "Those emails were part of the stolen discovery."

Valencia noted the accusatory tone but chose to ignore it. "Who's writing the story?"

"Tommy Sanzone," said Elizabeth. "He's a piece of shit."

"Don't know him," said Valencia. "But listen, I'm very good friends with the editor of the business section. Would you like me to call him and see if we can kill the story?"

"It's fucking printed," said Elizabeth. She sounded like she'd been drinking.

Valencia closed her eyes and tried to pinpoint the best way to proceed. "Liz, I understand that this—"

"Don't fucking patronize me."

"I'm sorry," said Valencia. "Tell me what you want me to do."

"I want you to relax," said Elizabeth, stressing the *x* sound. "I want you to relax and tell me why your Russian fucking friend would do this right now."

"Did the reporter say anything about Russians?" asked Valencia, moving her wrist, to loosen it, as if she were playing Ping-Pong.

"He didn't have to."

"Liz, there are hundreds of people who could have leaked those emails."

"You were supposed to recover them; you were supposed to get it all back," said Elizabeth. "How much have you billed us for this job? Fifty thousand? Plus the seven hundred and fifty thousand. That's almost a million dollars. What do we have to show for that? We're being fucking blackmailed for that."

For a moment, Valencia considered how her own mother used to get drunk and carry on with unfounded accusations. Arguing back never worked. "We shouldn't be having this conversation on the phone," said Valencia. She moved to the living room window and looked out at the park below her. "I can come to your house if you'd like?"

"I'm sorry," said Elizabeth. "This isn't . . ."

"I know," said Valencia, keeping the softness in her voice but staying clear of any condescension. They were silent for nearly five seconds. "Do you want me to come to you?"

"I'm at a party," said Elizabeth. "I just took a conference call with Scott and all of Calcott's in-house people. I'm by a pool right now, if you can believe that. Sitting by a fucking pool."

Valencia closed her eyes, relaxed her mind, and focused on Elizabeth's tone.

"My husband's talking to some short-haired intern, Louisa Eldrich's probing me for gossip, I have food poisoning—shrimp—oh God, hold on, Michael D'Angelo's calling."

The line went silent while Elizabeth answered the call. Valencia walked to her office and plugged her headphones in. She felt nervous, and, rather than fight against that feeling, she tried to embrace it. She'd been trained that way. *Draw the fear into your belly, accept it, appreciate it, own it.*

"They lost him," said Elizabeth, coming back on the line. "Tonight of all nights, they fucking lost him. My God, how hard can it be? These people are ridiculous."

"Lost who?" Valencia asked, playing dumb.

"Chris Cowley—fucking Chris Cowley," said Elizabeth. "The only reason, and I'm talking the *only reason* I haven't fired him was so we could keep our eyes on him."

"Now this," said Valencia.

"Now this," said Elizabeth. "At least we'll have him out of our hair."

Valencia took a moment thinking about what this would mean. "You have to do what you have to do," she said, finally.

"I'll tell you what I have to do," said Elizabeth, sounding drunk again. "Fire him."

After barely saying goodbye, Elizabeth ended the call.

The next morning at 8:42 a.m., Yuri Rabinowitz was woken by a loud pounding noise. It took a moment to realize someone was banging on the front door. It was hard to imagine a more unwelcome sound.

Yuri reached for his phone and saw four missed calls, all from his uncle's man, Grigory Levchin. The night before, Yuri and his brother had been out partying with their friends. They'd taken Molly, drank an obscene amount of vodka, and danced at a club in Greenpoint until five in the morning. Yuri was, to put it mildly, in pain.

He pushed himself out of bed and pulled on the shirt he'd worn out. It was a bright, button-up thing that—upon catching a glimpse in the mirror—now seemed utterly ridiculous. He hurried to the stairs. As he passed his brother's door, he called out "Isaac!" There was no response.

It occurred to him that it might be the FBI outside. He'd stay silent, of course. He wouldn't say anything; he'd wait for his uncle to arrange an attorney. Had Grigory been calling to warn them of an impending raid? Yuri cursed himself for not listening to the voicemail and he felt a sharp pain in his head. His stomach, in answer to everything, threatened to empty itself.

I'm in hell, he thought.

Before he reached the door, he recognized the shape and general color of Grigory Levchin's head on the other side of the frosted glass. Which wasn't to say he felt more relaxed. Good news never followed that kind of knocking. He was still in hell.

Yuri unlocked the dead bolt and opened the door. He tried to seem calm, and asked "What's up?"

"*Why the fuck didn't you answer your phone?*" said Grigory. He was wearing jeans and a sweater, an unusual outfit for him. He leaned in after he spoke, as though anticipating that Yuri's answer would be difficult to hear.

Yuri had never seen the man so upset. For a moment, he thought he was going to be told that Uncle Yakov had been killed. "I had it off," he said. "I was sleeping."

"*Get your brother, your uncle wants to see both of you.*"

Yuri gestured for Grigory to come in, but the large man just frowned, shook his head, pulled out a pack of cigarettes, and lit one. The smell of tobacco reached Yuri's nose instantly. Without closing the door, he turned and headed back upstairs.

His anger, as he went, became focused on Isaac. It was his brother who made them stay out all night. "One more drink," he'd insisted. As he approached the door, Yuri told himself not to start a fight. It wasn't what they needed right then. But when he opened the door, the first thing he saw was the shape of a sleeping woman. "Wake up, asshole," he said to his brother. His anger had returned.

"Huh?" Isaac leaned his head up. He looked even worse than Yuri felt. "What?"

"*Grigory's downstairs. He says we need to go with him,*" said Yuri.

"For what?"

"What do you think?" said Yuri. "Get dressed. Two minutes."

The woman in the bed groaned and pulled the covers over her head. Yuri couldn't help looking at the hill that her hip created under the blanket. I need a hill like that, he thought—kids, a family, the quiet life.

He turned and walked back to his room; he needed to dress more professionally. He didn't need this clown shirt. He pulled it off and exchanged it for a white oxford. When he stepped back into the hallway, he heard the shower running in the bathroom.

This fucking guy, he thought; an angry feeling sloshed around in his guts.

When he opened the door, he found his brother not in the shower, but instead sitting naked on the toilet. A horrible, fetid smell reached his nose. "*You can't—!*" Yuri yelled. He meant to say, *You can't shower*, but he couldn't even get that out.

His brother leaned forward on the toilet, groaned, and forced out an explosion of diarrhea. "What am I going to do?" he answered, looking like he might cry, but then smiling.

Yuri stepped back into the hall and slammed the door closed. He stood there for a moment looking down the hallway, then opened the door and slammed it again. He repeated this a few times, and then walked downstairs.

My toothbrush is in there, he thought. *My deodorant.*

The front door was closed when he got back. He found Grigory washing his hands at the kitchen sink. "*I can't control him!*" Yuri said.

Grigory turned. "*You need hand soap*," he said, nodding toward the sink.

Hand soap? Hand soap? These people are all insane, thought Yuri. He looked at Grigory and measured the man and wondered if he could be knocked out with a cast-iron pan. "*What does Uncle want?*" Yuri asked again.

"*He said, 'Call Yuri and have them come in,'*" answered Grigory, pulling paper towels from a roll and drying his hands. "*I tell him you're not answering. He says, 'Go get them.' I don't question him and say, 'First, sir, please sir, tell me the exact agenda of why you want to talk to them, Yuri might need to know'—come on.*"

Grigory went to the trash can and threw the paper towels away. "*You look like real shit, you know that?*" he said.

Yuri went to the same trash can, and with some difficulty, pulled out the white plastic bag. He spun it and tied it closed and carried it to the garage. Inside the garage, he turned the lights on and put the trash into a larger black bin. He then hit the opener and the garage door rumbled up. Yuri wheeled the bin to the curb with his eyes barely open against the sun.

When he was done, he turned and saw his Armenian neighbor Narek standing across the street. The man waved but put his head down and walked away before Yuri could wave back. Reminded of the man's son, Yuri turned and looked down the street for his van but didn't see any vans at all. He didn't want to wait with Grigory, so he spent a few minutes picking up trash that had blown into their hedge.

When he finally got back to the kitchen, he found Isaac standing there, dressed and looking fresh, telling a story that had Grigory laughing quietly and shaking his head. "What?" said Isaac, seeing his brother's face. "What was all that about?" he asked, pointing upstairs. "Why you gotta slam the doors?"

"We're late," said Yuri.

"Late for what?" said his little brother. "I'm ready to go." He held his hand toward Grigory. "We're waiting for you."

Yuri turned, went back upstairs, and took his toothbrush and toothpaste to his bedroom and brushed in there. *Own your choices*, he told himself in Russian while he brushed. *You made a choice to get into this.*

He changed shirts again, putting on a blue shirt that would hopefully make his face appear less pink. *Fucking pieces of shit*, he thought. *Bastards.* He went back downstairs and the three of them walked silently to Grigory's car.

When they got to Leo Katzir's office, they found the lobby—save one old man slumped in his seat—free of clients. Yuri noticed that a plant in a stand near the window had died. The girl he liked did not appear to be working that day, and the new one, a girl he'd never seen before, did her best not to look at the three men when they walked in.

"*May we go in?*" Grigory asked her.

"Yes, please," said the woman, standing up and opening the door for them.

Inside the lawyer's office, Yuri's uncle, dressed in one of his normal silk sweaters, sat in a chair facing Leo Katzir's desk. He turned as they entered, smiled sadly. He looked tan, clean, and well rested. Leo Katzir, meanwhile, sat behind his desk, hands folded, looking pissed off.

Their uncle waved the boys in. Yuri and then Isaac kissed him on the cheek, a gesture that he seemed to endure more than enjoy. "Sit," he said in English. "Grab a seat and sit."

Both brothers sat on a couch near the desk. Their uncle yawned and stretched his arms above his head. Grigory, ominously, stayed standing near the door. A phone in the reception area rang. Because of ongoing construction outside, the whole place smelled like tar.

Yuri looked at the lawyer, Leo Katzir, who shook his head and pursed his lips. *I get it, you're mad*, thought Yuri. *But please, for your own good, tone it down a little bit.*

"*Boys*," said their uncle. "*I'm going to ask you this only once, and I need you to be completely truthful with me.*"

Yuri felt his brother shift in his seat and saw him wipe his nose. For his part, Yuri stayed perfectly still and adjusted his face to reflect an appropriate level of concern. He felt ready to confess to whatever he was being charged with.

"*Did you have anything to do with this?*" asked their uncle, holding up a copy of the *Wall Street Journal.*

Yuri leaned forward to read it, but he couldn't make out the words from where he sat. "*What is it?*" he asked.

Their uncle lowered the paper, looked at the lawyer, and then looked back at Yuri. "*It is a story about this Calcott case. The story references documents. Emails.*"

"No," said Yuri.

"No," said Isaac.

"*Did you share the documents with anybody?*"

Yuri's heart galloped in his chest. He felt himself begin to blush, and he breathed in deeply to try to hide it. He wasn't guilty, he hadn't shown the documents to a single person; but he felt guilty. He couldn't stop blushing.

He shifted on the couch and faced his brother. "*We didn't do anything, right?*"

"*No, no, we didn't show the documents to anybody,*" said Isaac, sounding calmer and more composed.

"*Then say it!*" said Yuri.

"*I did say it!*" said Isaac.

Both brothers turned and faced their uncle. "We don't know," said Isaac.

The lawyer spoke next, "*Where is the thumb drive?*"

"*It's at the house,*" said Yuri.

"*Okay, then we are done here,*" said the lawyer, clasping his hands together on the desk. "*Give it to him.*" He nodded at Grigory Levchin.

"*I said they wouldn't do this*," said Yakov Rabinowitz, speaking to the lawyer, and apparently defending his nephews. He then turned and faced the boys. "*I said you wouldn't do this. But we have a very serious problem now. The American woman has said, 'If a story comes out . . .'*" He stopped speaking for a moment, looked down at his cell phone. "*Now here we are, a story is out. We must clean it up.*"

"*Kill her?*" whispered Yuri.

Yakov Rabinowitz rubbed his eyes like a tired baby, shook his head, looked back at the lawyer. "*They watch too many movies.*"

Yuri leaned forward. "*What do you want us to do?*"

"*Where is the money?*" asked Yakov Rabinowitz.

"*It's at Ossip's,*" said Yuri.

"*Bring it here,*" said Yakov Rabinowitz. "*The game is over. We're done with all that.*"

Yuri looked at the stretch of floor between them. He wasn't sad to hear his uncle's plan. He was relieved.

Chris Cowley sat hunched over his phone with the posture of a child. He was in his office, at his desk, scrolling through Instagram. His friends, each and every one of them, appeared to be living beautiful lives. A simultaneous vacation. They climbed mountains, lay on beaches, and gathered at fancy bars. They had babies, they accepted awards, made ironic jokes. Even their boring pictures—the lazy ones, selfies taken on couches in front of televisions—made him feel jealous. Boredom had never looked so appealing.

His hangover wasn't helping matters. Instead of doing the sensible thing, and going home after a drink or two, he'd stayed at the bar until one in the morning. He had met a couple in town from Denver. He drank two pointless martinis with them, bringing his grand total to five.

At that moment, Elizabeth Carlyle's assistant stepped into Chris's office and interrupted his phone scrolling. "Sorry," he said, looking at

Chris. "Liz wants to see you." The assistant's face offered no clues. It didn't matter; Chris knew what was coming.

He looked back at his phone, pressed the home button, and flicked Instagram closed. He turned to his computer, checked his email, refreshed it, stood, and adjusted his jacket.

"Are you okay?" asked Andy, looking at Chris.

"Hungover," said Chris.

When he got to Elizabeth's office, Andy stepped ahead of him, peeked his head in, and then turned and nodded to Chris. Inside, seated around the table, were Elizabeth, Pamela Ong from HR, and Scott Driscoll.

"How are you, Chris?" asked Scott.

"Chris, I'm sorry," said Elizabeth, not waiting for his answer. Even under these circumstances, she seemed pressed for time. "The partners voted this morning to terminate your contract."

Chris nodded. Tears came to his eyes, and he wiped them with the back of his hand.

"James from security is going to accompany you back to your office. You'll gather your personal belongings. Leave your work cell on the desk. Do you have any office laptops at your apartment?" asked Elizabeth.

"No," said Chris.

"Do you have any external hard drives, thumb drives, or any other devices carrying anything related to your work at CDH?"

"No," said Chris.

"Do you have any paper files, or notes at your apartment?"

"No."

"Sign this, then," said Elizabeth, nodding toward the HR person who pushed a clipboard forward.

Chris stepped closer, leaned down, and read the paperwork. It was the same questions he'd just answered. He signed at the bottom.

"Your prior nondisclosures, of course, are still in effect."

Chris nodded.

"I'm sorry this happened," said Elizabeth. "We're terminating you for cause, but we're going to pay two additional months. Help you get back on your feet."

"Okay," said Chris. "I'm sorry." He looked at Elizabeth; she was watching him closely. He thought about offering her a handshake but decided against it. Scott Driscoll sat there with his lips puckered. Pamela Ong didn't do anything but sit with perfect posture and watch him.

Chris turned and stepped out of the office. Elizabeth's assistant gave him a sad shake of the head, and mouthed the words, "I'm sorry, bud."

James, wearing his blue security coat and holding a walkie-talkie, was already waiting. He nodded at Chris, and then gestured that Chris should lead the way.

It was humiliating.

There wasn't much to gather in his office: a few suits, shirts, a fancy pen his father had given him. He had a plant he decided to leave. *Let it die*, he thought.

He went through his desk drawers, made sure he wasn't forgetting anything. Then he took his phone, held it up for James to see, and set it down on his desk.

On the walk to the elevator he passed a few colleagues who saw him with his suits folded over his arm, saw the security guard walking behind him, and either made sympathetic faces, or pretended they didn't see what was happening.

The elevator opened as soon as James pressed the button. Chris, followed by the security guard, stepped in. The guard pressed the M button and shook his head, acknowledging that this was indeed bad business.

As the elevator floated down, Chris looked at his blurry reflection in the brass walls. In his head, he sang a Madonna song: *Your heart is not open, so I must go.*

Walking across the floor of the lobby, he felt every single person in the room stare at him. He half expected paparazzi to jump out and start taking pictures. At the revolving doors, he stopped, looked behind one more time, then looked at James, who held his hand out for a final dry, limp shake. *This is it*, thought Chris.

Outside, Chris waved down a cab and was glad to see that it wasn't the shaved-headed guy driving. He got in and told the driver his address. As the cab made its way south, Chris stared out the window and looked at all the people coming and going. It occurred to him that he didn't feel particularly bad. He felt relieved. The last few weeks had been a kind of hell, and now he was finally going to be released.

Chris smiled. He could change his life. He could pack up and leave. Move out of the country, start a new chapter.

It felt like he was coming out of a strange fog. It wasn't just the current shit show he was in; it had been the last few years. He'd been living a life totally devoid of meaning. Being a corporate lawyer sucked. It was the worst. He was leaving that world, and in his core, he felt something he hadn't felt in years—happiness. Did he have his tormentors to thank for that? He shook his head at the irony of it.

My God, he thought. *What a life.*

When he got to his apartment, he paid the driver and gave him a seventeen-dollar tip. He didn't stop and look over his shoulder to see if anybody was watching him. He didn't scan the block for white vans. Those idiots had lost their power over him. They didn't matter anymore. Their spell had been broken.

As he entered his building his mind began organizing a list of tasks. The first order of business would be to go online and book a flight out of the country. He'd go somewhere sunny, Mexico or Brazil. Maybe Thailand. He got in the elevator and pressed five. As he rode up, his eyes settled on a spot of discoloration on the floor. It looked as though someone had spit mucus in the elevator. He couldn't stop looking at it. And just like that, his mood clicked back into pessimism.

In the hallway he heard the sound of a television coming from his neighbor's apartment. The voice on the show was saying, "Do you want to know who it is?" and an enthusiastic crowd was yelling back, "Yes!"

Chris reached into his pocket for his key, unlocked the door, and stepped in.

After setting his keys on the hook near the door, he carried his suits to the living room. As soon as he rounded the corner, he saw the man with the pitted skin. It was barely surprising. He sat turned on the couch so he could face Chris. The expression on his face suggested he was in a bad mood. He shifted on the couch to make room.

"I got fired," said Chris, shaking his head.

"So I heard," said the man.

"I'm sorry," said Chris, setting his suits down. "I did the best I could."

The man cleared his throat. "Sit down."

Chris walked to the couch and sat and looked at him. The man wore a fleece jacket over a buttoned-up plaid shirt. Chris looked at his feet—walking shoes, the kind worn by old men.

"Tell me your name again?" said Chris.

"Jonathan," said the man.

Chris put his hands on his knees. "So what are we going to do?"

"I'll tell you what," said the man, scratching his chin and looking up. "I just need an apology." He pointed at the coffee table in front of them and Chris saw a yellow legal pad.

"I'll give it to my boss," said the man. "Just write, 'Sorry'"—he held his hands up like he was apologizing—"'I did my best.'"

"I don't want to do that," said Chris. It occurred to him that he didn't want to put anything in writing.

The man's face darkened. "Just write, 'I'm sorry, I did my best.'"

"I don't want to."

The man sat there staring down at his own thighs. It looked like he was trying to reason something out. Chris noticed that his knuckles were hairy, and that he wore a wedding ring.

"I'm sorry," said Chris. He shook his head as though it was hardly worth negotiating.

The man leaned forward and grabbed Chris's own pen, which sat on top of the pad. He clicked it with his thumb, clicked it again. "Just write it," he said.

Chris realized the depth of trouble he was in, and his chest tightened. "I don't want to," he said. For the second time that morning, his eyes became wet, and he wiped at them with his hand. *I don't want to*, he thought.

"You want me to leave?" asked the man.

"Yes, please," said Chris.

"Then write the fucking note." The man wasn't angry; he seemed tired. But that provided little comfort. Chris's mind, like a cornered animal, started darting around looking for a way out. He could get up and run. He could run for his door and take the stairs; he'd run as fast as he could. He could walk. He could just walk out. But he couldn't.

"I did as much as I possibly could," said Chris. "I was never part of this. I never asked to be part of it. I never did anything . . ."

"Then just write the note. It's painless. Just write a note apologizing. Don't be so macho. You're all stiff." Holding his shoulders in rigidly, he imitated Chris. "We're all doing the best we can—get over yourself," said the man. "I got a boss, you got a boss. It's work. I have other shit I need to be doing."

They sat in silence for a moment, and then Chris held his hand out and the man put the pen in it.

"What do you want me to write?" Chris asked.

"'I'm sorry, I did my best.'"

"You'll leave me alone?" he asked.

"Yes."

Chris leaned forward and scrawled *I'm sorry, I did my best* on the paper.

"Now sign it," said the man.

Chris added his signature.

"See?" said the man. He leaned forward and squinted at the yellow paper. Chris watched the man's lips move while he read the short note. His hair was thin, and Chris looked at his scalp. He thought about trying to stab him in the neck with the pen.

The man looked straight at Chris. "Why are you so upset?" he asked.

"I got fired," said Chris. "I lost my job. You're here. I'm hungover. It's all bullshit."

The man closed his eyes and shook his head sympathetically. On the street, somebody honked their horn. Chris wiped his eyes again, took a deep breath. The honking stopped.

"Okay," said Chris.

"No," said the man. He pointed at a white paper cup that was sitting on the coffee table. Chris hadn't noticed it. "I want you to drink that."

Chris sat staring at the cup.

"It's medicine, to make you feel better. It's a painkiller. It will make all the pain go away." He leaned forward, picked it up, and held it toward Chris.

"I don't want to," said Chris. He closed his eyes and began crying in earnest. In his mind, unaccountably, he saw green leafy trees. "I don't want to," he repeated.

"What would your mother want?"

"She would want you to leave me alone," said Chris. "She would just—Please, can't you see that I'm not doing anything. I'm not a threat to you. I'm not going to say anything to anyone ever. I'm not going to the cops. I'm going to pack up and move out of the country. I'm never coming back to New York. Do you get it? I'm done with it all."

"It's all good," said the man. "That'll all be taken into account. Now drink it."

"I don't want to," said Chris.

"Just drink it," said the man, moving the cup closer.

Chris wanted to slap it out of his hand. He wanted nothing more in the world than to just slap the cup out of the man's hand. But he couldn't bring himself to do it. He couldn't move. All he could do was cry and beg. "Please," he said, through his tears.

"Drink it."

"What is it?"

"It'll help you," said the man. "Help your family. Help your mom."

Chris stopped crying and took the cup in his hand. He thought about dumping it—he could turn it over and dump it on the floor, he could throw it in the man's face—but he knew that wouldn't solve anything. He looked into the cup and saw a couple ounces of clear liquid. "What is it?"

"Just a little something to help you relax."

"I don't want to relax." He tried to hand it back, but the man pushed it back toward him.

"Just drink it. Don't be a pussy."

The tiny cup, oddly, was beginning to feel heavy in Chris's hand. He raised it to his nose and sniffed. Odorless. It dawned on him that this might all be part of some kind of sadistic joke. He put the cup to his lips, poured the liquid into his mouth, and swallowed. It tasted like water, with a hint of chemicals. A little bitter, like soapy water.

"There," Chris said. "Now fuck off."

The man smiled and took the cup out of Chris's hand. He stood up from the couch, and when Chris tried to join him, the man gently pushed him back down.

"Stay there," he said.

Chris watched him put the cup into the pocket of his fleece coat and zip the pocket closed. "Lie down," the man said. "Get some rest." He then bent down, gently lifted Chris's feet off the ground, swung them over and set them down. Chris was stretched out on the length of the couch. The man untied Chris's shoes and pulled them off. Then he sat down on the coffee table next to the note and looked at Chris. "Close your eyes," he said.

Chris closed his eyes.

He saw the same green trees as before. Leafy green trees, with sun coming through them. He saw a river he used to swim in when he was young. He'd swim underwater and dive down and grab smooth rocks from the river floor. It was colder near the bottom. He thought about all the times he'd been surrounded by happy people. He saw his family laughing, his parents in their kitchen before they divorced. He saw his grandmother dancing in the same kitchen. His shoulder muscles relaxed. The muscles in his face relaxed. His other muscles relaxed. It felt wonderful.

After picking up the thumb drive from the house, Grigory Levchin drove the two brothers to Ossip's Locksmith Shop. Construction on Neptune Avenue slowed their progress. Yuri stared out the window and watched two men carrying a mattress into one of the brick buildings on his right. He checked the side mirror for tails but didn't see any.

When they arrived, Grigory pulled into an empty spot, put the car in park, and hit the hazards. All three of the men looked at the shop. It appeared to be closed; the metal gate hadn't been pulled open yet.

They had called Ossip twice on the way over, but he hadn't answered either call. It was 10:39 a.m. Ossip always had the shop open by 10:00.

"What the fuck?" asked Isaac from the back of the car.

"*Go knock on the door,*" said Grigory. "*Wake that drunkard up.*"

Yuri stepped out of the car, and a gust of wind greeted him. Isaac got out and joined him on the sidewalk. Both men approached the front of the shop. Yuri found that the padlock, while set in its place, hadn't been locked.

He took the lock off and put it on the ground. Then he pushed the metal gate open, the sound of metal scraping on metal. Like a proprietor opening for business, he set it as best he could into its spot. Isaac moved toward the front door and began knocking on it.

Yuri joined him and looked over his shoulder. It was dark in the shop. "What the fuck?" whispered Yuri.

"Dude," said Isaac. "This shit is bullshit."

Isaac tried the door and found it unlocked. He walked in slowly, like he was afraid of interrupting something. Before entering, Yuri turned and looked at Grigory, who was watching everything from the car with a frown.

Standing near the door, Isaac was still in the front room when Yuri entered. "What are you doing?" whispered Yuri.

"I don't know," said Isaac.

Yuri stepped past him and hit the lights. The front room lit up. Hanging behind the counter on the wall was a collection of blank keys waiting to be carved. A seldom-used cash register sat on the counter. The shop was silent.

"Yo, Ossip!" yelled Yuri. He lifted the countertop and walked toward the back. When he got to the hallway he flicked on the light.

The workshop in back was dark, and Yuri had to feel along the wall like a blind man until he found the light switch. When he hit the lights, he saw Ossip's body facedown on the ground. There was blood pooled and smeared on the floor. The room, Yuri realized, smelled like shit and blood. He stepped back and hit a bucket near the door and stumbled, but didn't fall.

"What the fuck?" said Isaac, stepping to the body, but trying to avoid the blood. "What happened?" He turned the man over and they saw a dark gash on his throat where it had been cut.

Yuri, knowing full well what was waiting for him, walked over to the safe in the corner of the room. He found it open and empty. "Fuck," he said. *This can't be happening*, he thought.

"Let's get the hell out of here," said Isaac.

"No, no—"

"What?"

"Idiot, people saw us come in," said Yuri.

They both walked toward the front of the shop, and then stepped outside. Yuri stopped near the front door to make sure nobody else walked in. He watched Isaac walk over to the car and lean down to speak with Grigory.

Yuri looked down the street. There were people everywhere. A woman pushed a laundry cart right past him. Cars drove past in steady waves. Down the block, a child in a stroller cried.

"He doesn't want to come in," said Isaac, walking back to the storefront. Yuri bent his head and looked at Grigory, who was still in the car with his phone to his ear. "He's calling," said Isaac.

"The cops?" asked Yuri.

"Uncle," said Isaac.

Yuri looked at his hands; he hadn't touched anything but he wanted to make sure he didn't have any blood on him. He looked down and saw some junk mail scattered on the ground. *That mail was sent to Ossip, and it will never be opened.* He closed his eyes and breathed like he was crying, but no tears came out. *This is our fault*, he thought. *This is all our fault.*

"You know who did this, right?" Yuri asked his brother.

"Who?"

"Your fucking friend, that psychopath that was here. What's his name, fucking Dima?"

"Dima?" said Isaac. "Ossip's his uncle. He's not going to kill his uncle. For what?"

"For money," hissed Yuri. He looked back toward the car and Grigory beckoned him with his fingers. When Yuri walked that way, a group of black guys at a bodega watched him but didn't say anything.

He bent down by the window. "*He said to call the police,*" said Grigory.

"Fuck," said Yuri. "Me?"

"*Yes, you. I'm going to wait right here in the car.*" He pointed toward the bodega. Yuri looked that way and saw a camera directed toward the front of the locksmith shop. Grigory then pointed at Ossip's door. Yuri looked that way and saw a domed camera he'd never noticed before. "*That one doesn't work.*"

"*What do I say?*" asked Yuri.

Isaac joined them at the car.

"*Say that you came to get a copy of your house keys,*" said Grigory, "*that Ossip was a dear family friend, that you found the place as you found it, unlocked, dark, that you found him.*"

"*Throat cut?*" asked Yuri.

"*Throat cut,*" said Grigory, covering his eyes with his hands. "*Make the call.*"

Yuri stepped back toward the front door and dialed 911. He told the operator that he'd found his friend murdered. Yuri answered all of the dispatcher's questions with urgency, throwing in a curse word here, and a *please hurry* there.

As he spoke, he looked out at Neptune Avenue and marveled that people were running errands as though everything was normal. The sky was still blue, traffic kept moving, the world went on. He looked at Isaac and saw his little brother leaning against the back passenger-side door, staring at him with a flat expression.

Grigory, meanwhile, still seated in the driver's seat, was back on the phone, animatedly spreading word of what had happened.

When he finished the call, Yuri walked back to the car, and got in. "This is fucked," he said in English. Grigory nodded. Isaac got in the back and they sat in silence for a moment until Yuri finally said, "Dima."

Grigory looked at him. *"Why Dima?"*

"He was here when we made a withdrawal," said Yuri. *"Moishe had the money in a bag, but he saw it, he noticed."*

"What about Moishe?" asked Grigory.

"Never," said Yuri. *"He's in Jamaica. He left two days ago. It's not him."* After fussing with his phone, he held it up. *"See"*—on the phone was a picture of Moishe sitting on the beach, wearing sunglasses, and giving a peace sign—*"he's with Raya and Raya's wife and her sister. They left two days ago,"* he repeated.

Grigory's eyes went from the phone to the street in front of him. *"All days are bad days,"* he said. *"This day's the worst."*

The first sirens could be heard coming from the 60th Precinct.

"Don't mention the safe," said Grigory, turning to Yuri.

"What do you think we are?"

Grigory then told them what to say to the cops. He told them to give the statements they discussed, to be cooperative, and not to ask for a lawyer. *"Stick to the story: you came, you found, that's it."*

After the police secured the scene, the men were separated and told to stand in different doorways along Neptune Avenue. More people had gathered now. Word had already spread in the neighborhood.

One by one, the three men gave statements to the same uniformed female officer. She took notes on a small pad and watched them like she was looking for a crack in their foundation, but there was none. From there, they were ferried to the precinct. They were placed in their own small interview rooms along the same hallway.

As Yuri was led to his room, he spotted Grigory. The man sat with straight posture, his large hands placed on the table as if he'd just finished a piano recital.

Yuri's interview room was filthy; a balled-up Kleenex lay on the floor—maybe someone had been crying. The walls were smeared and dirty. Eventually, Yuri could hear the low tones of Grigory's voice coming from the next room.

Finally, a homicide detective wearing a loose suit, a black guy named Robinson, entered the room. He didn't treat Yuri like a suspect, but upon hearing his name he made a show of saying, "Rabinowitz," while raising his eyebrows, pursing his lips, and nodding his head like he knew who Yuri's uncle was.

The detective asked all the necessary questions, but he didn't press any issues. When he finished the interview, he shook Yuri's hand and seemed to take note of its clamminess. He gave Yuri a card and said to be in touch if he heard anything.

A different cop drove them back to Grigory's car on Neptune Avenue. Grigory sat up front and the two brothers rode in back.

Isaac was the only one who spoke. He kept repeating, "*I can't believe they killed Ossip.*"

"All right, gentleman," said the cop when he pulled next to the car. "Stay safe."

"Is he trying to be funny?" asked Isaac.

Grigory shushed him, and they got out. All three men watched the cruiser drive off, then together they turned and looked at Ossip's shop. A ribbon of yellow police tape hung across the front doorway. No cops were visible, but two empty squad cars and a city van remained in front of the building.

Grigory looked at his phone and told the brothers their uncle wanted to see them.

"Dude, this day is whack," said Isaac. "Start to finish."

Yuri shook his head, thought about saying that it hadn't even begun, but decided to stay silent. They all got into Grigory's car.

To avoid being followed, Grigory took Ocean Parkway all the way out to Sheepshead Bay and then zigzagged his way back to Brighton Beach. Slumping in the front seat, Yuri stared out the window and thought about all the times he'd spent with Ossip. He'd known the man his entire life. He'd always been there, cutting keys, acting as a bank, drinking, carrying on. He was a good man. Blood or not, he was part of their family.

Yuri also thought about Isaac, who'd looked like a teenager back there at the locksmith shop. As they drove down Avenue U and passed by all the Chinese stores, he felt a genuine affection for him. Yuri told himself he had to start acting better. He had to stop being so hard on his brother. He had to learn to control his anger. He had to be a better brother. It was time to start taking responsibility. It was time to grow up.

Yuri turned in his seat and looked at his brother. Isaac's eyes were red from crying. "I love you," Yuri said, holding his hand out.

Isaac grabbed his brother's hand and kissed it. "*I love you too*," he said in Russian. They all rode in silence for a moment; then Isaac reached forward and grabbed Grigory's massive shoulders. "*We love you, too, Big Angel*," he said.

Grigory's eyes became damp and he wiped them with his hand. All three of them bumped along, shaking their heads, looking at the trees in front of them.

When they got back to Leo Katzir's office, they found it closed. The secretary had been sent home for the day, and the front door had been locked. They had to wait for the lawyer to open it. When he did, he shook his head at Yuri like an angry grandmother. "Did I tell you?" he asked.

"Yes, you did."

In the back room they found their uncle on the phone, ending a call. "*Sit down, boys*," he said, pointing at the couch. He turned to Grigory. "*Close that door*."

Yuri and Isaac sat on the couch. As their uncle set a chair in front of them, Yuri tried to find some kind of self possession. He shifted in his seat, wiped at his jaw, and made a pained face. *This is the bottom*, thought Yuri. *This is rock bottom*.

Uncle Yakov, his eyes looking particularly blue, studied the two brothers. After a moment, he leaned forward, grabbed Isaac's knee, and gave it a little shake.

"*Boys, when we were young, back there*"—he spoke quietly—"*we had to do things because there was no other way to survive. We had to eat, and if you have to eat, and there is no job for Jews, then you make your own employment.*"

He leaned back, crossed one leg over the other. "*We've been talking,*" he said, looking at the lawyer, who sat at his desk, hands folded in front of him, shaking his head. "*It's different now. Yes, the world needs things. Things need to be shipped from here to there. Goods need to be sold. Orders need fulfillment.*"

He stopped speaking for a moment, looked first at Isaac and then shifted his gaze to Yuri. "*Your father was a good man. He never joined me in what we do, and I never held it against him. As you know, we remained very close. I loved that man. He's not here to watch over you.*"

His eyes went back and forth between the two brothers. "*Here is what I propose,*" he finally said. "*I'm going to pay the money back myself. We need to clean this up.*"

He turned and looked at the lawyer, and the lawyer nodded. "*And you boys are going to leave New York.*"

"*You can go wherever you want. Go to California. I tell you the world is whatever you want it to be. But you can't be here right now. You don't have to live this life.*" He sat there like he was trying to figure out what else to say, then looked at Grigory. "*It's unhealthy.*"

Yuri closed his eyes. He didn't feel any great relief, but he wasn't going to argue. "Yeah, I mean, I think we can do that." He turned and looked at his brother. "Right?" he asked.

Isaac said, "California," and nodded his head, like it was just one more fun thing they could do.

Yuri couldn't help staring at him.

It was settled: the Rabinowitz brothers would move to California.

That same afternoon, Michael D'Angelo received a text message from Elizabeth Carlyle: *Call your men off Chris C.*

He typed his response: *Really??* and hit send.

His phone lit up. *Yes, really.* Another message followed: *We fired him.*

D'Angelo was in a meeting at the time. He sat there for a moment, and then texted Paul Malone, whose team had been hired to watch Chris. He told him the job was over, to call off his men. He thanked Paul and told him to send his bill.

When the meeting ended, D'Angelo walked straight to his office, sat down at his desk, and opened the video of Chris Cowley's pickpocketing. He watched it in real speed, then slowed it down and watched it again. By this point, it seemed unquestionable that the attorney and the pickpocket had acted in tandem. It was right there on video: they looked at each other before the bump. In D'Angelo's mind it was a settled fact. He backed it up and watched again.

The pickpocket was skilled—he had to give him that. It didn't matter anymore. He closed the video player, then opened up his email and began responding to a message about his son's school.

D'Angelo finished work early and decided that instead of catching his normal cab, he'd walk to Penn Station. The walk didn't bring any relief. Midtown felt ugly; his bad mood seemed to be shared by everyone around him. A contagious, citywide bad mood had descended. *Florida*, thought D'Angelo. *The place for me is Florida.*

As he made his way across Bryant Square Park, he thought of Valencia Walker. Perhaps she could offer some closure. He stopped walking, took out his cell phone, and scrolled through his contacts until he found her number. While the phone rang, he moved toward the tables and chairs on the west side of the park.

"Michael, I was just thinking about you," Valencia said when she answered. Her voice was warm. Calling her had been the right decision, he knew it instantly. His mood was already improving.

After exchanging a few friendly greetings, D'Angelo came to the point. "You heard they fired Cowley?"

"I did," said Valencia.

"So what do you think?"

"Termination is never good," said Valencia, her voice still carrying that soothing tone. "It leaves a bad feeling."

"I mean bigger picture."

"Big picture," said Valencia. "The case is a mess. I think your firm's client is about to be in a lot of trouble. The thing needs to go away."

"Calcott?" asked D'Angelo. He was confused.

"Calcott."

"Yeah, well—"

"But don't tell Liz that," said Valencia, cutting him off. "You know she hates to hear bad news."

"Yeah, well—"

"I'm saying that based on a vibe in the air, not anything concrete."

D'Angelo's eyebrows turned in on each other; his head moved back an inch. He felt at a loss for words. It sounded so abstract coming from her. She didn't sound like an ex-intelligence officer, she sounded like a hippie. "Very New Age," he finally managed to say.

"I've been meditating," said Valencia. "Now tell me what you think."

"I think Cowley was in on losing that phone."

"Of course, he was," said Valencia. "He lost it."

"No, I mean, I think he lost it intentionally."

"Liz told me that," she said. "Seems plausible."

"You know we had men on him since it went down?"

"She told me that too," said Valencia. "Did they ever get anything?"

"Honestly, not really."

"I heard he lost them last night," she said.

"Yeah," said D'Angelo. "A real Jason Bourne."

"Last straw."

"That's it," said D'Angelo. "Hey listen, there was one thing that still bugged me."

"What's that?"

"The pickpocket."

"Oh God," said Valencia. "You don't know how long we worked on that. I called in a favor"—here her voice dropped down to a conspiratorial whisper—"from Fort Meade, mind you. Had them run the video through their facial recognition systems. *Nada*. For all we know, the dude might have been wearing one of those silicone masks."

D'Angelo found himself nodding while he listened.

"Also—well shit—I won't say his name 'cause you know him, too, but I had someone pull all the StingRay data from the Grand Central and the Bleecker Street stops. There were something like twenty-five numbers that seemed to hit the time frame right. I had my team track all—I'm saying *all*—those numbers back to their owners.

"Long story short, there were no good hits. We found four Asian fellas, but we looked into them and none was our target. I had my NYPD guy pull every sheet on every pickpocket in Grand Central and Penn Station for the last three years." She paused for a moment, then said, "The guy did a very clean job."

"You'd think Liz might have shared some of that information with me," said D'Angelo.

"Come on, you know these lawyers. They share what they think needs sharing. If it was up to me, we would've been coordinating the whole time," said Valencia. "I tried to let Liz loan you out to us when we first came on board, but she didn't go for it."

D'Angelo watched a college-aged couple walking hand-in-hand across the park. "Would've made more sense," he said.

"You got a good nose for this shit," said Valencia. "Ever since we worked on that Hammoud thing. I'm not saying this to be nice, either. There are some people who see it, and there are some people who don't. You *see* it."

"I appreciate that," said D'Angelo. "It's mutual," he added, feeling oddly sentimental.

"So, do you think you're going to continue looking for this Chinese dude?" she asked, sounding almost mirthful, like it would be a fun little escapade to get involved in.

"What am I, crazy?" said D'Angelo. "When Elizabeth Carlyle says you're done, you better be done."

"Well, if you ever do look into him, give me a call," said Valencia. "I'd do it for free. These things have a way of grabbing my attention."

"I'll do that," he said.

"We should have dinner sometime," said Valencia. "Go somewhere nice, drink some good wine."

"I'd like that," said D'Angelo, smiling.

They said their goodbyes and hung up.

D'Angelo stayed seated for a moment. He watched the workers walking home. Looked at the trees and saw that the leaves were about to emerge. It did make him feel better to speak to her. At least somebody in this godforsaken city appreciated him.

Even after the call ended, Valencia kept the phone up near her face and considered her best course of action. She'd just jumped in the back of an SUV for a rolling meeting. The phone call had been completely unexpected. The vehicle she was in continued down East Forty-Sixth Street. The traffic in Midtown was barely moving.

After a moment, when she felt fully composed, she turned her head so she could look into Jonathan Redgrave's eyes. "See?" she said. "He's got no imagination."

Redgrave's face didn't betray anything. "Has he ever called you before?"

"Not that I remember," said Valencia. She tried to read Redgrave's face to see what he was thinking, but the man had a facility for masking his thoughts.

"I'm not worried about him," said Redgrave, shaking his head and bending down so he could look out the windshield of their SUV. "The guy is zero on my list of worries."

Valencia had been instructed to leave CDH's office on foot at 4:10 p.m., walk up Madison Avenue to East Forty-Sixth, make a right, and continue on the north side of the street. If she wasn't picked up by the time she finished walking the length of that block at her normal pace, she was to understand that the meeting had been canceled and that she should wait for further instructions.

But they did pick her up. Before she'd made it halfway down the block, the SUV pulled to the curb and stopped fifteen feet in front of her. The back door popped open, and Valencia walked over. She looked in and saw Redgrave on the far side of the backseat.

Thirty seconds after getting in, her phone buzzed. Redgrave told her to put it on speaker. Now, with the call finished, Redgrave pointed out the windshield. "We gotta make a quick stop."

Valencia leaned toward the middle of the seat, but she couldn't see where he was pointing.

"He wants to find our guy?" said Redgrave.

"I guess so," said Valencia, shaking her head like they were sharing a joke.

"Good luck with that one," said Redgrave. He pointed to their left. "Here we are."

Redgrave's driver steered the SUV into a parking garage. Valencia had no idea where they were going. Her nervousness clicked up a level. The attendant, sitting in his booth, raised the boom barrier without checking any credentials. It appeared he was expecting them.

They drove to the very back of the garage, a darkened corner, and then—with wheels screeching quietly—made a few efficient turns before backing into a spot.

"Hop out," said Redgrave. Valencia got out. The driver joined her and told her to lift her arms. Then, looking for wires, he swept and scanned her with two separate handheld devices, one at a time. He frisked her—not in a rough way, but thoroughly.

While he did this, Valencia casually set about memorizing his face. The man looked Latino, but it was hard to say what country he was from. He had scars on his face, high up on his right cheek, near his temple. She noted his eye ratio, the pattern of his scarring, his nose type, height, weight, hairline, smell, and movement profile. She memorized it all.

When he finished sweeping her, he gestured toward the back door, and then opened it for her like a gentleman. She got back into the vehicle and saw that Redgrave had an open briefcase on his lap.

"Put your phone in here," he said. She placed the phone in the briefcase, and he shut the thing, snapped some snaps closed, and passed it forward to the driver, who put it on the floor in the front.

"So tell me," said Valencia, as they made their way toward the garage's exit, "who's number one on your list of worries?"

Redgrave studied her face in a lecherous way. He seemed to love this kind of banter. "You are babe. You know that."

Valencia couldn't help noticing a tiny speck of yellow discharge in the inside corner of his eye. The man was foul. Still, she batted her eyelashes at him and smiled.

When they emerged from the garage, the driver began looping back toward Madison Avenue.

"What about Chris Cowley?" asked Valencia, probing for information. "What number is he?"

"Shit, he's down there with D'Angelo," said Redgrave, shaking his head, squeezing his lips together, and holding his hand low on his chest like he was illustrating the size of a short man. "Down in the zero range. Subzero. Not a worry anymore. Debriefed him earlier. He's free and clear."

"And Elizabeth?"

"Now you're talking," said Redgrave. When he touched her thigh with the back of his hand, Valencia noticed a ring on his finger. She tried to imagine the woman who would marry this man, and the only thing that came to mind was a mail-order bride. She'd asked Danny to run a full background on Jonathan Redgrave, but none of the individuals he found were a match. There was nothing; the man didn't exist.

"Anyway, listen"—Redgrave adjusted his voice to signify that the joking and flirting were over—"the agenda for the coming week is simple. It's gonna move fast. More stories will come out in the press. I'm talking every day." He tapped his fingers on his palms. "The stories will make Calcott's stock fall. Did you have somebody short them for you?"

"That would be insider trading," said Valencia, aware that he might be recording this conversation.

Redgrave rolled his eyes, and continued. "Anyway, stock will fall, your girl Elizabeth will be blamed. And *you*—pretty lady—will nudge her all week long. You'll nudge all of them—Carlyle, Driscoll, Hathaway—the whole gang, until they decide that the only path forward is to go to Calcott's in-house and recommend withdrawing the case."

He paused for a second and looked out the window at a man screaming into his phone. "Listen to me, everyone needs to just stand down. Case needs to be withdrawn. I'll leave the approach to you. Handle it however you see fit. That's why we hired you. You're the best, right?"

"Best nudger in the business," said Valencia, smiling, shaking her head, and pressing her thumbnail against her finger.

"You brought your shit?"

She reached into her breast pocket and handed a small envelope to Redgrave. Inside the envelope, scrawled in her neat handwriting on a greeting card, was her thirty-four-character address for Bitcoin deposit.

"What if they won't drop the case?" asked Valencia.

"Then the stories will get worse and worse and their stock will continue to fall until they bottom out and get chopped up and sold for parts. It's not a question of if they'll drop it—it's when." He shrugged and shook his head like he didn't care.

"And Emerson?" asked Valencia, glancing out the window and watching a masked delivery man on an electric bike riding next to them. "What if they don't drop their side of the case?"

"Shit, we're way further along with them, right?" Redgrave asked the driver.

The driver looked in the rearview mirror, shook his head by way of an answer, and looked back at the road.

Redgrave turned his attention back to Valencia. "Don't worry about them. We're all just little pieces, doing our little parts." He sounded like he was imitating some singer. The reference was lost on Valencia.

Redgrave continued: "Elizabeth Carlyle—that's all you have to worry about. Make her see the light. Preach to her. Tell her stories. Isn't that your thing? Didn't you say that somewhere?"

Valencia couldn't recall if she'd ever said that.

"She respects you," said Redgrave. "That's why you're here. That's why you get paid the big bucks."

Valencia pretended to yawn. The vehicle came to a stop. They all stared at a taxi that had stopped and was blocking their way.

Valencia felt her blood pressure tick up a few bars as she prepared her next question. "And this is still authorized by the colonel?"

"You keep asking the same question, and the answer remains the same: yes," said Redgrave. "Authorized, fully DS7'd all the way up. Straight from the colonel."

Colonel Pollock was the U.S. Army full bird colonel in charge of N14—Redgrave's group. N14, as far as Valencia was able to find out, was operating out of NORTHCOM. It was a Department of Defense group and had no crossover coordination with Langley. Her sources told her that N14 was set up for quote-unquote domestic operations. The "quote-unquote," when she heard it, implied true, high-level black bag operations inside the United States. None of this was remotely public information; it was, as her source told her, "Stovepiped, DOD bullshit."

When she asked her old boss about Colonel Pollock, she was told, "He's Montana—not Colorado—that's all you need to know." She understood this to mean that N14 was fully off the books, completely unrecognized, unknown to Congress. Even the House Permanent Select Committee on Intelligence wouldn't have any idea who they were.

"Can you do me a favor, and I mean this seriously," Valencia said, mirroring him and touching his thigh the same way he'd just touched hers. "Can you please tell Colonel Pollock that if he ever comes to New York I'd like to have a drink with him?"

"I'll do that," said Redgrave. "Or you can call him yourself. He's listed in the phone book."

Valencia smiled at that.

"Any problems, leave your bathroom blind open and Manny-boy will reach out." He looked at the driver. "Right?"

"That's right, sir," said Manny, looking in the rearview mirror.

"If you need immediate attention," said Redgrave, "call the messenger service. Ask for Raul. They'll say wrong number, and you'll hang up. That's emergencies only. We'll reach you within thirty minutes."

"Sounds good," said Valencia.

"One other thing," said Redgrave. "No more asking about us. No more talking to Stockton or any of them. You did your due diligence, now you gotta shut the fuck up. Do you understand what I'm saying?"

She smiled. The conversation she'd had with her old station chief, Bildad Stockton, had been face-to-face. She'd traveled, unannounced, to his house in Georgetown. She hadn't sent any emails or made any calls. She was being warned that she was under surveillance. "Had to ask," she said.

"But you're done asking."

"Message received," she said.

"Good," said Redgrave. "We'll get rolling then."

Redgrave spent the rest of the drive bragging about his sailboat and the brave solo trips he'd made. Valencia listened, smiled when it was called for, and asked questions to keep him talking. She felt—even as he carried on about his boat—that he was really trying to tell her something else, that he was playing some other kind of mind game.

Her attention would shift to Manny occasionally; she'd try to catch his eye and read his feelings, but he was too focused running surveillance-detection maneuvers, second-lane turns, and mid-block stops and starts.

By the time they got near her apartment, she was feeling claustrophobic and hot. She pointed at a wine store, two blocks from her front door. "Drop me right here, please. This is good."

After getting her phone back and saying goodbye, she got out and watched the SUV drive away. She resisted the urge to look up and instead looked at the red mark she'd made on her finger. For good luck, she spit on the ground, something her grandmother used to do, and then she went into the wine store.

Two hours and forty minutes before that meeting, Valencia's underling, Billy Sharrock, had left his cell phone on his office desk, grabbed a walkie-talkie, and set out for the Bronx. He took a circuitous route and ran surveillance detection the entire time. First, he hopped on a downtown A train and jumped out right before the doors closed at Fulton Street. He skipped up the stairs to the exit. From there, he walked south on Broadway for a few blocks, dodging slow-moving people as he went.

At a light, he hopped into a taxi without waving at it and passed sixty dollars forward to the driver. "Drive around for a little, I want to lose some asshole who's following me," he said.

"You want me to drive around?" asked the cabbie. He counted the money and then turned and looked through the dirty partition.

"Yeah, yeah, just go," said Billy, waving him forward.

"You want me to go fast?"

"Yeah, yeah, but not so fast you'll get a ticket, just loop around down here for a little bit. Keep the change."

The driver pushed the gas and hit a hard right on Cedar Street. The little street was free of cars, and the driver raced down it. He rolled a stop sign and cranked a left. They sped past a construction site. With his hand on the ceiling, Billy had turned in his seat and was watching out the back window. He couldn't see anyone following him. "Okay, okay, slow down."

The driver didn't seem to hear his passenger. He ran a red and made a left onto Rector and a quick left onto Trinity Place. After a bicyclist yelled at him, he finally slowed down and looped back toward the station. Before getting out, Billy pulled on a beanie and took off his coat, folded it up, and tucked it under his sweatshirt. He then sped down the stairs into the station, swiped his way back in, using a card previously purchased with cash, and caught an uptown 4 train.

In the train, he sat next to an old Indian woman who was eating a piece of corn on the cob. Billy, breathing slightly more heavily than normal, took his time examining every passenger. He felt un-followed.

During his ride uptown he thought about Valencia and wondered what the hell she was getting them into. Eight days earlier she'd told them that they were in "war mode." She instructed them to be careful on any phone and to assume they were being monitored at all times. She said it wasn't a big deal—they just had to keep their eyes open. Thinking about it now, Billy had to shake his head. He'd hate to see what counted as a big deal.

At Eighty-Sixth Street, he got out, exited the station, ran a four-block surveillance-detection route, and then went back into the station and got on an uptown 6 train. He got off in Mott Haven in the Bronx at 138th Street.

A few blocks from the station was a lube shop. A windowless Sprinter van was parked in front of the shop on 138th Street. Billy approached it slowly and knocked on the back door. A second later, the door slid open.

"You made it," said Colter Jacobson. He looked over Billy's shoulder, then stepped out. He pointed to the front of the van. "Let's go," he said. Billy walked to the passenger door and waited to be let in.

A kid rolled by on a BMX, rapping about how many guns he had. When Billy got in, Colter told him to buckle up.

They drove a few blocks over to a self-storage lot that sat right next to the Harlem River. The gate had a keypad and Colter got out, bent down, and punched in the code.

When he got back, he told Billy he was friends with the owner, and that one of the best signals in New York City could be found there. Billy took out his walkie-talkie, found the appointed band, and tested it: "Blue Dove, Blue Dove," he said. A moment later, he heard Milton answer, "Blue Dove, Blue Cat."

They parked near a clearing that faced the river, hopped out, and got in the back of the van. Billy looked at the floor and admired the rubber matting. He stepped to the shelves and looked at the welding. Every tool had its place. Billy could only shake his head with jealousy.

They had about forty-five minutes to kill before the operation started, and they spent it talking first about the Knicks, and then a little bit about Billy's time in Afghanistan. Then they talked about the weather.

Colter's pilot was back in White Plains. When the drone was up, Colter told Billy that they had to keep it at about 4,400 feet to avoid the NYPD. They watched on the monitor as the pilot flew it above

Harlem. Colter took control of the camera from his computer, and he zoomed in on different practice targets.

"Good camera," whispered Billy.

"This thing," Colter answered modestly, like he was embarrassed by any kind of praise. He then tapped the back of his head, and they both stared at the monitor.

The pilot flew toward Midtown, and Colter set the camera on Carlyle, Driscoll, and Hathaway's building. They had ten minutes before Valencia was supposed to walk out. In order to make herself easy to spot, she'd worn a bright yellow coat that day. They looked at everyone who emerged from the building. Twenty seconds after 4:10 p.m., Colter spotted Valencia. He zoomed in and pointed at the screen.

Billy took his walkie-talkie, and in prearranged code told Milton that Valencia was on the move and headed north: "Blue Dove, South, North, East, West." He repeated it once.

The drone's camera stayed on Valencia as she walked. Billy sat on the edge of his seat and watched her.

When Valencia turned right onto East Forty-Sixth, Billy called in an update to Milton, who was soft-following from a few blocks back.

They watched Redgrave's vehicle stop in front of her. "Here we go," said Billy. On the monitor they saw her stop at the door, and then get in.

Billy took a little notepad out of his jacket pocket and searched for the code for Escalade. When he found it, he raised his radio and spoke into it: "Blue Dove—Blue, Green, Black, Michigan." He repeated that, and Milton copied.

Billy got nervous he'd mistaken the car model, and he asked Colter, "That's a Suburban or an Escalade?"

"Escalade," said Colter. "Looks like a 2016, but it could've been a '14, '15, or '16."

Then Colter spoke into his own headset and asked his drone pilot to angle on the plate. Fussing with the camera's remote, Colter leaned forward and read from the screen, "'New York HWY 4120.'"

Billy jotted the number down but held off on radioing it. They watched the vehicle drive two blocks east and then saw it enter a parking garage. This led to an extended period of nervousness because they had no idea what was happening. Billy consulted his paper map and took some time jotting down call signals into his notepad.

"Park-Lex, Park-Lex, Mad-Broad, Mad-Broad, 4-6, 4-7, 1-9, 2-9, 3-8, 3-3," Billy said into his radio, reading from his notes. He then repeated the same message.

Milton copied.

The vehicle reemerged a few minutes later and continued on East Forty-Sixth before circling around and heading west. Nobody knew whether Valencia was still in the SUV. Billy jotted down the directions in his notepad and read the code to Milton.

Then Billy switched the band on his radio and called Danny Tsui, who was on his computer at a Starbucks in Midtown to avoid any potential listening devices in their office. In code he asked Danny whether Valencia's phone appeared to be headed west on East Forty-Seventh.

A few moments later Danny's voice came over the radio and said they'd lost her phone signal.

"They took it," said Colter.

"Yep," said Billy.

They watched the SUV make its way back to Madison Avenue. Colter pulled the camera back and they tried, unsuccessfully, to see if they could spot any other cars trailing their target. He tried to find Milton, but he couldn't even see him.

After Valencia hopped out near her apartment, Colter zoomed in on her for a moment; Billy could almost make out the expression on her face. Then Colter moved the camera back to the target vehicle.

This was the whole point. They wanted to track him. They needed to know who Jonathan Redgrave really was.

The SUV made its way to the West Side Highway, looped around and headed downtown. Billy sat poking his tooth with his tongue and wondered where the hell they were going. He spoke into the radio and told Milton to loop back to Columbus and soft-shadow south from there. The SUV made a few countersurveillance moves, but nothing fancy.

Billy looked at Colter and asked, "Where do you think they'll go?"

The older man thought about it for a moment, then, referring to the NSA's Manhattan spy hub, said, "probably Titanpointe."

"That would be fucking hilarious," said Billy, shaking his head.

They watched the Escalade travel down through the West Village into Tribeca. When it finally stopped, Colter zoomed his camera in, and they saw Redgrave hop out and walk straight into a building. The Escalade took off.

"Which building is that?" asked Billy.

"That would be"—Colter flipped a switch on his control and white HUD characters popped up on the monitor—"99 Hudson Street," he said.

Billy rubbed his hands together like he was cold. "What the hell does he want in there?"

"That's your job, not mine," said the drone man.

Milton Frazier pulled his SUV over on Varick Street and put it in park. He'd been told their target had entered 99 Hudson Street, and that he should sit tight. He took the opportunity to peel and eat an orange. After the orange, he ate some raw cashews, one at a time. He drank water and stared at a passing woman. When he was finished, he put on lip balm, examined his face in the mirror, and checked his teeth for food. Then he leaned back in his seat, thought about Valencia, and told himself she was safe at home.

His walkie-talkie sounded, and Billy told him to take a look at the target building.

Milton pulled back into traffic and looped around to Franklin Street. He parked in a loading-only zone and set his NYPD placard on the dashboard. After changing bands on his radio, he called Danny Tsui, and asked him for a list of businesses in the building.

Inside the glove compartment Milton pulled out a paper envelope that held five thousand dollars. He separated eight hundred dollars from the rest and put that into his pants pocket. A minute later, Danny radioed back and listed some of the companies in the building: a law firm, a film company, an environmental organization, a real estate agent, and a PR firm.

Milton got out, grabbed his suit coat from the back, put it on, took the cash out of his pants pocket and transferred it to his inside jacket pocket. He took a moment to fix his tie in the reflection of his SUV's window. He pulled at his shirtsleeves, flapped his coat, and then started walking toward the building. He felt a controlled kind of nervousness.

Milton studied the building from across the street. He stamped the impression on his mind: fifteen floors, nothing too fancy, a little gold trim, art deco. Valencia would ask for the details: *Tell me more.*

When he peered in through the glass door, he was happy to see that the doorman was black, that he had dreadlocks, and that he was the only person in the lobby.

Milton opened the door and walked toward the desk. "What's up with you, sir?" said Milton, smiling when he got there.

The doorman squinted at him, let his head fall to the side, and said, "I'm good man, you?"

"I'm all right man, but"—he lowered his voice a little—"working all day."

"I hear that," said the doorman.

Milton looked down at the sign-in sheet, but the last signature was a woman thirty minutes earlier. "Summer's coming," Milton said.

"Gonna be the hottest in years," said the doorman.

Milton looked up like an idea had just occurred to him; he tapped his knuckles on the desk. "Listen—I was supposed to give one of my pitches to that white brother that just came in a few minutes ago. You know the dude I'm talking about? He's got little pimple scars on his face? Skinny guy? Brown hair a little thin up here?"

The doorman nodded, "Mmm-hmm."

"He works here, though?" asked Milton.

"Yeah."

"I feel stupid," said Milton, like he was confessing something, "but I forgot the man's first name. What's his name? Jonathan?"

The doorman dropped his head and made a pained face. "I'm sorry, brother, I'm not supposed to give out that kind of info."

"I hear you," said Milton, dropping his voice a little to match his register. "We all gotta do our jobs."

"I'm sorry about that," said the doorman.

"It's all good," said Milton. He reached into his coat pocket and palmed the eight hundred, flashed it, and whispered, "I got eight hundred dollars if you tell me the dude's name and where he went to."

He put the money on the desk, his hand still covering it, and slid the cash forward. "It's worth that much to me, and nothing more."

The doorman smiled, reached for the money, didn't count it, and slipped it into his own jacket pocket. "What's that dude," the doorman said. "That dude Jack Glasser, works on the eighth floor, solar place?"

"He just came in?" asked Milton.

"Yeah, but ten minutes ago."

"He got them little pimples on his cheeks, hair pushed back like an Italian dude?"

"Skinny dude?" asked the doorman.

"Yeah, skinny dude with the pitted skin, about fifty." They were both whispering now.

A white woman stepped out of the elevator and the doorman said, "Okay now," to her. They waited for her to leave and when the front door closed, the doorman said, "Yeah, that's him—Jack Glasser. He's up there in the Solar Solutions."

"Works here?"

"Yeah."

"Dude just came in. He's like six foot one?"

"I'm telling you. He just came in ten minutes ago. Only other person came in was two white ladies on the second floor."

"I thought he was called Jonathan Redgrave?"

The doorman made a face like Milton was crazy. "I don't know who that is. The dude's Jack Glasser—he works here. Been here ever since I have."

"All right then," said Milton, taking a step back. He touched a finger to his lips, a *Be quiet* gesture, and then pointed at the doorman. "I appreciate you, sir."

"Appreciate you too," said the doorman.

The following morning, Michael D'Angelo woke from a nightmare. In the dream, he'd been visiting his mother's house outside of Buffalo (she actually lived in a nursing home). There was a disturbance outside. When he looked out the window, he saw a dead deer. He went outside to look closer and saw that the yard was littered with dead deer. They'd run through the fence, leaving deer-sized holes where they entered. Some of the deer had tree limbs jammed through their heads.

It was disgusting, and he woke in a panic. His bedside clock read 5:11 a.m. He had an hour before his alarm was set to go off. Next to him, his wife slept soundly. He touched her back and then got up.

The Maplewood train station in New Jersey was a ten-minute drive from his house. He arrived there at seven thirty. Everyone waiting on the platform seemed to be in a bad mood; they frowned, they clenched their jaws. People coughed, a man spit. When the train pulled in, they all jockeyed for seats. D'Angelo found a spot near the window. The man who sat next to him looked like a banker. Overweight, he breathed through his nose like a bulldog. D'Angelo was just thinking of moving seats when his phone buzzed in his pocket.

He cringed when he saw it was Elizabeth. "Good morning," he answered, staring out the window at a traffic-jammed freeway.

"Michael, shit, hold on—excuse me, no, thank you. Okay, sorry—Michael? Are you there?"

"I'm here," said D'Angelo, pulling the phone from his ear and grimacing.

"I need you to go to Chris Cowley's house and collect his laptop. He told us he'd returned all CDH-issued computers and phones, but now Lauren from IT says he checked out a laptop and we can't—"

"Shit."

"Yep. Can you go directly there?"

"Yeah, I'm on the train, I'll jump in a car when I get out."

"If he doesn't open the door, see if you can get the super to give you access."

D'Angelo made a face but said, "Okay."

When he got to Chris's building, he stared up at it and cursed the young man under his breath. Of course Cowley lived in a building like this, fancy, and all glass. He was about to press the buzzer, when he decided that this conversation shouldn't be conducted over the intercom system. He stepped back to the sidewalk and looked up again.

After a few minutes, a young, wet-haired woman exited, and D'Angelo was able to catch the door before it closed. On the elevator ride up he realized he was feeling nervous. He worried that Chris might cause some kind of a fuss. *No, you can't have my fucking computer*, he imagined Chris saying. *This is harassment. I'm filing a claim against you.*

When he got to Chris's apartment, he knocked on the door and stood there waiting. His mouth was dry, and he wanted water. When he didn't hear anything, he put his ear near the door and pressed the bell. A soft chime could be heard coming from inside. He straightened up from the door and pressed the bell five times in a row.

God damn it, Chris, he thought. He tried the knob and found it unlocked. After pushing the door open, he looked back down the hallway toward the elevator, then leaned his head into the apartment and called out.

"Hey, Chris, it's Michael D'Angelo, I need to talk to you." His voice sounded pinched.

After stepping into the apartment, he closed the door without latching it and called out again. "Hey, Chris, you here, buddy?" The walkway from the door to the living room was only about ten feet long. He sniffed at the air and smelled a cleaning product. "Chris?"

When he saw keys hanging on a hook by the door, D'Angelo stared for a moment and considered how he could use one of those in his own house. Then he realized that the hanging keys suggested Chris was there. He walked farther into the apartment toward what he assumed was the living room.

As soon as he rounded the corner, he saw Chris lying on the couch. He was fully dressed. D'Angelo said, "Oh, Chris . . ." but he let the sentence trail off. He stood there staring at him.

"Chris?" he repeated, and moved closer; but he already suspected that the young man was dead. There was a stillness in the room, and Chris's skin looked pale.

D'Angelo stepped even closer and looked down. The young lawyer had an odd look on his face, and his eyes were closed. His arms lay flat next to his sides, both his hands squeezed into fists.

When D'Angelo touched his neck, he found it cold and without pulse. There was a fecal smell in the air, and D'Angelo stepped away from the couch and held his hand in front of his nose. He looked over the scene and saw a piece of paper on the coffee table. On it, he read: *I'm sorry, I did my best, Chris Cowley.*

D'Angelo took out his phone and snapped a picture of the note. He figured Liz would want to know exactly what happened, so he stepped to the other side of the room and took a picture of Chris's body. After looking more closely at the picture on his phone, he saw an empty orange prescription bottle on the floor. He used a pen to lift it and set it on the bar near the kitchen. There was no label.

He sniffed it, but it only smelled like plastic. When he looked at it more closely, he could see a white residue inside. He took a picture of the bottle, then used the pen and set it back where he'd found it.

D'Angelo walked around the back of the couch and looked at Chris's shoes on the floor. They were untied and laid out neatly in the direction they'd be pointing if he was still wearing them. It looked odd, and it made D'Angelo feel sad. "God damn it, Chris," he said. He felt a wave of heavy grief, but then it faded, and he went back to feeling almost nothing. He took out his phone and was about to call 911, when he realized that Elizabeth would ask him why he didn't grab the computer. Stepping away from the couch, he moved toward the kitchen to think about it.

He played out the scenario in his mind: *Came by to get computer, did a wellness check, found him dead, took the property.* It didn't feel right. *Fuck you Liz*, he thought.

He dialed 911 and reported that he'd found an apparent victim of a suicide. While he spoke, he moved into Chris's bedroom; staring out the window he answered all of the dispatcher's questions.

After the call ended, the investigator found the computer sitting on top of a dresser. He checked the bottom and saw a *Property of Carlyle, Driscoll, and Hathaway* sticker.

When he called Elizabeth, he reached her voicemail. "Elizabeth, you need to call me right away, it's urgent," he said, sounding depressed.

When the option was given, he thought about rerecording it, but decided against it. His mind went to Valencia: What would she do? She'd take the computer before the cops even showed up. She'd tuck it into the front of her pants and walk it out to her car so the security cameras wouldn't record her.

He moved a stool to the kitchen and sat there reading the *New York Times* on his cell phone. After a few minutes, a second wave of grief crashed over him. D'Angelo cried. He thought about Chris and sat there on the stool and cried. The kid had looked so lonely lately. He thought about the time he'd walked in and found him talking to his mother on the phone. *Stupid kid*, D'Angelo thought, wiping his eyes and trying to get a hold of himself. *Stupid fucking kid. It's just a job; there are plenty of jobs out there.*

When the cops showed up, he told them why he'd stopped by. He explained that he entered the premises because the door was open, and he wanted to do a wellness check. He pointed out the pill bottle, and the note.

The cops were babies; they both seemed to be about twenty-five years old. They had slightly dazed looks on their faces. D'Angelo informed them he'd been an FBI agent for eighteen years. One of the cops, a female, raised her eyebrows and nodded when he said it, but she didn't seem otherwise impressed.

When the time came, he showed them the computer, pointed to the "Property of" sticker, and told them that he was going to have to take it with him. He didn't ask, he simply told them. The cops exchanged glances and shrugged.

Before he left, D'Angelo took one last look at Chris's body. There was something almost religious about the way he was lying there. For a second, looking at him, D'Angelo felt a strange moment of peace.

But it faded, and he became angry at the kid again. He gave the cops his business card and walked out. By the time the elevator had delivered him to the ground floor, his anger had transformed into a kind of dull despair.

Elizabeth Carlyle sat in a conference room on the nineteenth floor of their office building. Her mentee, Sujung Kim, was in the middle of explaining some new case law to a cadre of attorneys. Elizabeth only half listened; most of her mind occupied itself by plotting moves in the Calcott case: *As soon as the judge ruled against their motion for summary judgment, they'd engage in settlement talks for a while; this would cause a string of delays that would—*

Henry Blatt, who happened to be sitting next to her, tapped her on the thigh and interrupted her thoughts. It seemed inappropriate for him to touch her, and her eyes went down to the spot of the foul. When she looked up, Henry nodded toward the door. Standing there, with his head poking into the room, was Michael D'Angelo. It was only then that she looked at her phone and saw she'd missed three calls from him.

"What's up?" she asked, joining him in the hall.

He led her away from the door. "Liz, I'm sorry," he said, looking down at his feet. "Chris committed suicide."

"What?" she asked.

"He took pills. There was a note. I took pictures."

He seemed to be preparing to show her something on his iPhone, but Elizabeth took a step back from him. "My God," she said, closing her eyes and putting her hands to her forehead. "When?" she asked.

"I just found him."

"What did the note say?"

"It said, 'I'm sorry, I did my best,' and he signed it."

"Okay," she said. "Fuck." She stepped back.

Another lawyer, walking by in the hallway, seemed to sense what was happening. She made a concerned face and drifted toward them. Elizabeth waved her away.

"I got the computer," said D'Angelo.

Elizabeth wanted to say, *Who the fuck cares.* All she could manage was, "Okay." She moved away from him and headed for the elevator. Over her shoulder she said, "Thank you."

As she made her way down the hall, her heart raced so wildly in her chest that she worried she was suffering a heart attack. She put her hand above her breast and breathed deeply through her mouth.

Oh fuck, she thought. *This is where I'm going to die.*

By the time she reached the elevator, her heart rate had dropped back down to a safe level. She pressed the button and started compiling lists of tasks. They would need to call an office-wide meeting.

First, she'd have to call all the partners in. She'd have to contact Chris's parents, which might present some legal issues. She'd have to talk to Ed Oasa, who represented the firm in these types of situations, to sort through that mess.

After the elevator dropped her one floor down, she walked straight to her office. Hearing her approach, her assistant Andy glanced up to see if she needed anything. "Hold my calls," she told him.

She went straight to her desk and checked her email. She simply didn't want to deal with what needed doing. Instead, she went online and raced through the headlines on different news websites, as if the answer to her problems might be embedded there.

I need a moment, she told herself. *I just need a moment.*

A memory from Chris's initial interview passed through her mind. Someone had questioned his feelings regarding long hours. His answer had been something to the effect of, "I'm not exaggerating, I love working all the time. I know exactly what I'm getting into, and I'm choosing to do it." He'd stopped for a beat, looked at each of his interrogators. "I'm choosing to do this work."

The answer may have been out-and-out bullshit, but Elizabeth remembered being impressed by his composure. She remembered thinking at the time, *Well, he's a decent actor.* Now, sitting at her desk, all she could do was shake her head.

Interrupting her reverie, Andy knocked softly on the door and poked his head in.

"I have Jimmy Hipps on the phone," he said.

"I said, hold my calls."

"He says, 'Code red emergency.'"

"Jesus Christ," she said. She touched her hairline on her forehead. "Thank you, Andy."

She picked up the phone. "Code red?" she said. "What is code red?"

"New story coming out," said Jimmy. "I just got a call from a reporter at *Bloomberg*. More emails."

"What emails?" asked Elizabeth.

"Hold on, we're trying to match the quote to the exact document, but I believe they come from discovery group D28, or D30, whatever batch, it's about the"—here, absurdly, he dropped his voice, as though that might shield it from a wiretap—"it's about the bond-fixing stuff."

"Who's writing it?"

"Becca Greenfield. She says the emails were sent to her anonymously. For what it's worth, I know her and I trust her."

"Meaning what?" asked Elizabeth.

"Meaning I believe her when she says it was an anonymous tip."

"How long is she giving us to respond?"

"End of the day, but the story's running tomorrow with or without comment."

"And what's Ted say?"

"Ted and Leo are in D.C. We're trying to have a meeting in our office in half an hour. We're going to phone them in. Can you possibly come here and join?"

Elizabeth closed her eyes, breathed in deeply. "Yes," she said.

"Can you bring your Scott, Sarah, and Vishal?"

"Yes," she said. "Jimmy, listen to me. When you talk to this reporter again, you have to try to make your voice sound like you're not having a fucking nervous breakdown. Pretend you're bored."

"That's what I did."

"I can hear your heart in your throat. I can practically smell how scared you are. You have to calm down. Pretend it's all boring."

"I will," he said.

When the call ended, Elizabeth sat at her desk for a moment and studied her nails. She felt a strange sense of calm. Her mind had become perfectly focused. Funny way to stop a panic attack, she thought.

She dialed her assistant and asked him to come in. When he did, she told him to summon Scott, Sarah, and Vishal. She said to tell them they had an urgent meeting at Calcott in half an hour, and that they'd go there together in fifteen minutes.

Then she looked at her clock and told Andy to gather all the partners for a meeting at 4:15 p.m. Andy nodded and jotted down her instructions. She thanked him, and he left.

She picked up her desk phone and dialed Valencia.

"Chris Cowley committed suicide," she said when Valencia answered.

"What?" asked Valencia, sounding alarmed. "How?"

"We think pills. Michael went there this morning. He found him. He took pictures."

"Tell him to send me the pictures."

"For what?"

"I want to see them."

"Okay," said Elizabeth.

"You all right?" asked Valencia.

"Strangely, I am."

"Do you want me to come over?" asked Valencia.

"You won't believe this. That's only part one," said Elizabeth. "Part two is that another story is about to come out. A reporter at *Bloomberg* got some kind of anonymous tip email bullshit that apparently includes part of the material from Chris's phone. This kid is everywhere. Who would have imagined—Chris Cowley."

"Jesus," said Valencia. "Why would he do that?"

"We're headed to the Calcott office for an emergency meeting."

"Case is turning into a real doozy," said Valencia.

"It certainly is."

"You'll let me know what you need," said Valencia.

"Of course," said Elizabeth.

"What a nightmare," said Valencia. "If I were you, I'd tell the in-house over there to find a way out. Fucking settle this thing, drop it, withdraw it, whatever. It's messy, it's a reputation destroyer, and it's going to spread. Nobody is going to win."

Elizabeth sat there for a moment with her mouth slightly open. Valencia's speech seemed inappropriate, but at first she didn't say anything; then she just agreed. "I know."

After they ended their call, Elizabeth sat staring at her desk. The case did need to go away. They needed to find a way to stand down. It was rotten to the core. It needed to be put out of its misery. It needed to be withdrawn.

Right then Scott Driscoll came into her office. "What's happening? Is Calcott going to fire us?"

"Something like that," said Liz. "There is a new story coming out. *Bloomberg*, bond-rigging emails." She stepped to her mirror and fixed her hair.

Then she put on a fresh coat of lipstick. "Where the hell are Vishal and Sarah?" she asked. "We gotta get this show on the road."

"They're coming," said Scott.

When she finished putting on her lipstick, she told him that Chris Cowley had killed himself.

"What?" said Scott.

* * *

Later that night Valencia sat in her kitchen looking at the pictures that Michael D'Angelo had texted her. He only sent four images. One was of the note, one was the empty prescription bottle, and two showed the orientation of Chris's body from about fifteen feet away.

None of it looked right.

The first thing she noticed was that the handwriting on the note looked too large. It took up almost 40 percent of the page. It wasn't conclusive, it wasn't evidence, it just looked off. She closed her eyes and tried to picture how a real note from Chris would be written. The handwriting would be measured. He would write carefully. He'd want to exhibit how in control he was. Look at the way he dressed. Look how he carried himself. The man was neat.

This note had been scrawled, as though penned by a serial killer or a lovelorn teen. Or, thought Valencia, like a man under duress.

The shoes caught her attention too. They were laid out at the end of the couch. It looked composed. It looked set up. Her gut told her it was wrong. She could picture Redgrave setting them there. Making a little art exhibit of his work.

She looked at the pictures of Chris's body. He was still wearing his tie. Would he come home after being fired and not take off his tie? Would he choose to commit suicide in the uniform he'd been wearing when he'd been fired? She didn't think so. He'd probably put on that leather jacket he wore in the video. Something that he'd want to be remembered in.

Hanging over all these speculations, shaping them, of course, was Redgrave. He'd just told Valencia that Chris was not a worry anymore. What did he say? Not a worry anymore? Debriefed him earlier? He's free and clear? The message he was sending couldn't have been more clear.

She put her hands over her eyes and thought about it. She could see the whole thing. The pickpocketing had been a smoke screen. The stolen documents, the park, the Chinese guy, the Africans, Avi Lessing, Chris Cowley, the Rabinowitz family—even she, herself—all of it had been arranged to provide cover for Colonel Pollock's group.

Eventually someone—whether it was the FBI, the SEC, or Congress—would look into this. What they would find would be stolen documents, an untraceable Chinese man, Russian gangsters, bribery, and a payout of $750,000.

It wasn't hard to imagine what Colonel Pollock wanted. He wanted the case to go away. He wanted, as Redgrave put it, "for everyone to just stand down." Valencia almost had to smile. It was exactly what Elizabeth wanted too.

Right then, her phone rang. She felt sure it would be Elizabeth. Instead, the caller ID showed Utah Sandemose's name. She hadn't been expecting a call from him. She took a second to get into character and answered. "You calling to ask me out on that dinner date?"

"Not quite, although that does sound more tantalizing than what I've got planned," said Utah. "How busy are you?"

Valencia looked at her wine, wondered what he was going to ask her. "That depends," she said.

"Well, I tell you—you made quite the impression on our little Russian friend."

"Is that right?"

"He liked you."

"Well it always feels good to hear something like that," said Valencia, intentionally mimicking Utah's speech pattern. She closed her eyes and pretended to be him. She adjusted her body to stand like him. "I was impressed with him, too, he was a fine fella." She had considered adding a *bless his heart*, at the end of the sentence, but that seemed like too much.

"He wants to see you."

"Oh, my," said Valencia, moving from her kitchen toward the living room. "I've already taken off my dinner dress and put on my house slippers," she lied. "I was just settling in."

"Says he wants to give something back to you. I have no idea what the hell you two are up to, and I don't want to know, but he says all this is good news, whatever the hell that means. Same place—Uzbekistan," said Utah. "You got the stuffed cabbage last time?"

"I did," she lied. "It was, quite simply, the best I've ever had."

"I told you."

"You did, indeed," said Valencia, stepping back to the kitchen. Pinning the phone to her ear with her shoulder, she carefully poured her glass of wine back into the bottle. "What time does he want to meet?"

"He's already there," said Utah. "Says whatever time works for you."

She pictured Utah standing there with Mr. Rabinowitz right then. "You sure you don't want to join us?"

"Shit, I'm gonna have to sit this one out, but I will take a rain check on our one-on-one."

After hanging up, Valencia texted Milton Frazier: *Our friend just asked for another meeting. I'm going back to that same place, just FYI.* She was perfectly aware that Redgrave would have someone monitoring her phone calls and texts. It didn't matter. She wasn't doing anything out of line.

A moment later, Milton texted back: *I'll take you.*

She responded: *Sit tight, it's a friendly call.*

In the bathroom, she looked in the mirror, brushed her hair, and searched her face for any imperfections. After peeing, she changed into a different pantsuit, a black one, soft and velvety. Then she dotted a tiny bit of perfume on her finger, touched the finger to her wrist, rubbed her wrists together, smelled them, and then touched the wrists, one at a time, to the sides of her neck.

Riding down in the elevator, she thought about all the times she'd been called out for emergency night meetings. It made her feel strangely gleeful. On the street, she waited for a taxi. When it came, she got in, gave the driver the cross streets, closed her eyes, and started getting herself in the right headspace.

She pictured Yakov Rabinowitz. *I want to help you*, she thought. She'd found that approaching these meetings with a desire to help rather than a desire to win got better results. *I really want to help you.*

The driver made his way down the west side of the park. Valencia stared at the dark trees on her left. She looked at the joggers running by, and she brushed her eyebrows with her fingertips. When the driver turned toward Columbus Avenue, he put the radio on and hummed along to a pop song.

A few weeks earlier she'd received an odd phone call from an ex-colleague from the Agency, Spencer Newman. She thought about that call now.

Spencer, like Valencia, had left the CIA about eight years ago and joined a law practice in D.C. They remained friendly, and occasionally had turned to each other for advice. During the call, he asked if they could meet in two days. At the time, her brain and body had offered no misgivings. Simply put, her intuitions failed her. She said yes.

Spencer told her to meet him in Central Park at the Heckscher softball field. He told her to sit behind home plate at field number five, that he'd find her there.

At the time, Valencia wondered why—if he was taking all these precautions—would he even talk about it on the phone? But she didn't say anything.

When the time came, she went to the field. It had been raining that day, which added to the sensationalism of it all. It felt like the good old days. She sat behind home plate, hiding under her umbrella, checking her email on her phone, and tried not to become grumpy at the rain.

When Spencer arrived, she knew almost immediately that something was off. He greeted her in a friendly way, but he seemed jittery.

He scanned the area while he spoke, kept his shoulders tense, and avoided her eyes. It didn't take him long to get to the point. "Remember Colonel Pollock?"

"From"—she wracked her memory—"Soft Music?"

"That's right."

Colonel Pollock had run a joint task force between the CIA and the Department of Defense that used Pentagon money to fund and arm Sunni Awakening Councils in Iraq. It was a highly sensitive operation. Valencia hadn't been involved, but she remembered Colonel Pollock gaining a reputation at the time as something of a wild card. Since then, Valencia had heard rumors here and there. Her understanding was that Pollock was still deployed in the Arabian Peninsula.

"He's in charge of a new group," said Spencer.

"Pollock?"

"N14, officially DOD—totally off the books."

Valencia studied Spencer's face. He was nervous, but there was something vacant in his affect, like a man who hadn't slept in days. "Never heard of it," she said, confused where this could possibly be going.

"They want to meet," said Spencer. "They have a job for you."

"I don't think they can afford me," Valencia said in earnest.

Spencer's eyes appeared to moisten. "They can afford you," he said. "It's a simple job, but they want you."

"What is it?"

"They didn't tell me. They asked for an introduction. I said, you know"—he sounded like he was reading from a script—"I wanted to check with you."

Valencia watched his face while he spoke. She noticed a slight tic in the muscle above his eye. The man was definitely lying. She should have refused right then. In retrospect, it was a staggering lapse of judgment. Instead, she asked when they wanted to meet.

"Right now," he said.

Curious about what they could want with her, and slightly flattered that the army would think of her, she agreed to meet. Spencer walked her deeper into the park.

After a few minutes, he pointed at a man, seated on a bench with his back to them. "That's him," he said. "He goes by Redgrave."

"Redgrave?"

Spencer whispered, "The guy is weird. You'll see. Not typical Army."

"You're not going to come with me?"

"They want to talk to you alone."

Valencia grabbed his arm, pulled him toward the bench. "Come on, this is ridiculous," she said, trying to lighten the mood by smiling—as if he were being silly.

"I'm sorry, I can't," said Spencer, twisting his arm free. "Call me next time you're in D.C." With that, he walked away.

Valencia turned her attention to the man on the bench. His back was to her, and she assumed she was unobserved. She began walking toward him. When she got within twenty feet, he stood and stepped to the side, so the bench wasn't between them. He wore a navy blue ski jacket: a boring thing to be wearing, she thought. He dressed like an Upper West Side dad. His pants appeared to be soaked. He lowered his hood and waved shyly, like a man on a blind date.

"I've wanted to meet you for a long time," he said, smiling, walking toward her, and holding out his hand. "Redgrave, Jonathan Redgrave."

He was an ugly man: pitted skin, thin hair, close-set eyes, but he moved with confidence. Valencia said, "Nice to meet you."

They shook hands, and he moved her toward the bench. They sat facing a meadow and for a few minutes he carried on about work she'd done for the Clandestine Services. He mentioned specific assignments she'd been involved in, secret assignments, some that were never put on paper. She took this as a kind of credential-proving, and she stared out at the green grass while he spoke, nodded vaguely when he looked at her, and wondered just how big of a mistake she'd made in accepting this meeting.

It had stopped raining. They both sat in silence for a moment, and then, after shifting on the bench to face her more directly, he brought up what he wanted. "Carlyle, Driscoll, Hathaway," he said.

Valencia didn't say anything.

"They work for the Calcott Corporation," he added. "Calcott is in the midst of a civil suit against Emerson Trust Bank."

Valencia told him she was aware of the case, and that she read the newspapers. He smiled at that, dropped his head to the side. "National security," he said. They sat in silence for a moment. "The case has been deemed a threat to the security of the United States. It needs to come to an end."

"Deemed by who?"

"Colonel Pollock."

Valencia explained that she didn't work for Carlyle, Driscoll, Hathaway, that she certainly didn't choose what cases they worked on, or how they were handled—and that she was only occasionally called by them to take care of thorny situations.

"Well, this is as thorny as it gets," he said. "The case is getting into some uncomfortable—"

She interrupted him, "I'm sorry, with all due respect, I actually don't want to hear any of this," she said.

"Colonel Pollock needs a friend on the inside, someone close to Elizabeth—"

"I don't work for Carlyle, Driscoll, Hathaway," she said. "And I don't work for Colonel Pollock. I don't work for Langley." She looked at him and wondered whether he might be mentally unstable. "I'm sorry."

"Elizabeth Carlyle is going to call on you. You'll do what she asks you." He stopped her from protesting by raising a hand. "After that, you will politely suggest that Calcott withdraw their side of the case. That's it. It's simple. Two steps. Clean as a whistle."

Valencia's mind spun out a few quick calculations about the risk of simply refusing, thanking him for his time, and walking away. The risk wasn't minimal.

Still, she said, "I'm sorry, I won't be able to help you on this one."

She started to get up, but Redgrave put his hand above her waist—he didn't make contact, but the gesture stopped her progress. "We're already fully operational," he said. "At this point, you gotta ask yourself if it's safer inside or out." He moved his hand away from her waist.

She turned her gaze back to the field in front of them. The man had just threatened her. It was absolutely breathtaking; it was unprecedented. She sat there blinking for a moment, searching her mind for the appropriate party to report this to.

He wasn't done. "Think what Demet would do."

Demet Harmanci was one of Valencia's oldest friends. They'd been roommates in college. They'd just spoken on the phone that morning.

"Think what Amanda Bautista would do," he said, raising his eyebrows.

Valencia had just returned an email to Amanda. She'd done it while she was waiting for Spencer to join her in the park.

You are fucking insane, she thought. *Who the fuck do you think you are?* She shifted on the bench so she could look directly into his face. *You want to start a war with me*, she thought. *You want to start an unprovoked war with me? Do you have any idea who I am?*

"Don't worry, you'll be paid," he said. He rubbed his eyes and pretended to make some kind of mental calculation. "Three hundred and forty thousand. It's already budgeted. Bill them whatever you want. We'll pay you on top—Bitcoin." He held his hand out. "Are we good?"

In the space of a single breath cycle she concluded that any pushback would have to come later. Refusing right there wouldn't be the best move. First, she'd have to fully assess the situation. She wasn't in a place to make a rash decision. Her heart was beating like she was in the middle of an actual physical fight.

She swallowed her anger, reached out, and took his clammy hand in her own. "Yeah we're good," she said. She smiled warmly and they shook. "If that's the extent of it, we're good."

Her memory from the park was interrupted by the taxi driver asking if he should drop her on the corner. "You want?" he asked, looking in the mirror.

"Can you loop around, please? Pass by once." She pointed toward Thirty-Sixth Street. "Loop back over to Eighth Avenue and pass it again."

When they drove past the restaurant, she saw that butcher paper still covered the windows, and that they again weren't open.

"Keep going," she said, pointing down the block. Nothing else caught her attention; still, she questioned her judgment in not having Milton drive her. She told the driver to cross Ninth Avenue.

After paying and getting out, she took a moment and looked at the sky. There were no stars visible, but the moon was above her and it looked about three-quarters full. She took a deep breath and started walking toward her meeting.

Inside the restaurant, at the same table as before, Yakov Rabinowitz sat reflecting on the state of his own mental condition. What the hell was wrong with him? It boggled the mind to think he'd given the green light for this incredibly stupid plan. Was his brain softening? Was he becoming senile?

He frowned at the thought, and then checked the time on his cell phone. The lawyer had sworn the woman would come—where the hell was she? He glanced at Grigory Levchin, who sat across from him.

Newark—thought Yakov, squeezing his eyes closed—*to put Newark at risk! And for what? For the boys to run some kind of prank? What would Vadim Vertov say if he found out about this? My God, am I losing my mind?*

His thoughts jumped back to the locksmith. *Ossip dead! Because of this! Because of me!* A memory of Ossip back in Russia, drunkenly standing on a table, passed through his mind. It must have been forty years ago.

I'm sorry old friend, thought Yakov. *It was not supposed to end like this.*

Right then, the proprietor of the restaurant appeared in the doorway. "*She's here*," he said in Russian, rubbing his hands together in front of his chest. The silence of the place seemed to make him nervous.

"*Bring her*," said Yakov, speaking to Grigory. The large man stood and walked toward the front. "*Ask for her phone. Leave it in front.*" Left alone in the back room, Yakov rubbed his nostrils, dug his finger into his ear, and brushed at his face with his hands.

A moment later, Valencia entered the room with Grigory. Yakov stood as she walked toward the table. She looked prettier than he'd remembered, more glamorous. She was perfect. Her black velvet triggered a wave of nostalgia. Yakov signaled to Grigory to leave them alone.

"I wasn't expecting a call from you tonight," said Valencia.

He felt himself squint at her English, ran a few test responses through his mind, and came out with, "Are you hungry?"

He didn't know if he should offer to kiss her cheek or shake her hand. Finally—awkwardly—he decided to pull her chair out from the table. He felt like a teenager again. *Even as an old man*, he thought. *Even still, to this day.*

He smelled perfume in the air. "Vodka, whiskey, wine, vermouth?" he asked.

"Are we celebrating?"

Yakov sat down in the seat next to her. "Not celebrating . . ." He searched his mind for the right phrase. "My lawyer . . ."

He stopped speaking and tried to arrange what he wanted to say, but his thoughts were not easily corralled. "I want to tell you, before anything else: the *Wall Street Journal* story—not us. We have nothing to do with that."

He molded his face into a look that he hoped conveyed concern. "I want to be clear." He shook his head and put his hands on the table in front of him. He watched the woman's eyes narrow.

"You could have called and told me that," she said.

Yakov put his hand to his chest. "I want to apologize for everything that happened."

"You're so sweet," she said, but her face remained impassive. "Apologies are good."

"This should have never happened," he said.

In his mind, Yakov saw his boss, Vadim Vertov, the man who truly ran the business in Newark. He looked away from the table for a moment, let his eyes settle on a painting of a beach. Then, quietly, like he was telling a secret, said, "We're returning the money."

With her raised eyebrows and dropped chin, she looked genuinely taken aback. "Well, Mr. Rabinowitz, I don't know what to say to that," she said. "I'm at a loss for words. I really am."

Yakov considered telling her the money had been stolen and that he was paying it back from his own pocket. Instead, he asked, "But it makes you happy?"

"It will make my clients happy, which always makes me happy."

A weight lifted; Yakov smiled. "People do such stupid things," he said. His relief was such that he felt for a moment like standing up and dancing. "Cheers." He lifted his glass. "People do crazy things."

"Indeed, they do."

"I always say the easiest path is the one you should take. Fix things if you can. Don't be stubborn." The vodka was making him feel poetic. He breathed in deeply, thought about saying something more, but stopped himself again.

"I think I like you," she said. "I felt it the first time we met. I said to myself, 'I like this man, he's a man who thinks like me. He sees the world like I do.'"

There was something charming about the way she spoke, and Yakov found himself nodding along.

He poured another glass and they drank. "The money's in the kitchen," he said, waving his hand in that direction.

The woman seemed to study him for a moment. "Everything will be okay," she said.

Yakov thought of his friend Ossip, and his eyes filled with tears. "So many problems," he said, shaking his head. "The best we can hope for nowadays is friendship, family, and quiet times." He worried he was babbling and frowned into his empty glass.

"I feel the same way," she said. When he looked up he saw that her face had become serious. "Sometimes you meet someone, and it feels like you've known them for a long time."

"Are you Jewish?" asked Yakov.

"No, but I feel like I am."

"I feel like you are too."

Valencia reached out, grabbed the bottle, and filled their glasses again. "May I propose a toast?"

"Please," said Yakov.

"No matter what happens down the road, I want to propose that I will help you, and you will help me. We'll be friends. Can we toast to that?"

"It would be my honor," said Yakov, raising his glass.

The next morning Valencia woke with a hangover. Her mind went immediately to the night before. At some point, the owner of the restaurant had come out with a bottle of expensive scotch; soon, both he and Rabinowitz's bodyguard had joined them at the table. They drank many rounds.

By the end of the night Grigory Levchin was reciting poetry from memory, and Rabinowitz was translating and dabbing his eyes with his napkin. After their final drink, Rabinowitz offered her a ride home.

When she refused, he insisted on personally hailing her taxi. Once she was settled in the cab, he put the bag of money on her lap. She remembered him leaning in and kissing her cheek. He tried to pay the cabbie, but she waved him off. It had been one of those nights.

As soon as the cab turned onto Tenth Avenue, Valencia—setting wheels in motion—sent a coded text message to Billy Sharrock: *Good morning Billy, I have a meeting at Horowitz Barnes tomorrow at 9:00 am, so we'll have to reschedule lunch.*

He responded a moment later: *Sounds good.*

When she got home, drunk, and humming a tune, she deposited the $750,000 into the safe in her office.

In the morning, after taking four painkillers and putting coffee on, Valencia grabbed a garment bag out of the far left-hand side of her closet. The bag held a blue pantsuit, a white shirt, a khaki trench coat, and a paisley silk scarf. Underneath were a pair of black suede flats. She checked the pocket of the trench coat and confirmed her sunglasses were in it.

At 8:35 a.m., dressed in that outfit and carrying a small tote bag, she took the elevator down to the ground floor. She stopped and made small talk with the doorman for exactly one minute and twelve seconds. Then, she stepped outside and waved down the first taxi that appeared.

Sitting in the back of the cab, squeezed down on the floor like a stowaway, was Sonya Radovani—Billy Sharrock's girlfriend. She was dressed in the exact same clothes as Valencia and wore a brown wig that had been specially made in Valencia's image. She wasn't wearing the sunglasses, but she had them in her hand. The driver of the taxi was Nawaz Khan, a real cabbie they paid for jobs like this. He'd make $2,500 for an hour's work. Sonya was more expensive; she'd get $6,500.

After Valencia told the cabbie the address of Horowitz Barnes—a law firm she worked with—the cab started moving. Valencia put her hand on Sonya's back and gave it a reassuring rub. Sonya turned her head, looked up, and made two silent kisses at her. Valencia then took her phone out and called Milton, and for the purposes of appearing normal to listening ears, she started a mundane conversation about some business matters.

The driver made his way through Central Park toward the east side. While they rode, Valencia kept talking to Milton. As they approached the first tunnel, Valencia patted Sonya three times on the back. When they passed under the tunnel, Valencia popped down to the floor, and Sonya popped up.

Valencia—finding Sonya's hand and giving it a squeeze—kept the phone conversation going from the floor. After ending her call with Milton, she handed her phone to Sonya. The cab bumped along. Then she passed her wallet up.

Sonya meanwhile slipped Valencia a large manila envelope that Billy had given her. After that, Sonya, as she'd been instructed, opened the browser on Valencia's iPhone and began reading a story from the *New York Times*. If anyone was monitoring the phone's activity, all would appear normal.

Horowitz Barnes was on Lexington Avenue, not far from CDH's offices. When they arrived there the cab stopped and Sonya used one of Valencia's credit cards to pay. It wasn't cold enough to justify wrapping the scarf over her head, but with sunglasses on, she got out and entered the building. At the front desk, she announced herself as Valencia Walker and said she had a 9 a.m. meeting with Lynn Duggins.

She gave the security guard Valencia's driver's license and he swiped it on an ID scanner.

Lynn Duggins, a lawyer at Horowitz Barnes, had no idea what was going on. But she'd been prepped for this type of scenario. Billy had alerted her that same morning by calling to confirm Valencia's meeting.

When Sonya arrived on the twenty-third floor, the lawyer was waiting for her. Playing her role, Lynn said, "Good morning Ms. Walker," and accompanied Sonya to a reserved meeting room, usually used by interns, in the back of the office.

Before entering the room, she asked for Sonya's coat, which held Valencia's phone. There would be no listening in to this meeting.

Sonya accepted Lynn's offer of coffee and then was left alone in the small conference room. She sat with her back to the door, pulled out her Anne McCaffrey novel, and began reading.

In the taxi, Nawaz Khan, ignoring a man waving at him, looped over to Third Avenue and made his way through traffic toward Forty-Second Street. On the floor of the cab, Valencia opened her tote, pulled out a black wig and a hooded black nylon jacket. She pulled her trench coat and suit jacket off, folded them together, and stuffed them into the tote. She left the tote on the floor, she'd collect it later from the driver. Then she put on the jacket. After that, she pulled on the wig and set it right. It was awkward changing down there, and she was slightly out of breath when she finished.

As the cab approached Grand Central, Nawaz Khan, in order to alert Valencia, began whistling a tune. As soon as they were under the Park Avenue Viaduct, he stopped the cab. Neither drone, nor satellite would see Valencia exit the taxi and enter Grand Central. Six months had passed since Valencia, Nawaz, and Sonya had practiced these maneuvers. Still, everything ran smoothly.

She swiped her way in with a card that had been purchased with cash. Then, blending in with the crowd, she walked straight to the downtown-bound 6 train platform. It occurred to her that it was the same train the pickpocket had taken. She only had to wait a minute.

During that time fourteen people joined her on the platform from the same direction she'd come. None of them looked like Redgrave's men, but she couldn't be certain. All she could do was take note of them. As the train rolled into the station, she felt her stomach cramp with nervousness.

Inside the train, advertisements for online dating services were plastered all over the car. Despairing-faced passengers sat in their seats with their eyes either closed or on their phones. Valencia checked her reflection in the window and pushed her wig back half an inch.

She got off at Fourteenth Street and spent the next hour getting on and off trains, leaving stations, and running countersurveillance moves. Finally, at Queensboro Plaza, convinced she wasn't under human surveillance, she jumped on a downtown-bound N train and returned to the city.

The car was still crowded with late-morning commuters; she eased her way to the front of it so she could watch all the passengers. Two of the three that boarded in Queens were African American women: Valencia felt fairly confident they weren't with Redgrave. The third was a bespectacled older white man; he looked eccentric, and he got off two stops later.

During the ride from Queens through Manhattan, she thought about what she was about to do. She'd never ordered a hit before. During her time abroad, she'd been involved in plenty of operations where people were killed, but she'd never given the order herself. She noticed that she wasn't particularly bothered by the prospect, at least not overly so. It simply had to be done.

She rode all the way to the Kings Highway stop in South Brooklyn. After getting off the train, she took a moment to look at the blue sky, then fussed with her bag until she was sure she'd be the last person walking down the stairs. The MTA attendant in his glass booth was the only person who watched her leave.

Outside a black car sat waiting for fares. After approaching it and exchanging thumbs-up signs, she opened the door and got in. The car smelled, not unpleasantly, like cocoa butter. The driver, an older Jamaican man, asked her where she wanted to go.

"Can you please take me to 2783 East Sixty-Sixth Street—Mill Basin," she said.

"Sixty-Sixth, out there in Mill Basin?" he asked, with his accent.

"Yes, sir."

They made their way east on Kings Highway, passing beauty salons, hardware stores, Chinese barbecue places, perfumeries, jewelers, and pharmacies. As they went, Valencia turned in her seat and looked out the back window. All that she saw was a bus. Nobody appeared to be following her.

She then pulled out the manila envelope and checked it one more time. It was all the information that Danny Tsui had found regarding Jack Glasser. There was a bio pulled from the Prexius Solar Solutions website that showed a picture of Jack Glasser—unquestionably the same man as Jonathan Redgrave. The photo showed him smiling; he wore on oxford shirt. His bio stated that he had received his master's degree from Stanford and earned his PhD from the University of Texas.

It said he'd worked for eight years at a firm in Boston and six years in China. It didn't mention anything about the army or the Department of Defense. The rest of the paperwork was database material for the half dozen John and Jack Glassers in New York, New Jersey, and Connecticut. That's all Danny could find. Valencia put the papers back in the envelope and placed the envelope back in the bag.

After a few minutes of riding in silence, the driver—apropos of nothing—said, "It's my birthday today."

"Seventy-one years old."

"You don't look a day over fifty," she said.

He squinted in the rearview. "I drink my water and eat my greens."

They rode in silence for the rest of the way. When the driver stopped in front of the address, she asked how much.

"Ten dollars," he said, looking like he was ashamed to ask for anything.

Valencia dug money out of her pants pocket, pulled off two twenties and passed them forward. "Keep the change," she said. "Happy birthday."

She let the car drive away and then turned and walked eight doors down to the actual address. During the walk, she pulled off the wig, brushed her hair with her hand, and then stuffed the wig into the pocket of her jacket. The house was larger than she imagined, almost a mansion. The metal gate surrounding the driveway had been left open, and Valencia couldn't help interpreting that as a good sign.

There was a black Mercedes SUV parked in the driveway. The blinds in all of the first-floor windows had been drawn. Valencia walked up the driveway and headed toward the door. When she pressed the doorbell, a series of low gongs sounded. She took a final deep breath.

After a few seconds she heard the sounds of locks being turned, and then she watched as the door opened. An older, Filipina-looking woman stood at the threshold with a questioning look on her face.

Valencia smiled. "Is Mr. Rabinowitz in?"

The woman's eyes went up and down Valencia, like she was wearing something scandalous. She made a face like she was upset, and then called out behind her, "Maestro, a woman here to see you."

Valencia leaned forward so she could peer into the doorway, just as Yakov Rabinowitz came walking toward her. He was drying his hands on a towel and squinting at the light. He had a suspicious look on his face. When he saw it was Valencia calling, he smiled widely.

270

After exchanging greetings, and still standing at the door, Yakov asked her what she was doing.

"I'm sorry to drop by unannounced," said Valencia. "But I have to return what you gave me. I'll have one of my assistants bring it to you."

Yakov Rabinowitz looked over her shoulder at the street behind her, confirming she was alone. "Come in," he said.

She stepped past him.

As they walked down the hallway, Valencia reached into her tote bag and pulled out the manila envelope with the Jack Glasser bio. "There is something I need to talk to you about, though" she said.

That same afternoon, Elizabeth Carlyle was in the middle of reviewing a colleague's motion to enforce judgment when Scott Driscoll marched into her office. "Look at this," he said, holding his iPhone out to her.

She pushed herself back from her desk, took the phone out of his hand, held it at a readable distance, and saw a story on CNN's website. The headline read "Emerson Trust Bank's Unseemly Swaps." She skimmed through to the second paragraph: *Recently leaked discovery from the civil suit shows that Emerson Trust Bank has been engaging in a practice of sham defaults, bringing back memories of the 2008 financial crisis.*

"Are we in this?" she asked.

"Only in relation to the lawsuit," said Scott.

"Jesus," said Elizabeth.

"Yeah," said Scott. "Mutual and total destruction."

Elizabeth's intercom sounded. "I have Jimmy Hipps on line one," said her assistant.

Elizabeth picked up her phone, pressed the button for line one, and turned her eyes to Scott. "Hi, Jimmy," she said.

"There is an article on CNN's—"

"I'm reading it right now," said Elizabeth.

"It's worse than ours. Sandoval's gonna have a stroke," he said, referring to the judge.

"Jimmy, I have Scott in my office," she said. "I'm going to put you on speaker."

"Scotty, how are you?" asked Jimmy Hipps.

"I'm fine, but this is not good."

"What hurts my enemies—"

"No, Jimmy, please, listen," said Elizabeth, interrupting him, and motioning for Scott to shut his mouth. "Jimmy, all roads lead back to the same place, and none of it is good. You guys were doing the same shit. This is an industry-wide problem. Tell Nathan and all of them to be expecting calls. Listen to me. This is the script: 'We are in the middle of a lawsuit and we've been instructed by the judge not to comment.' That's it."

"Is this from your kid's phone?" asked Jimmy Hipps. She'd told Jimmy about Chris's suicide during a call the previous night.

"Hold on a second," said Elizabeth. She jabbed the mute button, looked at Scott. "This Emerson stuff wasn't on Chris's phone, was it?"

"I don't think so," said Scott.

"Call Sujung, ask her, and tell her to join us." She unmuted the phone. "Sorry Jimmy—we are checking on that, but we don't initially think so."

"We got a ship that's leaking from top to bottom," said Jimmy Hipps.

Elizabeth looked at Scott, who was speaking to Sujung on the phone. Scott covered his phone and said, "She says, no."

"None of this was on Chris's phone," said Elizabeth.

"Judge is gonna say this is retaliation for the *Bloomberg* story," said Jimmy Hipps.

"Yeah, well, it isn't, so he can say whatever the fuck he wants," said Elizabeth.

"I'm sorry?" said Jimmy Hipps.

"I said, it isn't, so he can say whatever he wants."

Right then Sujung Kim came into the room. She was out of breath and looked frightened.

Elizabeth's cell phone buzzed. She picked it up and saw Ben Alden—another in-house counsel from Calcott—was calling. She texted him: *Talking to Jimmy, call you right back*, and hit send.

Elizabeth couldn't help but smile. "Ben's calling on my other line," she said into the phone.

"Jesus, I'll get him in here," said Jimmy Hipps. They listened while he yelled at his secretary to get Ben Alden into his office.

"Chris Cowley only had D1 through D44, E, M, MM, and part of Q on his phone," said Sujung, reading from a notepad. Elizabeth noticed a dark area around the woman's armpits. She made a mental note to tell her to get them botoxed.

"Jimmy, why don't you call us back when Ben joins you?"

"Okay, two minutes," said Jimmy Hipps.

Elizabeth hung up, looked at Scott, shook her head, and said, "I'd like to see how they're taking this over at Emerson."

"Welcome to the jungle," said Scott.

"Tell me about it," said Elizabeth.

Later that same evening, Valencia joined Elizabeth at a French restaurant in Midtown.

"Madame is waiting for you," said the maître d'.

Valencia followed him into the place and saw Elizabeth seated near a window, texting on her phone. The restaurant was only half full, the lights were dim, and it smelled like butter.

"Sorry I'm late," said Valencia, touching Elizabeth's shoulder and gliding toward her seat.

"I ordered wine," said Elizabeth.

Valencia sat down and studied Elizabeth's face. "Look at you," she said. "Unflappable."

"When things are at their worst," said Elizabeth. She poured Valencia some Bordeaux and then refilled her own glass. "Cheers."

They touched glasses and Valencia made a show of smelling the wine and tasting it carefully. She puckered her lips, shook out her napkin, and placed it on her lap. She looked outside the window, noticed a white van parked across the street, and memorized the plate.

"You saw the CNN thing?" asked Elizabeth.

"I did," said Valencia.

"You know," said Elizabeth, dropping her head to one side, "I never asked you if anybody ever approached you about this case."

Valencia felt her autonomic nervous system kick on, a small army of nerves being summoned to battle. "Anybody like . . . ?" She squinted.

"Anybody like anyone from the press, or you know, how do I say this?" Elizabeth pretended to think. "Interested parties."

"You know I'd tell you if anybody did that."

Elizabeth, who had seemed buzzed, now appeared suddenly sober. "I know you would, but I never asked," she said.

"Well, in that case, the answer is still, no."

"Enemies on all sides," said Elizabeth. "Within and without."

"So, what're you going to do?"

"With what?"

"With the case," said Valencia.

"Prepare for war." She made a face and peered over Valencia's shoulder, searching for a waiter.

Valencia looked at her glassy-eyed friend and smiled. "Don't you wish it would just go away?" she asked.

"No," said Elizabeth. "I'm just getting warmed up." She shifted in her seat. "They can smell desperation."

"Who?" asked Valencia.

"Everyone. So, no, I don't want this case to go away—not ever. I want it to go on and on, and I want it to go to trial, and I want to take it to a jury, and I want the jury to say that we won, that we are the best, and then I want to get a very large bonus at the end of the year."

Valencia leaned forward, looked her dead in the eyes, and whispered, "It just seems like this might be one where it would be better if everybody would just stand down. Just walk away. It feels like this might be bigger than Calcott"—she paused for a moment, searched her mind—"and Emerson."

Elizabeth squinted like an act of treason had occurred. Someone in the kitchen dropped a platter.

Someone outside honked. "You're a naughty girl, aren't you?" Elizabeth said.

Valencia smiled, leaned back. "What are you going to order?"

"The rib-eye, rare."

"Me too," said Valencia.

Elizabeth filled their glasses. "To Chris Cowley," she said. They clinked glasses. Elizabeth kept hers raised, so Valencia did too. "He was—rest his soul—an obnoxious kid. But he was a kid. He should never have died over any of this."

It almost seemed that Elizabeth was accusing her of something. They drank, and Valencia shook her head and looked outside the window and saw an older man, dressed normally, carrying on and talking to himself like a schizophrenic.

She looked back at Elizabeth. "It's horrible," she said. For a moment Redgrave came into her mind; she saw his face, and in her mind all the veins in his face became blue and visible and she could see a road map running across his cheeks and forehead and chin. "Horrible," she said, again, shaking her head.

The waiter came, and they ordered their steaks.

Six days later, on a Tuesday, Elizabeth Carlyle and her team appeared with their opposing counsel in court. Both sides submitted motions whereby the Calcott Corporation and Emerson Trust Bank withdrew their lawsuits against each other. There would be no trial. Judge Sandoval seemed satisfied.

The story was picked up immediately. "Toxic Case Comes to an End," read the *Times*'s headline.

Inside his office at Prexius Solar Solutions on Hudson Street, Jack Glasser, feeling something like a narcotic high, was reading the stories as fast as he could find them. He finished the first, then jumped to the next. "Mega Suit Ends, Wall Street Sighs in Relief."

When he was finished reading all the articles, he stood up from his desk and walked toward the door. The secretary, a woman named Luz, pretended not to see him and began typing on her computer. He knew she didn't like him; it didn't bother him in the slightest.

You have no idea who I am, he said in his mind. *I'm the most powerful man in New York.*

He went to the bathroom and peed a yellow stream into the urinal. In his mind, he practiced what he would say when the colonel called: "Yes sir, very good sir, thank you."

Everything had worked out fine. They had their money in Oman; they could arm their friends in Yemen. They could be a self-sufficient machine. No more begging Congress and the Pentagon for every tiny penny. Everything was good. The colonel would be happy.

When he finished peeing, he went to the sink and looked at his face in the mirror. *You are fifty-one years old*, he told himself. *You need to wear sunscreen.* Then his mind shifted, and he remembered a chore that needed doing.

He had to pick up Charlie's new hockey skates. *Fuck*, he thought. *Fucking Helen, it's called Amazon, you can order things online now.* He left the bathroom and headed for the elevator. He'd celebrate today's victory with a cappuccino and a chocolate chip cookie.

When the elevator came, it smelled like cigarettes. On his way out of the lobby, he raised his hand in a peace sign to the doorman. *Getting coffee, I'll be back*, he said to himself.

The doorman, a black guy with dreadlocks, said, "All right then."

It was cooler outside than he expected, and he regretted not bringing his coat. The traffic, headed for New Jersey, had already started; and a flurry of honking began a block away and spread toward him. Glasser jammed his hands into his pants pockets, walked north, and rehearsed how he'd order from the coffee girl: *Gimme a single cappuccino. A single cap. Single cap. Hey, just a single cappuccino, please.*

Because of the honking, he didn't hear the footsteps coming up behind him until the very last second. In the reflection of the building's window, he saw a skinny man in a motorcycle helmet limping toward him.

He didn't have time to turn. His mind sensed what was coming, though, and it screamed accordingly. He didn't hear a gunshot, but he felt the air around him change. He saw the ground—gray and dirty—and a flash of light. His head snapped forward like he'd been punched and his feet felt yanked back. The ground came rushing up to meet him and knocked the air out of his chest and hurt his chin and jaw.

Then there seemed to be a long moment where he was lying on the ground and trying to run but nothing was happening. He could see people's feet and the sky, and the clouds above him were gray and white, and his chin hurt and his head felt cracked open and the screaming in his head became a low kind of humming.

There had been some kind of great mistake.

Acknowledgments

First and foremost, I'd like to thank my agent, Charlotte Sheedy. As always, I lack sufficient words to express how thankful I am to her. She's simply the best!

This book was edited by Patricia Mulcahy and Morgan Entrekin. I'd like to thank both of them for their insight and wisdom. Additionally, I'd like to thank Briony Everroad, Sara Vitale, and all the wonderful people at Grove Atlantic.

Walter Greene designed the cover. What a guy!

Ryan Gattis, Jason Schwartz, and Ezra Feinberg were all early readers and provided invaluable feedback.

Joshua Dubin recommended me for a private investigation job that led directly to this book. That's all I can say about that.

Rebecca Young, Emma Freudenberger, Haeya Yim, and Jenny Ma answered my endless questions about lawyers and the law.

Chris Brown and Rodney Faraon fielded my spy questions. I am very thankful to them.

Benjamin Roberts and Dave Hoffman answered my questions about banks and finance.

Reyhan Harmanci, to whom the book is dedicated, did everything including urging me early on to change Valencia's gender from male to female. Yes, I'll admit it. But that was just one of a million things. Thank you!!! Love you!!!

I lost some very dear friends and family during the writing of this book. RIP Nicky B. RIP Christine Poldino. RIP Noelle Tenedou-Levine. And RIP to my mom, Kathy Coyne.